DELICIOUS

DELICIOUS

Mark Haskell Smith

Atlantic Monthly Press
New York

Published simultaneously in Canada
Printed in the United States of America

ISBN 0-87113-884-0

Atlantic Monthly Press
an imprint of Grove/Atlantic, Inc.
841 Broadway
New York, NY 10003

For Diana, my designated driver

DELICIOUS

The End of the Story

One

"I'm gonna dig an *imu*."

He couldn't think of any other way. So the night before, Joseph went out and gathered as many large rocks and hunks of lava as he thought he'd need. He'd spent the morning collecting banana stalks and chunks of koa wood from a farm near Waiahole, filling the bed of his pickup truck with as much of the stuff as he could, all the while telling the farmer that, yes, he was making kalua pig but, no, he wasn't having a luau. It wasn't a party for family and friends. It was a business thing.

He drove the long way around, past Kahuku and Waialee, past Sunset Beach, and the Banzai Pipeline with its horde of roughly glamorous surfers, their bodies bronzed and articulated like Roman statues, their long hair curling from hours of salt and sun, attended by young girls with tight bodies in tighter bikinis.

Joseph had often wondered what it was like to ride the big waves on the North Shore. To feel the ocean swell and build underneath you until it rose up, three stories high, rumbling and pushing with a primeval force, beginning to reach out over you, cutting off the sun and sky, wrapping around you in a seething roil of heavy foam. Joseph had seen it, all that pressure building inside a tunnel of water until it suddenly collapsed, like a building falling down, the air pressure exploding like a cannon, shooting a surfer out of the tube in a blast of salt spray at fifty miles an hour. He had heard it was an unbelievable rush. Better than sex, better than any drug. But he couldn't do it. Leave it to the crazies from Brazil or the rad Cali dudes to risk getting shredded on the coral just beneath the waves.

Joseph didn't like to go out into the water. He didn't surf in it. He didn't swim in it. He didn't even like to ride in a boat. Whenever he was in the water the hair on the back of his neck would stand up. The fear of joining the food chain. A distinctly sharky vibe.

He liked the beach. Liked to kick back, drink a beer, watch the girls, feel his skin go from brown to really brown. As long as he didn't have to enter the water, the beach was fine.

Joseph stopped for gas and an energy bar in Haleiwa before turning inland, driving past the sagging homes and rotting little farmhouses that dotted a desolate countryside filled with scrub grass and clumps of wild sugarcane.

Most of the land was owned by Dole or some other agribiz that zealously guarded its pineapple fields, putting up gates and patrolling the rutted roads in pickup trucks. But that didn't bother Joseph. He knew where to go.

He turned off the pavement and onto a dirt road, the red soil rising up in a cloud behind his truck like a brush fire. He jounced down the road for a few miles, seemingly in the middle of nowhere, and then stopped, the truck disappearing for a moment in a thick swirling cloud of dirt.

Joseph let the dust settle and then backed the pickup down a deeply rutted and pockmarked trail through a dense thicket of sugarcane near an abandoned sugar mill. He drove slowly, careful not to bottom out the springs on his truck, the rocks and firewood clunking and lurching in the back.

The main house and crushing mills stood faded and falling apart, ruins from another time, left over from the days of C & H, Claus Sprekels, and the sugar boom, when hundreds of Japanese and Filipinos, wearing heavy clothes to keep from getting lacerated, had hacked down cane in the fields to sweeten cakes, cookies, and coffee on the mainland. It had been a big business on the island until the company found a cheaper place to grow and harvest sugar. Now it was a wasteland, the sharp canes growing wild, like a forest of green razors, waving in the breeze.

Joseph rolled his window up; he didn't want to get cut.

He reached the edge of the thicket, a small clearing by a decaying outbuilding, and pulled to a stop. He climbed out and looked around. He could turn his head in any direction, and all he could see was tall green sugarcane bobbing in the breeze.

It was hot, so Joseph took off his T-shirt, revealing a lean body with taut muscles and light brown skin. He looked Hawaiian but, like most people on the island, his lineage was a mixed bag. His father was half Samoan, half Hawaiian, his mother a slender blend of Thai and Danish. He looked like everyone else in Honolulu, brown skin, Asiatic eyes, and dark hair, but with a kind of beautiful mash of a face, his Thai and Northern European DNA fighting it out on a handsome Hawaiian canvas.

He had a Samoan last name, Tanumafili, but he was never mistaken for a Samoan. When asked what race he was, he always referred to himself as chop suey: a crazy mix of left-overs jumbled up and thrown together. Chop suey. Fill that in on the census form.

Joseph dropped the gate on the truck and began chucking hunks of wood into a pile. Bright red dust, looking like something from Mars, rose up in little blooms with each thud and thunk as he emptied the truck bed.

He fished a bag of newspaper and some small sticks out of the cab of the truck—stopping to take a long drink of cold water from the battered Igloo cooler in the front seat—dragged the bag over to a clear spot, squatted, and began to form the material into something combustible.

Sweat, dripping from his forehead, put out the first match. The second one reached the crumpled newspaper without incident. Joseph watched as the paper caught fire, sending tentative licks of flame up into the twigs. He picked up a couple of large hunks of koa and, using an ax, split them and threw them on the fire.

Now came the hard part.

Using a stick he marked out a large rectangle on the ground, about six feet by four, bigger than your average *imu*. Joseph spit into his palms, plucked a shovel out of the truck, and drove it into the ground along the line he'd made. The blade bit into the soil with a crunch, and he heaved the loose red dirt, pocked with dark pebbles of volcanic rock, off to the side.

As he dug, Joseph thought about what his uncle had told him. They were being invaded. They had to do whatever they could to protect themselves, their island, and their way of life.

It reminded him of all the old stories, the folktales of brave warriors, island kings, and angry volcano gods. But Joseph didn't need the old stories, the tribal warfare, the myth of Pele, or the arrival of Captain Cook to convince him that his uncle was right. He had seen the consequences of invasion with his own eyes. Rich Caucasians from the mainland were buying up property on the cheap, displacing local families, and then turning around and selling to even richer Japanese. Companies were building factories, employing hundreds of locals, and then shifting the business farther west to Asia, where cheap labor flourished, leaving the islanders unemployed, living with debts they could never repay.

Life was hard enough. The cost of living in Honolulu was far higher than what the average person could afford, and most of Joseph's friends had to work two, sometimes three jobs just to make ends meet. Those without steady employment often found themselves fishing for dinner. An empty net and their children went hungry, while overstuffed pink-skinned tourists ordered room service and drank mai tais on the beach.

The mainlanders, the haoles, had come and taken what they wanted. They had abused the islands and the people who call them home, perverting the spirit of aloha and turning it into a marketing catchphrase for bare-breasted hula girls and rum drinks in tiki mugs. They didn't give a rat's ass about the local traditions, the culture, or the Hawaiian people. All they wanted was money. Profit at the expense of the natives.

Joseph had seen it happen before, but it was always to someone else. Now it was happening to him and his family, his *ohana*. So he was digging an *imu*. He couldn't think of any other way.

...

Joseph stopped digging. He stood up in the hole, now almost four feet deep, and cocked his ear. He heard the whine of an engine reversing down the dirt road, the crunch of tires, the soft putter of exhaust. He climbed out of the hole just as the rear of a plain white van appeared in the clearing. Joseph had to shout to keep the driver from backing into the fire. The van skidded to a stop and then lurched forward in quick little hops, as if stung by a bee.

Joseph directed the van next to his truck and watched as the dust settled and his cousin Wilson climbed out of the driver's seat. Wilson stood and stretched, blinking in the sunlight. He was a lot bigger than Joseph: strong, with a large barrel chest and huge bulging biceps ringed with tribal tattoos. Wilson's shaved head looked like it was planted on his shoulders, his neck disappearing in a mass of thick muscles bulging out at extreme angles like flying buttresses. He wore shorts and flip-flops, revealing legs that looked like smooth tree trunks, knotted with thick blue veins.

Wilson had turned down a chance to play defensive end for the University of Washington Huskies, preferring to go right into the police academy. But police work was tedious and he never made it onto the force, dropping out of the academy and settling into a life working for his father's company. Occasionally, Wilson would take a job as a bouncer at a local disco. He liked that job, enjoying the music, the girls, the free crank. He held the record for tourist tossing, having once flung a rowdy Japanese man over a parked car and into the middle of Kalakaua Avenue. He came back the next day and measured the distance from the disco's door to the bloodstain still on the street. Twenty-four feet seven inches. Untouchable.

Joseph, his body slick with sweat, stepped forward and embraced his cousin.

"Cousin."

"How's it?"

"Getting close."

Wilson broke from the embrace and looked at the hole. "Wow, brah. You almost done."

"We might need some more rocks."

Wilson checked the pile. "Looks like enough."

"Did you bring any food? I'm starving."

Wilson nodded. "No worries. Nana cooked us fried fish and rice."

Joseph looked at the fire. "Let's put the rocks in and eat."

. . .

As the rocks began to heat and smoke in the fire, Joseph and Wilson sat in the shade of a large banyan tree, eating from Tupperware containers of fried fish and rice.

Wilson spoke with his mouth full. "How long you think this gonna take?"

"All night."

Wilson didn't like the sound of that. "All night?"

"Better to be on the safe side, don't you think?"

"Seems long."

Joseph snapped at his cousin. "I don't want to be going back and starting over because we didn't give them the extra time, man. I don't like this as it is."

Wilson shrugged. He generally let Joseph take the lead. Joseph was the smart one in the family, the ambitious one, the one who went to college. Unless it was one of Wilson's areas of expertise—football, primarily—he deferred to his cousin.

"You da boss."

Joseph stuffed a chopstick load of food in his mouth and exhaled. "Sorry. I'm just tired."

"No worries. You da best cook in da family."

Joseph looked over at the van parked next to his pickup at the edge of the thicket. "They in there?"

Wilson nodded. "Dey not goin' nowhere."

Joseph nodded thoughtfully. For some reason, he looked up at the sky. He saw blue. Nothing else, not a cloud, not a bird, just a wash of vibrant color. He didn't know what he expected to see: God looking down on them? Not that he, or anyone in his family, was particularly religious. Occasionally his grandmother would make a *kakuai,* an offering to the gods. But that was usually associated with someone's marriage or the birth of a new great-grandchild. She never made a big deal out of it, once pitching an overripe banana out the kitchen window and saying it was a *kakuai* because they needed rain. No one else in the family even bothered to do that. Who has time for old myths and stories when you've got to go to work? But Joseph couldn't be persuaded to disregard the local beliefs. Why should he? As far as he knew, the world was full of *akuas.* Maybe there really was a volcano goddess, shark god, waterfall god. We got loads of gods and goddesses around here. It was the Christian God who was always causing all the problems, with his absolute decrees of good and evil, right and wrong. The Christian God just didn't understand that sometimes—well, circumstances arise where good and evil become relative terms. The local gods understood what Joseph and Wilson had to do. They approved. For some reason the Christian God always sided with the mainlanders: the haoles and butter-stinkers.

Wilson finished his food and let out a belch. "Da rocks look ready."

...

They laid down a good four-inch layer of beach sand in the bottom of the hole. This helped insulate the ground and kept the heat from dispersing too quickly. Joseph chopped the banana stalks in half, soaked them briefly in water from a well near the abandoned outbuilding, and put a layer over the sand while Wilson pushed the white-hot rocks out of the fire toward the hole. Together they shoved them onto the banana stalks, steam bursting from the stalks the moment the hot rocks hit them, and then tossed another layer of wet banana stalks on top of them.

Now came the meat.

Joseph followed Wilson over to the van. Wilson opened the doors to reveal two large, naked, and very dead Caucasian men slumped in the back. There were nasty-looking wounds on their chests, the skin blackened and burned around the puckering bullet holes.

Joseph recoiled. "Fuck."

"Dey not dat big. C'mon."

"Do they have to be naked?"

"Wot difference?"

Joseph considered that. There was no difference. Nothing was going to make this any easier.

"You get the feet."

They carried the first body, a thin, reedy guy with a bushy mustache and sandy hair, cut in a kind of seventies style with the hair coming halfway over his ears. Joseph thought the guy might've believed he looked like a bad-ass Texas Ranger type, but he really looked more like a car salesman. They lowered his body onto the hot rocks, and the skin instantly began to spit and sizzle. Joseph and Wilson both covered their noses.

Without a word, they went back and got the second body. This guy was big, almost as big as Wilson. Wilson let out a grunt as they hoisted him.

"Dis cat used steroids."

"Why do you say that?"

"White guys don' get dis big."

Like his partner, the big guy had a bushy mustache. Wilson didn't know what to make of that. Maybe they were in a cult.

Joseph and Wilson struggled with the second guy, eventually laying him next to the hole and rolling him in. A burst of steam rose out of the pit as soon as the body hit the hot rocks.

They quickly got to work finishing the *imu,* throwing wet banana stalks on top of the bodies and then rolling more white-hot rocks on top of that. These rocks they would keep replacing with other rocks from the fire, rotating them to keep the *imu* as hot as they could for the next ten or twelve hours.

Joseph walked to the shade of the banyan and collapsed in a heap. He was soaked through with sweat, red dirt sticking to his hair, his face, his arms and legs, his chest, and his back. His sweat had turned the dirt to mud; the sun was starting to bake it into clay. From a distance he looked like one of the mud men of New Guinea: a ferocious clay-coated island warrior. A mud-caked cannibal.

Wilson walked to his van and pulled a couple of cold beers from a cooler in the front seat. He carried them back and handed one to Joseph without a word. Joseph gratefully took the beer, cracked it open, and felt the cold bitter taste wash the dust out of his throat.

The two cousins sat together in the shade, drinking their beer, watching the smoke rise up from the *imu* and drift in the wind.

...

Joseph had been dreaming. He'd dreamed he was on a raft at sea. In every direction there was no sign of land, no sign of another boat, nothing. Just big, blank vastness. It was a moonless night, or at least in the dream he didn't see anything as comforting and normal as the moon. The sky was clear and starless. The ocean rocked with malevolent swells, the dark waves churning with jellyfish, *pololia,* the water almost solid, like black glass, with sharp jagged edges.

The raft wasn't a Robinson Crusoe job—it wasn't bamboo lashed together with vines—it was one of those yellow rubber inflatable things that fishing boats and pleasure yachts keep for emergencies. Joseph bobbed up and down in the waves, unable to move, trapped in the marshmallowy rubber like a man drowning in a condom, a grubby prophylactic spinning and swirling as it's flushed down the toilet.

Joseph woke up and blinked. The sky was warming, the morning sun somewhere off to the east, just cresting over the sea. Birds flitted from branch to branch in the banyan tree above him. Joseph didn't need a shrink to analyze his dream. He knew what it meant. Something bad was hiding under the black waves, something that was sucking him down, keeping him stuck in place. It was obviously an anxiety dream. But the jellyfish: What did that mean?

He cranked his head to one side and saw Wilson snoring on a blanket.

"Fuck."

Joseph jumped up and moved quickly to the fire. It had been Wilson's turn to watch the *imu,* so Joseph was relieved to find it still hot, the rocks still cooking. Joseph took a stick and bent over the pit. He poked at some of the meat, watching as it fell away from the bone, white, steamy, and tender. Just the way a kalua pig is supposed to look. Alarmingly, his stomach let out a ferocious growl. Somehow, in the night, the horrible stench of burning hair and roasting flesh had turned into—well, it smelled like bacon.

Joseph shuddered and walked back over to his sleeping cousin. "Wake up."

Wilson rolled, rubbed his eyes, and groaned. "What's it?"

"They're done."

Wilson sat up. "You check?"

Joseph nodded. "Yeah."

"How dey taste, brah?"

"Stop fucking around."

Joseph turned, walked back to the van, and began pulling out long kitchen tongs and large metal pans. Wilson joined him.

"I need coffee. I no can fo' wake up."

Joseph didn't respond; he just kept pulling out stuff, organizing the work that had to be done.

"Serious, brah."

"I don't have any coffee."

"Let's go into town, get somethin' fo' breakfast."

"It's too dangerous."

"Get somethin' to take out, den. Dere's gotta be some-place fo' grind near da freeway. I'll stay an' make work."

Joseph thought about it. He realized Wilson was right. They'd probably be here another four or five hours; they'd need some food.

"All right."

"Right on. Get me two—no, three—breakfast san'wiches an' two extra-large coffees wit' milk an' sugar. I need lotsa sugar."

Joseph brushed himself off and started to get into his truck.

"An' some fries. Fo' later."

"Make sure they're all the way done."

Wilson saluted as his cousin drove off, jouncing down the red dirt road.

...

Joseph headed back toward the sugarcane fields with several bags of takeout riding on the seat next to him. Even at this early hour he'd had to wait in a line of cars in the drive-thru as commuters grabbed their steaming sacks of the fried egg, pork sausage, mayonnaise, and molten-cheese sandwiches before taking the Kamehameha Highway to the H2, racing into Honolulu like it was the Indy 500.

A couple of papayas, picked up at a roadside stand, tumbled around on the floor. Joseph rolled his window down, letting the cool morning breeze blow in and carry the stench of congealing grease out the window, across the ocean, and back to the mainland where it came from. He looked at the bags on the passenger seat. The paper was growing incrementally darker, wicking the grease from the bottom to the top of the bag. It reminded him of his youth.

He'd spent his childhood eating grease. Raised on the "plate lunch," a deep-fried chunk of protein, a scoop of macaroni salad, and two scoops of rice, Joseph had gone through his adolescence and early adulthood constantly overweight. He hadn't been big enough or strong enough to use his weight as a defensive lineman like his cousin, so he spent much of his time sitting under a tree reading books, eating potato chips, and listening to Hawaiian pop singers like Israel Kamakawiwo'ole.

In retrospect he realized it hadn't been so bad. Sure, he felt left out and lonely, but then he was the only person he knew who'd read Proust's body of work in one summer-long marathon. He didn't go to the prom or to the school football games; instead he would go to the library and, if he found an author he liked, he'd work his way through their collected works. Steinbeck, Poe, Dostoyevsky, Arthur Conan Doyle, Victor Hugo, Mark Twain: He devoured them.

When he discovered pulp fiction, it got worse. The Hardy Boys led to Mickey Spillane, to Raymond Chandler, to Ross MacDonald, and on and on. He'd read a book a day, sometimes forgetting to sleep. Paperbacks rose like stalagmites next to his bed, reaching toward the ceiling, collapsing into heaps, collecting like snowdrifts in the corners of his room.

This sedentary lifestyle came crashing to a halt one day. Sitting in his underwear on an examining table at the ripe age of seventeen, weighing in at a robust 275 pounds, a well-worn library copy of Shakespeare's *Julius Caesar* in hand, Joseph heard the doctor tell him about the "Hawaiian diet." It was based on one simple fact. The Polynesian body had developed for centuries subsisting on a diet of roasted fish, greens, fruits, and taro root. The introduction of oils, and in particular the hypersaturated fats used in fast foods, had caused a weight explosion among islanders because their bodies couldn't process the stuff. They just didn't have the chemistry.

So Joseph began his freshman year at the University of Hawaii the same way he ended his senior year of high school: sitting by himself, reading a book, oblivious to the ebb and flow of pheromones and hormones, the pitch of tight biceps, or the pull of a heaving bikini top. Only now he was intensely interested in food. He began reading cookbooks, searching for new ways to cook things. And his diet changed drastically. Instead of a bag of potato chips or a cheeseburger, he ate fresh papaya and pineapple; instead of steak or meat loaf, he ate fresh fish. Sometimes he'd go for days only eating raw foods: sashimi and melons. Other days he might roast fresh seafood on the beach, just like his ancestors.

It didn't take long for his body to adjust. The weight dropped off him, like peeling out of an oversized suit, and he soon found himself filled with a strange new energy. He began walking everywhere, walking for hours. He'd let his mind drift on these walks, daydreaming. Occasionally he'd find himself strolling on the beach with a large boner rising up inside his pants like the periscope of a submarine reaching through the murky ocean toward the bright light of day.

If his life was like a book, something he could easily relate to, then Joseph thought of his early years as one chapter, the greasy lonely chapter, and his college years as the next.

When he was younger he never paid much attention to girls and, for their part, they never paid much attention to the pudgy little nerd with his head in a book. So he had never done the things that drive most adolescent boys crazy. He'd never been to a school dance and held a girl close while a cover band blared some crappy ballad by Billy Joel and his penis throbbed like an outboard motor in his pants. He'd never felt the ache and pang of a first crush, never experienced the flush of adrenaline, the bloom of blood rushing to his face as he played Spin the Bottle around a fire pit on the beach, never knew the awkwardness and excitement of a first date.

In his sophomore year of college, all that changed. He chose to major in something called Hawaiian Oral Traditions, because he liked stories and thought someone ought to remember how to speak Hawaiian. When he wasn't jogging on the beach or hanging around the campus learning, through trial and error, his way around the female anatomy, he was working. He got a job in a restaurant, starting out as a dishwasher and working his way up to prep cook and then line cook. Even though it wasn't necessarily the healthy Polynesian food he himself ate, Joseph enjoyed preparing all kinds of things—even the goofy dishes that the tourists craved, like macadamia-crusted *opakapaka* with mango salsa or pork braised in *haupia* milk.

With the responsibility of employment came some financial freedom. Joseph found himself with more spending money than most college students, and he invested that money in his culinary education. He'd take women out on dates, but only to restaurants he wanted to try. He ended up becoming something of a regular at Alan Wong's. He'd sit at the counter facing the kitchen and watch the cooks throw together a kind of inspired mélange of tropical, French, and Japanese.

It was during these dinners that he realized what he wanted to do. He wanted to be a chef.

His dates didn't understand. Why didn't he want to sit at a table and look into their eyes? They wanted to talk to him, to tell him what they were interested in, what things they liked to do, what they thought about others. They wanted to find things in common. They wanted to communicate.

Joseph didn't want to talk, he wanted to cook.

. . .

He swung his truck off the main road and turned back down the rutted red trail. He drove slowly, creeping along between the sugarcane, so as not to make too big a rooster tail of dust.

As he pulled into the clearing, he looked over and saw Wilson, squatting near the smoldering *imu,* a human leg on the ground in front of him, picking meat off the thigh, putting it in his mouth, and chewing thoughtfully.

. . .

Joseph jumped out of the truck. "What the fuck are you doing?"

Wilson looked up, his mouth still full of freshly roasted human flesh, and held up a finger. "Wait a sec."

Joseph stood there, feeling a bubble of stomach acid rising inside him, and watched as his cousin finished chewing and swallowed.

"Are you insane? You can't eat people!"

"I just wanted a taste."

Joseph turned and retched. Bitter fluid spewed out of his stomach and onto the ground. Feeling his knees go weak, he collapsed, letting the red dirt rise around him, and began to cry quietly.

Wilson looked at him. "I just tasted it, brah. Don't freak."

Don't freak? That's all he wanted to do. He'd been doing all this, digging the *imu* and cooking the corpses, on a kind of autopilot. He hadn't felt anything toward the two men: not hatred, not pity, nothing. But now, seeing Wilson squatting on the ground munching on a thigh? "Don't freak" was kind of an understatement.

He looked up.

"That's a person's leg. A human being. You can't eat a human being."

"Yeah. But, like, when am I ever gonna get a chance to try dis again? You know wot I'm sayin'? It's not like it's gonna be on the menu at Sam Choy's."

Joseph didn't say anything.

"It's not dat bad. A little stringy."

"You're an Ai-Kanaka."

"Dat's just a story."

Joseph wiped tears from his eyes. "Those stories come from somewhere."

Wilson shook his head. He looked down at the leg still steaming on the ground. Joseph thought he saw a strange look flicker on his cousin's face. Not a look of revulsion or repulsion at what he'd done. No. It was the look of a young boy staring at the cookie jar. A look desperate for one more taste.

Joseph jumped up. "Stop. Just—fucking—stop!"

Wilson looked hurt. "I stopped, okay?"

"Move away from that leg!"

Wilson stayed put and looked up at Joseph. "I'm sorry, okay?"

Joseph got up and walked shakily back to the truck. He reached into the cab and pulled out the bag of fast food.

"Here."

"All right!" Wilson leaped to his feet and stuck his face in the bag. "I was starvin', brah!"

He pulled out a breakfast sandwich—a cold, congealed artery bomb coated with mayonnaise, decorated with two strips of fat-marbled bacon, and smushed between two English muffins—unwrapped it, and took a huge bite. He held it out for Joseph. Joseph looked at the sandwich and at his cousin, who was chomping relentlessly, little blobs of mayonnaise and grease squirting out the side of his mouth; then he looked over at the leg on the ground. Cooling now, it was beginning to attract flies. Joseph shook his head.

"You gotta eat somethin', man. We got a lotta work ahead of us."

Joseph sat on the bumper and watched as a fly landed on the leg and began doing its fly thing. He wanted to give up, to surrender, just lie down and sleep until someone came and arrested him. Let the authorities lock him away or, better, treat him like the old Hawaiians treated an Ai-Kanaka and pitch him off a cliff to his death. He watched as another fly landed on the leg. He heard his cousin's lips smacking wetly as they worked over the breakfast sandwich. A bird chirped.

"It's not dat bad."

"What's not that bad?"

"Wot we did."

Joseph looked at Wilson. "It's bad, okay? There's nothing good about it."

The anger in Joseph's voice made Wilson defensive.

"Dey were gonna do it to us."

Joseph nodded. What could he say? Yeah, they were going to do it to us. We were just defending ourselves. Protecting the islands, defending our *ohana,* our way of life. We aren't murderers and cannibals, we're just scaring the conquerors away with some Polynesian craziness. Knocking them off before they take our land and destroy our culture, just like they did to the Cherokee, Crow, Shawnee, and Navaho. Yeah. We're innocent. We're just keeping them from corrupting our culture.

But Joseph wondered about that. How innocent were they? How justified? Who was really responsible for corrupting the culture? Out of necessity the natives had converted their culture into a commodity and sold it so they could afford to live in their own homes. But had they sold out or become subjugated? Why were they spending all their effort and energy welcoming the conquerors, serving them pineapple and poi, offering them leis and mai tais, giving them the spirit of aloha, when what they'd really like to do is feed them to the sharks?

What was the alternative? Should they just give the island land to the haoles and let them turn it into golf courses? Speak only Hawaiian and keep to themselves? Was it better to live in squalor on a reservation than become an Ai-Kanaka? What does it mean to be Hawaiian?

Wilson was well into the second sandwich. He looked at Joseph.

"You gotta eat, brah."

Joseph wiped some dust off his sunglasses. "I had some papaya."

Joseph watched Wilson sitting there, devouring a sandwich as a couple of corpses steamed in the *imu* next to him. He hung his head in dismay. Maybe it really was time to walk away from paradise. Maybe it wasn't paradise anymore.

The Story Begins

Two

"Put your pussy right in my face."

Strobe lights flashed. Raunchy hip-hop music scratched and throbbed. The lap dancer, encased like a sausage in a fishnet bodysuit, moved up and down, in and out, simulating some kind of strange mix of musical chairs and fucking. She twitched and swiveled around the chair as the old man stared at her, his body listing to the left like a sinking ship. His pale blue eyes bugged out of a face tanned tobacco and leathery from years in the Nevada sun as they watched her curvaceous ass sling from side to side. He licked his thin, chapped lips, feeling the scraggly whiskers of his mustache hanging down, and shifted in his seat. Using his right arm he moved his left arm out of the way. He reached up and adjusted his bolo tie, a large chunk of turquoise embedded in a web of Indian silver. While his left hand was limp and unadorned, his right hand sported several chunky gold rings and a Rolex watch that was so expensive it might have been made from plutonium.

"I wanna smell your bush, baby."

"Will that get your motor runnin', honey?"

"My motor's always runnin', cupcake."

That part was true. Ever since the stroke, all Big Jack Lucey could think about was fucking. When he was healthy he hadn't had time for sex, he'd been too busy running his business, but now that half his body was useless, his left arm and left leg hanging off him like an oversized clown suit, sex obsessed him. Whether it was a case of wanting what you can't have or a deep fear that women would now find him repulsive and cut off all contact, he didn't know. One doctor had theorized that the stroke had caused some damage to one of his glands, causing the other glands to compensate and become overactive. Whatever the cause, the stroke had left him oversexed and impotent.

This frustrating and unfortunate dilemma led to a chain of medical mishaps that left him with a constant aching hard-on, courtesy of the inflatable air bags inserted into his penis. The doctors had sold him on the air-bag thing; he was supposed to be able to inflate them when he wanted an erection— there was a little valve and pumper—and deflate them when he didn't. But the gizmo got stuck and Jack found himself with an erection that would never go down.

The doctors decided it was too dangerous to take out the air bags—there might be permanent damage—so they just left it the way it was. He'd just have to adapt, they said. Adapt to the useless limbs, adapt to the persistent raging boner.

The stroke made Jack relearn how to do simple things like wipe his ass and brush his teeth. The malfunctioning air bags meant Jack had to learn how to piss in an arc.

It had changed him, all this adapting and this hard-on 24/7. He used to be a bit of a cutup, a man who was quick to buy a round of drinks for his friends or invite people over for a poolside barbecue. But now he was plagued by an insistent, demanding urge, like an itch that won't stop, an itch no amount of lotion will ever quench and no amount of scratching will ever satisfy.

A permanent boner is a blessing and a curse.

So here he was, watching a twenty-two-year-old blond girl from Irving, Texas, dance around him like she was a harem girl and he was the Grand Poohbah.

"What's that in your pants, baby?"

"What do you think it is?"

"Oooh, it looks like an anaconda."

The lap dancer moved his walker, custom made by a retired bicycle racer, a few feet away so she could get down to business. She sat in his lap, thrusting against his thighs, finding his inflated cock and running her ass against its ridge.

"Can you feel it?"

"Oh, yeah, baby, I can feel it."

Jack leaned forward, almost getting his eye poked out by one of her stiff little nipples protruding through the fishnet. He put his face down by her thrusting belly and inhaled deeply.

"I love the smell of that."

The music changed and with it the dancer's rhythms. She got serious. She crawled close to him, right on top of him, and began to pump her crotch pneumatically against his lap as she swished her hair around in a circle and pressed her breasts an inch from his face.

"Are you gonna get your nut for me?"

Jack didn't respond; he was at a loss for words.

Her soft hair whipped across his face as her body ground against his inflated cock until he thought the air bags might pop. A spasm slowly worked its way up his spine and through the right half of his body. His face contorted and he let out a little grunt. The dancer stood up.

"That fun?"

Jack nodded. He realized she was speaking to him as if he were hard of hearing. Sometimes people did that: assuming that if you needed a walker you were deaf or retarded. Normally it made him angry, but he was still a little stoned from the pheromone tsunami that had just washed over him, so he let it slide.

She picked up his walker and brought it next to his chair. "I hope I see you again, real soon."

Jack looked at her, finally croaking out a sound. "You betcha."

She stood there, expectant, as he fished around in his pants pocket and pulled out his now soggy money clip. Jack peeled three hundred-dollar bills out of the clip and handed her the clammy currency. She took the money gingerly, holding the bills by a corner.

"Thanks, Mr. Lucey."

"Thank *you*, Brenda."

"Barbara."

"Thank you, Barbara."

He watched her walk out of the room, flapping the bills in the breeze to dry them.

...

The doorman, an ex-UNLV lineman named Baxter, big and brawny with a shaggy mullet and matching mustache, held the door open as Jack lurched his walker, his body slowly trailing in painful little half steps, out into the parking lot. Jack looked down and saw a sticky, wet smudge slowly seeping through his pants leg. He turned and smiled at Baxter.

"Beautiful night."

"You have a good one, Mr. Lucey."

"Thank you, Baxter."

Jack hobbled toward his specially built van. In the distance he could see the sun going down behind the strip, the neon lights and big-screen billboards of the casinos coming to life. He inhaled deeply, the dry air tinged with the scent of burning meat from a nearby steakhouse. He loved Las Vegas. It was paradise.

Three

Francis cracked the neck on the tiny bottle of scotch. He watched as the amber liquid coated the ice cubes and slowly rose up the angled sides of the little plastic cup. Fucking terrorists. They'd succeeded, hadn't they? Changed his life forever with their mayhem.

Whatever inspiration their God-demented brains gleaned from the Koran had served them well. All that time on their knees, foreheads planted in the dirt, bowing to the east. All that Allah, Allah, Allah had really paid off. They took on the evil, bloated, and gluttonous West. They gave their lives to it, which, discounting the virgins and rivers of wine in everlasting Heaven, was the ultimate sacrifice. They'd become martyrs, rock stars for the new millennium, and they'd succeeded beyond their wildest fantasies. The world was changed forever. Now, post–terrorist attack, cocktails in first class were served in cheap plastic cups. Like anyone could hijack a jet with a fucking tumbler.

Still, the scotch tasted good. He needed it to taste good. He'd be drinking three or four of these, maybe more, if the little idiot next to him kept yakking away. Francis took another sip and looked over at the young woman like he was interested in what she was saying. He saw her lips move: flap, flap, flap.

Funny, he'd always thought Japanese women were beautiful—next to Thai women, the most exquisite in the world. But not this one. Short and scrunchy featured with adult acne erupting across her forehead like some kind of bacterial archipelago. Big eared, bad breathed, and completely flat chested.

And, my God, she wouldn't shut up. She even talked over the captain's announcements. Francis would never know what altitude they'd be flying at and what speed, he'd never know the temperature to expect when they arrived. Instead, he was treated to discourse on the benefits, both psychological, physiological, and something to do with some kind of sexual chakras, of belly dancing. Francis nodded and sipped his scotch. He smiled to himself as she blabbed on. Bend over and grab your ankles. I'll open your sex chakra.

The belly dancing turned out to be the tip of the iceberg. There were conga lessons and contact movement improv, whatever that was. There were Pilates classes, self-hypnosis workshops, and afternoons spent passing out free condoms at the local clinic. All at the behest of something called a life coach.

Francis watched as her lips kept moving. She was disappointed that she'd have to put all that self-improvement on hold, but she had to make a living. Francis nodded and wondered why he hadn't read her résumé a little more carefully when he hired her as his production assistant.

Francis cracked open another tiny bottle of scotch. He made a little promise to himself. If she starts talking to me about my drinking, I'm going to set her on fire.

But she didn't. She talked about how excited she was to be working in the film industry. She had studied auteur theory in college and had written several screenplays that her friends said were really good. She couldn't wait to be on the set watching the magic happen—to actually be a part of it, a member of the creative team. She couldn't wait to watch the director work with the actors. She wanted to observe and learn because someday *she* was going to be a director. Not a director of corrupt and soulless Hollywood studio product but a director of important independent films. She had things to say, powerful, important, life-affirming observations of humanity. That's why she was going to Honolulu. She was on her path. She was following her bliss. Her life coach had been a big help.

Francis didn't want to burst her bliss bubble. She'd find out soon enough that the only magic that happened was getting done with the day before midnight. Instead of artistic concerns and aesthetic choices, they would spend hours trying to find, and then get permits for, parking spaces for the giant pop-out trailers that the director and stars demanded. It would break her heart to know that the only work with actors she would see would be filling out time cards, making sure that star A didn't have to work more than eight hours according to his contract and that extras were sent home before any kind of overtime, golden time, or bonus meals had to be paid.

Any insights into human nature would come at the bar, trying to numb your way through another day.

He poured his scotch over the ice and picked up a few barbecued almonds from the little dish. He thought about his boyfriend back in L.A. She asked him if he was allergic to nuts.

Francis wasn't looking forward to being part of the magic. He couldn't care less about magic. He was going because he could work on his tan, drink mai tais, and forget about Chad.

Chad was a producer, a big shot with a studio deal. He and Francis had been living together for almost fifteen years when Francis first learned about the other man—or men. That was just a month ago. The information didn't come out in a big messy talk-show revelation; it dribbled out, one sad confession after another. First it was the dentist after they'd both gone in to get their teeth bleached. Then the guy at the tanning salon. Chad's assistant, Jason, was sprinkled in there somewhere, along with a well-known director, an agent, and the dog walker. And this was just the last year. There were dozens more. Party planners, masseurs, a couple of guys he met at the gym, a postman, a construction worker . . . eventually Chad's confessions started to remind Francis of the Village People. All he needed was an Indian Chief and a Policeman and he could've fucked the whole set.

Having his heart broken was bad enough, but what made Francis angry, really deeply pissed off, were the sacrifices he'd made for Chad. The diets he'd stayed on, the countless hours in the gym with the personal trainer (yes, Chad had fucked him too), the liposuction to get rid of a tiny double chin, all at Chad's insistence, all to make him desirable.

They tried couples therapy, but it seemed to Francis that Chad and the therapist had a thing going, so he stopped.

One morning Francis stood in the bathroom and looked in the mirror. He saw a handsome man in his late forties, his face still slightly boyish with flashing blue eyes and a cute nose. Sure there were some wrinkles around the eyes, but he still had a full head of hair, a great body, a blinding smile. What was missing was not cosmetic.

Francis realized he needed to get some space, some perspective. He had to get out of town. So he picked up the phone, made a few calls, and took the first job he was offered.

He made a promise to himself. He was going to eat, drink, and adventure with abandon. All those years of holding back, denying himself simple pleasures in the hope of earning his boyfriend's love. What had he been thinking? Now he was going to have that cocktail, snort that line, dance with that cute guy, ride that motorcycle. He was going to eat chocolate. He'd been monogamous for fifteen years, and all he'd gotten out of it was humiliation. He had some catching up to do. He was going to screw the first ukulele player he saw.

The multiple scotches were working wonders, untying the knots in his neck and shoulders better than any deep-tissue massage he ever had, slapping a goofy smile on his face, filling him with a warm and contented feeling he hadn't known in years, putting a song in his heart. A disco song. Francis took two of the empty bottles and, animating them with his hands, pretended they'd just met at the first-class airplane discothèque. The little bottles cruised each other, and then one made a move. Soon they were dancing the hustle on Francis's knee. Yeah. Get down tonight.

The annoying woman interrupted him. What was her name, Yuki? She was saying something about the air quality on the plane. There wasn't enough fresh air in the mix; germs were multiplying in the heat; pestilence was fermenting in the vents. Francis shrugged and watched as she got up and went to talk to the flight attendant. From behind, her flat ass and slight body looked boyish and attractive. The scotch acted as a conduit to Francis's brain as he watched her. Maybe she wasn't so bad after all, he mused. Maybe if I just flip her over she'd be all right.

Four

J ack looked out his front window. It was an impressive view. His lawn stretched out lush and verdant across a swath of land—interrupted only by the double-wide circular drive made out of pink flagstones from Arizona and a large flagpole where Old Glory snapped back and forth in the swirling desert winds—until it butted up against a high security fence at the end. A quiet residential street edged his property, as straight a line as any urban planner could draw, a sun-smoldered asphalt moat dividing his plush bluegrass from the great nothing on the other side.

You could see the nothing. There was a whole lot of it. Rocks, dirt, tumbleweeds, and bits of paper blown by the wind, a line of telephone poles receding into the vanishing point, and, if you squinted, distant train tracks heading north. A million miles of brown that ended flush with Jack's sprinkler-soaked grass.

He smiled smugly and lit a cigarette. He knew it was bad for him, one of the many culprits that caused his stroke, but, fuck it, he only needed a couple of drags, just to get his bowels moving. One of the good things about always having a hard-on, you wake up ready to take on the world. Jack wanted to get to the office early this morning. He'd been reading *Daily Variety* and had come up with an idea. He had work to do.

Providing the food and beverage service—it was called production catering—for movie and TV shoots is always an iffy proposition. In the good times, when you were feeding hundreds of cast and crew members at seventeen bucks a head for months at a time and you had three or four trucks rolling out on different shows, you could make a couple million bucks a year. And because of an arrangement with the Teamsters, where most of your cooks are paid hourly as if they were truck drivers, it was almost all profit. In the lean times, when months would go by without as much as a car commercial coming through town, it sucked. You still had to make loan payments and pay insurance on the trucks, and those babies were worth about a quarter million each. Jack knew that the key to success was to keep as many trucks working as possible. It didn't matter if it was a huge star-studded feature film or a crappy commercial for dog food.

Jack had made a habit out of expanding his business into areas without too much competition. There was no way he was going to break into the business in L.A. or the Bay Area. Those markets were supersaturated. He'd had high hopes for Seattle when he moved into that market two years ago. It had been easy to muscle out the little guys there, really just a couple of roach coaches run by some grunge-rock schmos. They didn't have the connections, the guts, or the wherewithal to keep Jack out.

But Seattle wasn't such a hit. Most of the film and TV work went up to Vancouver, where the studios got a 30 percent discount on every dollar they spent, courtesy of the

Canadian government. Seattle, except for a couple of low-budget horror films, had been a loser, a slow bleed on his cash flow. He'd managed to pick up the occasional shoot in Portland, but it wasn't the bonanza he'd hoped for. Then he'd chanced upon an article about the Teamsters in Honolulu.

The islands were hopping with work; they always had been. Dinosaur movies, Vietnam jungle flicks, and then you had the whole *Beach Blanket Bingo* thing with teenagers shouting "Surf's up!" and racing off with big slabs of wood under their arms. Jack had always liked those movies: cute chicks with big hair doing the Watusi in front of tiki torches. Maybe they'd make a comeback. And then there were the TV shows like *Hawaii Five-O,* another of Jack's favorites, and the commercials; dozens of zippy new pickup trucks from Japan were filmed careening through the mud every week on Oahu.

Jack knew he had to move fast. There was only one production catering company on that island. With so little work in the rest of the country, it was only a matter of time before someone else got the same idea.

...

A young man, looking like a slightly haggard Bible salesman, entered the living room. He wore brown slacks and a robin's-egg-blue shirt with a brown-and-red striped tie dangling too short from his neck. Even though he was only twenty-nine he looked decades older. His hair was thinning dramatically—he kept it looking good with a slick comb-over—and he wore reading glasses that made his eyes look gigantic, like some kind of freakish desert insect. Only his shoes betrayed his youth and his interest in rap music. He liked to wear expensive multicolored basketball shoes.

Despite his nod to phat style, Stanley Lucey was as white as Wonder Bread. Possessed by a supercharged energy, he was always looking around with an anxious expression, waiting for something bad to happen, like a missionary who'd just arrived in Nairobi, hoping help would arrive before the Hottentots took him captive.

Stanley carried two cups of coffee.

"Dad, you know you're not supposed to smoke."

Jack turned and faced his son. "And you know you're supposed to mind your own fucking business."

He took a cup from Stanley, slurped some coffee down, and handed the cup back to his son.

"Hold this. I gotta take a dump."

...

After efficiently eliminating the waste product of a New York strip, baked potato with sour cream and chives, Bac-Os-bits, some iceberg lettuce swamped with ranch dressing, and a peach cobbler à la mode, Jack headed to the garage. Stanley followed. He stood back as his father negotiated two short steps with his walker. Stanley thought about helping, thought better of it, and then finally stepped forward to lend a hand.

"Here, Dad."

Jack snapped at him. "I'm fine. You treat me like I'm some kind of fucking retard."

"I'm just trying to help."

"I don't need your fuckin' charity."

Stanley didn't push it. It didn't matter. They'd had this same exact argument countless times. It always ended the same way.

Jack lurched down the steps with his walker and then, with some effort, climbed into his specially built van.

"You coming? We got work to do."

"I'll meet you there."

"Great. The way you drive, you'll get there just in time for lunch."

Jack nodded as the garage door automatically opened and blinding-white sunlight blasted the dark and oily room. Stanley stepped back as his father started the van. Jack never looked where he was going when he backed out. He just threw it in gear and hit the gas. Mirrors were for pussies.

Five

Francis woke up. The intense midmorning sun was raging outside, its white heat muffled to a greenish glow by the heavy blackout curtains covering the hotel room windows. Francis blinked. Even with the curtains pulled tight, the light was excruciating, searing his eyeballs like a red-hot knitting needle. His mouth felt dry and cottony, as if he'd slept all night with a sock stuffed in it. His muscles ached, his bones were throbbing, and his nose was clogged with what felt like great crunchy globs of dried blood. He couldn't remember a time in his life when he felt so abused.

He looked around the room, trying to make some sense of it. It looked like his room. But then, all hotel rooms look the same, as if they were mass-produced in a gigantic building, windowless and whitewashed, with the word HOTEL plastered on the side. Identical rooms rolling off a conveyor belt, each outfitted with the same lamps, the same beds, the same art, the same ice buckets, the same terry-cloth robes. All designed to offer comfort and stability to the generic businesspeople who stayed in them between meetings with other generic businesspeople. A place to rest and recover from strategizing, selling, teleconferencing, or whatever it is those people do.

Francis imagined the men and women in their tailored suits with monogrammed leather briefcases and stylish hair-cuts coming back to these rooms to celebrate some kind of deal. Did they break open the minibar and drink the pint-sized bottles of Something-Crest-Rock chardonnay? Did they eat the barbecued almonds? A couple of candy bars? How did the straight business world celebrate? Did the women lie on their backs with their legs spread while missionary-minded salesmen closed the deal?

Thinking about it hurt his head.

Francis shifted and felt the fluid in his brain slop from one side to the other, painfully trickling through his pons like ice-cold turpentine, making him feel slightly nauseous. He fought the impulse to puke, laying his head back down on the soft pillows. That was when he felt the warmth of the body in bed with him. And then he remembered.

Oh, yeah. The lifeguard.

Suddenly, Francis was feeling a little better. He propped himself up on an elbow and admired the young man as he snoozed. Francis couldn't remember specific details about the tan young man, like his name, but he did remember some-thing about his being an ex-competitive surfer. Francis thought his name might be Dick, but he wasn't sure. It didn't matter. Who needs a name when you've got a chest like that, hairless and rippling with muscles, rock-hard biceps, and buns so tight you could bounce a quarter off them?

Francis grinned to himself, a big canary-gobbler of a smile, and wished he had a digital camera so he could take a picture and e-mail it to Chad. Francis thought about how he'd art-direct the photo so the pineapple tattooed on the humongous bicep was clearly visible. That, coupled with the broad shoulders and shaved head, would be enough to send Chad into a spasm of jealous rage.

He wrote the e-mail in his mind. *Dear Chad: Look what I just fucked. Sorry you couldn't be here to watch! Aloha!*

Francis realized he had to take a piss so, trying not to wake Dick, he crawled gingerly out from under the covers and tiptoed toward the bathroom. Feeling a sharp pain in his foot as he stood up, he looked down at the floor and saw a coconut-shell bra and a plastic grass skirt strewn on the carpet. Around them were the shattered remains of what looked to have been a cheap ukulele. Francis sat down on the bed and picked the ukulele splinter out of his foot. He stretched his neck from side to side and tried to remember. Had he been wearing a hula outfit? How did the ukulele get smashed, had he fallen on it?

Careful where he stepped, he went into the bathroom, flicked on the light—which was much too bright—and studied himself in the mirror. He didn't remember partying that much—a half a Quaalude, a couple of mai tais, and a bottle of wine with dinner—but man, he looked like he'd been run over by a truck. Francis was suddenly struck by a horrible thought. Maybe he was too old to be doing this. That would suck, wouldn't it?

He fished a couple of Advils out of his Dopp kit and washed them down with some Evian provided by the hotel. He wasn't too old. He was just out of shape. He hadn't been carousing in years. And when was the last time he'd been fucked like that? Possibly never. When was the last time he dressed up like a hula girl and had a lifeguard save him?

Definitely never. No, he wasn't too old. He just had to get back in the swing of things.

He was sitting on the toilet when the phone rang. It was his assistant, that Asian girl, reminding him, in an insufferably chipper voice, that they had brunch with the union reps in a half hour.

Six

Waimanalo Beach was empty. It was too far from the big hotels on Waikiki for tourists to bother with and most of the locals were already at work, so Joseph had the place to himself as he jogged on the hard wet sand near the edge of the water. He liked the way the cool sand felt on his bare feet, enjoyed the occasional slap and curl of sea foam around his ankles. He looked out at the water, clear and blue and mottled green and dark and sparkling, all at the same time. He was surprised there were no surfers out, but maybe they were all up north riding the monsters at Pipeline or even better, to his thinking, in school.

A large wave rolled up onto the beach, slamming into an outcropping of rocks and sending a thick foamy spray fifteen feet up in the air. Joseph jogged through it, letting the water rain down on him, feeling its cool salt caress. This was something he'd miss. Actually, there was a lot he'd miss: the air, the fresh fish, the pineapples and papayas. He realized he could find tropical fruit in New York City, quite possibly fresh fish as well. But you couldn't buy this quality of sunlight or smell the salt spray, no matter how exclusive the boutiques in Soho.

Joseph was ambivalent. Sometimes he felt claustrophobic, living on a small island where everyone knew everyone; other times he couldn't think of a more beautiful place to be. So he waffled and flip-flopped, debating the pros and cons in his mind until the weight of the decision became too much and he had to push it out of his brain. But this was the chance of a lifetime. Working at one of New York City's top Italian restaurants, cooking with the finest ingredients available, honing his skills, gleaning secrets, and learning how to run a real kitchen. For Joseph it was like being plucked out of obscurity to play shortstop for the Yankees.

It was his lucky break. The chef, a large and boisterous American who'd spent several near-monastic years cooking in the Italian countryside to perfect his skills, had been in Honolulu to film an episode of a Japanese TV series that pits celebrity chefs against each other in a cooking battle. Joseph and his uncle were handling the catering for the crew. Joseph was in the truck grilling fresh *moi* when he noticed the chef watching him. *Moi,* it turns out, is similar to *branzino,* and the chef was impressed with Joseph's skills. He tasted one of the fish and offered Joseph a job at his Manhattan restaurant on the spot. Joseph told the chef he'd think about it, and to be honest that's all he'd been doing ever since.

Not that he'd made up his mind. He had a good job, a job he loved. He had a girlfriend. He had his family and the friends he'd known all his life. He had everything that anyone would ever want, and yet he was anxious to leave.

Joseph had thought about seeing a psychiatrist. But that's just the problem, isn't it? Oahu is a small island. Everyone knows everyone. As soon as he told the shrink he was thinking about leaving, his nana and his uncle would be all over him to stay. And what about Hannah? Shouldn't he marry her? Didn't he owe it to her after all this time?

Thoughts of scents, flavors, and tastes beyond the Pacific horizon taunted him. He wanted to eat Mexican food in Mexico. Curry in Bombay. Green papaya salad from a street vendor in Bangkok. He wanted to go to Paris and have a twelve-course dinner at a three-star restaurant. He wanted to drink cava in a bar in Barcelona. He wanted to taste the world. How could he be a great chef if he didn't explore the world? And how could he explore the world if he was stuck on this tiny little island? Yet why would he want to leave such a unique and beautiful place where he lived surrounded by friends, family, and loved ones?

...

Yuki hung up the phone and shook her head. Why was her boss such a raving asshole? Why did he have to be so snide, so dismissive? Was Francis one of those homosexuals who carried his animosity toward the straight world like a big flaming chip on his shoulder? Maybe he was just self-absorbed and hostile, but either way it hurt her feelings. She considered herself very open-minded regarding matters of sexual preference, and she had lots of gay friends to prove it.

She tried to think of anything she might have done to upset him. She was nothing but professional. Well, maybe she had been overly enthusiastic on the plane. Maybe she'd talked too much. But she was excited. This was her first big job. She remembered that he snapped at her when she went up and complained to the flight attendant about the lack of fresh air. But that wasn't just for her, that was for everyone. Somebody had to make a stand.

Yuki picked a couple of strawberries off her plate as she walked to the balcony and looked out at the sea. It was a beautiful day, maybe the most beautiful day she'd ever seen. The air was superclean, sunlight bouncing off the silver-blue water. She couldn't believe the clarity of the light, the way it made the colors so strong. The grass was the purest green, the sky Superman-blue. Even the sand was an amazing fresh wheat color, like really good bread. The few specks of clouds on the horizon were whiter than bleached cotton.

The palm trees jiggled in the breeze. A little black bird with a vibrant scarlet head landed on her balcony and pecked at some crumbs. Yuki inhaled deeply, an oxygen rich, cleansing breath. She exhaled. So this is paradise. How could Francis be such a jerk when outside his room was heaven on earth? She found herself growing agitated and reached for the phone. Her life coach would know what to do.

It took her a few minutes to detail what had happened on the plane to David. Even her life coach had to admit that Francis had behaved badly when he made her take a shuttle bus from the airport to the hotel while he drove off in a rental car. But he told her to look at it from all sides. Maybe Francis had somewhere to go and didn't feel comfortable taking her with him. He reminded Yuki to be compassionate, like the bodhisattva. If she could understand the forces that made Francis the way he was, she could learn a lot from him. David reminded her of something the Dalai Lama said: *Sometimes the greatest teacher is someone who treats us badly. Then we can learn about ourselves as we try to overcome the obstacles in our path.* David suggested that she remain as positive as possible and use aromatherapy oils to cleanse her aura every night.

Yuki thanked him and hung up. Maybe he was right about Francis. Maybe having an asshole boss was her karma. She had to deal with it and learn from it before she could have a breakthrough.

Francis was a piece of work. Yuki could tell he was filled with negative energy. But where had it come from? No one is born like that. She'd have to be wary, careful not to let his negativity infect her. She went to her suitcase and pulled out a crystal necklace and some aromatherapy oils. The crystal would charge and protect her heart chakra while perhaps a dab of lavender on her neck would send out a soothing vibe.

She also decided to toss some rosemary oil in her hair to help cleanse her aura, a little ylang-ylang on her wrists, and a splash of peppermint on her blouse to give her energy and patience.

She wondered if it might be too much.

Yuki lit some incense and gave herself an affirmation. She set a goal. She was going to do whatever it took to turn Francis to the light. She would get him to embrace his positive Buddha nature. This was her mission.

...

Jack couldn't help it; her ass was just too fine. He kept his eyes glued to the sweet round chunk of booty as the flight attendant bent over, handing some guy a couple rows up a drink with a paper umbrella and a piece of pineapple dangling off the edge. Jack traced the outline of her panties against the blue sweep of her skirt with his eyes. It's not like it made him hard. That was a given.

Jack's eyes followed her as she worked her way through the cabin. Stanley sat in the next seat, complaining about flying first class.

"Slippers? What are they for?"

"Comfort, you nimrod."

"It's such a waste. We paid triple coach for slippers?"

Jack wondered about his son. Who complains about flying first class? It wasn't just the slippers that made it better. Check out the flight attendants in the front of the plane: young, blond, and looking like they were poured into their uniforms. You want to fly with frightening-looking biddies with hairy moles sprouting out of their chins? Take a seat in economy.

The flight attendant came up to Jack and looked down at him. "Would you like a cocktail? Mai tai or piña colada?"

Jack smiled up at her. "Fruity drinks are for fruity fellas. Gimme a beer."

As he said that he adjusted himself on the seat so a blind person would've noticed his enlarged and turgid cock straining against the fabric of his pants. The flight attendant noticed.

"Are you having trouble with your tray table?"

Jack grinned at her. "It won't go down."

She smiled at him, a detached, slightly condescending smile that indicated she'd had about enough of assholes like him and would quit tomorrow if only her husband hadn't lost all their money in the stock market.

"Let me."

The tray table banged down, the drink and tiny bowl of mixed nuts soon after, and then she was gone.

Stanley looked at his dad. "Why'd you do that?"

"What?"

"Flirt with her."

"I had a stroke, Stanley. I'm not dead."

"You offended her."

"That's what you think."

"She forgot about me because you bugged her."

"He who hesitates becomes lunch."

Stanley hated when his dad said that. A pout spread across his face. "I'm thirsty."

Jack turned away; he couldn't stand the whining. Stanley was never a good traveler. Even in first fucking class he was whining about not getting a drink when all he had to do was push the little button on the armrest and the chick with the sweet ass would be hustling down the aisle to attend to his every whim. Why couldn't Stanley figure that out? A monkey could do it.

Jack sipped his beer. It was cold and slid gently down his throat, cleaning the airplane air out of his mouth, leaving a sweet and sour aftertaste on his tongue. He was happy. This move was genius. Sure, it'd been a big investment, almost a million bucks. But he'd done it before and—except for the disappointment of Seattle—it'd worked out well. You had to take a risk if you wanted to grow. What was the cliché, break eggs to make an omelet? Jack didn't like omelets—steak and eggs was more his kind of breakfast—but he knew that pussies stood pat while the gambler hit—except on seventeen. It was the only way to beat the house. Sometimes you just gotta lay your ass on the line. That's how he took his father's lunch truck business in Detroit and made it the success it was. He spent years feeding Teamsters on construction sites until he discovered the big money in feeding Teamsters on a movie set.

Jack's dad's relationships with the AFL-CIO paid off when Jack moved the company to Las Vegas. He muscled out a little guy—not without a fight, of course. The little guy turned out to be resourceful and have some connections himself. They were mostly Hollywood connections—something Jack hadn't developed at the time—and for a while there Jack was worried. But then he hired a fixer, who took care of things the old-fashioned way. The scrappy little guy died of carbon monoxide poisoning in his catering truck, and that, as they say, was that.

After Las Vegas, Seattle and Portland had been a cinch. Moving into Honolulu was just the next logical step in Jack's long-term business plan.

Jack had had to take out a loan for most of it, using his house as collateral. But it was worth it. The trucks and gear had landed two weeks ago and been stashed in a warehouse. No one knew what was in them; no one knew what they were for. He had put Lucey Truck Sales on the manifest. Any long-shoreman or AFL-CIO member taking a casual interest would think Jack was opening a truck dealership on the island. That was how he liked to do it. Stealthily. In the dead of night. Don't let the competition know you're there until it's too late. Before they knew what hit them, Jack and Company would be out of the gate: locking up jobs, hiring the best drivers, and basically showing the locals how the big boys did things.

Stanley waved to the flight attendant. Jack watched her breasts heave as she walked toward them.

Stanley ordered a glass of skim milk.

...

Wilson drove his father down the road toward Honolulu. Verdant hills, deep green and jungled up, rolled along, spilling down from the Kolekole Pass heading for Pearl Harbor and the ocean. Sid Tanumafili, a man with a body built like two linebackers gone to seed, adjusted his bulk in the seat of the Ford Explorer, brushed some donut crumbs off his XXL University of Hawaii sweatshirt, and turned to his son.

"What you know den?"

"No one can get in."

"We bust in."

"Alarms."

"Since when did dat stop anyone?"

"And dey got dogs."

"Give 'em some Spam an' Seconal."

"It's just some fuckin' trucks, Dad."

Sid Tanumafili knew it wasn't just some fucking trucks. He wasn't born yesterday. He didn't maintain his grip on the business through blind luck. He knew who Jack Lucey was, and he had a pretty good idea what he was up to.

"You talk to Joseph?"

"He went out fo' a run."

"What he say den?"

"Nobody gonna drive fo' dem, man. Nobody gonna cook fo' dem. Dey're fucked."

"He say dat?"

Wilson shifted in his seat. "Not exact like, no."

"What he say den?"

Wilson's face flushed. "How come you only care wot fo' Joseph say? Don' I count?"

Sid didn't answer. What was he going to tell him, *No, you're my son but you're an idiot?* Better not to say anything. Sid pulled his cell phone out of his sweatpants and speed-dialed his nephew.

...

Francis could smell her from down the hall. What was she wearing, burnt patchouli? It made him want to light a clove cigarette just to counter the stench. He watched as Yuki came bounding down the corridor, a bright smile on her face and some kind of grotesque chunk of rock dangling from her neck, banging into her flat chest. Francis checked to see if she was wearing Birkenstocks. She was.

"Good morning!"

Francis grimaced. Only a retard is this cheerful. "Let's go."

"Sleep well?"

Francis didn't respond.

"Is your room comfortable?"

"It's fine."

"I slept great. Must be the fresh air, all those ions from the ocean. Did you see the ocean? Can you believe the view? Isn't it fantastic?"

It was going to be a long morning.

They entered the hotel restaurant, with its sweeping view of the ocean and landscaped lawn, and sat down in a blindingly sunny booth. Francis couldn't take the brilliance while his brain was still struggling to escape the full nelson of a World Wrestling Federation–sized hangover, so he popped his sunglasses on. That was better. He toyed with the idea of ordering a Bloody Mary for breakfast, hair of the dog, but thought better of it. That would be like admitting he had a problem.

The smelly girl pushed her menu away and looked at him. "I already ate. I had some fruit in my room."

Francis looked at the menu.

"After I do my meditation, I like to eat fresh fruit."

"That's nice."

"It's good for your body, you know? Gives you a fresh feeling."

Francis wondered if he could fire her. Send her home with a severance package and a couple of pineapples. Take her high-fiber, low-fun, sunshine-fresh feeling and send it packing.

"Don't you just love it here?"

He looked over at her and forced the sides of his mouth to rise up in a creaky, painful imitation of a smile.

"It's great."

Although it was an almost superhuman effort, Francis was glad he'd done it. It made her day. She positively twinkled, like a disco ball.

"The papayas are superdelish. Try one."

"Okay. I will."

...

Hannah pulled her long black hair back into a ponytail and wrapped a rubber band around it to keep it that way. She turned, revealing the golden-brown nape of her neck, faced the blackboard, and wrote the word KAMAPUA'A on the board. She immediately heard titters from her class of ninth-graders. It was like that every year she taught this section of the

Kumulipo, the Hawaiian creation myth. Certain stories in Hawaiian mythology were funny, but the myth of Kamapua'a, the Hog God, was the one that got the kids going. Hannah knew why. The Hog God had been a playboy. Naughty and hedonistic, licentious and lustful, allegedly endowed with a "snout of great size," he was the one—along with Kanaloa, the evil-smelling Octopus God—that captured their imagination.

Hannah wasn't that much older than her students, and she remembered her own grueling hours spent attempting to memorize the lineage of the Hawaiian gods. Who gave birth to whom and when and what form of animal, vegetable, or mineral they became. It was complicated, difficult. She was glad they could laugh and enjoy it.

Hannah had studied Hawaiian history and language in college; it had made her feel special, proud to be Hawaiian. She decided to make it her personal mission to keep the culture alive and that's what she was doing; she was teaching Hawaiian. Her father, a former navy pilot who had gone on to fly commercial jets for Aloha Airlines, was always offering to put in a good word for her, and frankly she could've earned twice the money working as a flight attendant. But she believed her work was important, which gave her a feeling of satisfaction a big paycheck couldn't match. All the classes at Ke Kula Kaiapuni'o Anuenue were taught in Hawaiian. It was a pilot language-immersion program, one of only a handful in the state, and she was one of the dedicated teachers working to make the experiment a success.

Hannah turned just in time to see Lisa Nakashima, the troublemaker, trying to pass a note to Liliana Morrison, her accomplice in class disruption. Hannah intercepted the note and unfolded the paper to reveal a crude drawing of Kamapua'a, the Hog God, looking a lot like Porky Pig with a gigantic erection. Hannah couldn't help herself; she smiled.

...

The union reps arrived, one of them looking like that guy in *Goldfinger* who throws the hat—oh, yeah, Oddjob—the other some weasely Caucasian dude in a shirt that looked like it was made out of irradiated hibiscus blossoms. Francis was glad he'd kept his sunglasses on.

"You Frank?"

"Francis."

"People call you Frank?"

"Not really."

The two men stood there, Teamster tough, glaring at the faggot from Hollywood and his smelly assistant.

Francis pointed to Yuki. "This is my assistant."

He kicked himself for not remembering the smelly girl's name. But she helped him out; she stood up and extended her hand.

"Yuki Sugimoto."

The Caucasian spoke. "Joe Ward."

They all shook hands. Then it was Oddjob's turn.

"Ed Huff."

There was nothing friendly or open in the greetings. It wasn't nice to meet them. It wasn't a pleasure. Joe and Ed came with one mission in mind: to get the full hourly rate for their union members. They were sick and tired of constantly cutting deals and dropping overtime or—worse—eliminating golden time, where the union members made double their hourly rate. This time they were going to dig in their heels. Pay full freight or film your stupid movie-of-the-week in Thailand.

Francis wasn't intimidated; he had dealt with men like these many times. They represented the grunts, the boots-on-the-ground of movie production. The men who drove the trucks, unloaded the equipment, and then sat around eating and playing cards until it was time to pack everything up and drive off to the next location. They were the first to arrive and the last to leave. You couldn't do a shoot without them, and if you didn't keep them happy they could really fuck you over. They could start running late; there could be a problem with the trucks; they could get lost or, worse, just slow down. These kinds of things could cost a production tens of thousands of dollars in lost days. The last thing a producer like Francis—a line producer whose job was to see that everything is where it should be when it's supposed to be—wanted was to lose a day of shooting because of grumpy grips and pissed-off Teamsters.

"Please, have a seat."

Yuki got up and moved around to sit next to Francis, the proximity to her fragrance sending a volcanic rush of bile into his throat, almost killing him with aromatherapy, as Joe and Ed squeezed into the booth.

"Hungry? It's on me."

"Just coffee."

Joe leaned in. He didn't want to waste time. "What're we lookin' at?"

"Six weeks prep, twenty-eight-day shoot."

"How many trucks you think you're gonna need?"

The coffee arrived. Francis ordered half a papaya to start and then, figuring he'd need some protein to replace what he lost last night, ordered an omelet and a side of bacon. He sipped his coffee and smiled to himself. The side of bacon had been an afterthought, a little fuck-you to his psychic nutritionist, his personal trainer, his dermatologist, his cardiologist, and best of all to Chad. Chad had a fear of pork. As if a little plaque in the arteries or an extra decimal point of body fat was the worst thing that could ever happen to a person.

"A full complement. We're going to put a lot of your men to work on this one."

Joe and Ed were instantly suspicious. "Yeah?"

Francis nodded and sipped his coffee. Joe and Ed sipped their coffee. Yuki took out a notepad and a mechanical pencil.

Joe shot her a look. "What's that for?"

"I thought I might need to take notes."

Joe turned to Francis. "We're not making any concessions."

Francis smiled. He'd been waiting for this. "I'm not asking for any deals."

"You're paying full freight." It was not a question.

"Absolutely."

Francis thought he saw Ed's shoulders relax.

"The last time your studio was here they killed us with concessions."

"That was last time."

Joe continued to eye him suspiciously. Francis sipped his coffee.

"Look. I'll level with you guys. This is a short job, an easy job, and the studio decided they didn't want any headaches. This thing goes to series and we're here on a permanent basis—well, then I'd imagine someone from business affairs would come and renegotiate."

Joe and Ed nodded conspiratorially, as if they'd just been let in on some valuable corporate secret.

"What about overtime?"

"Overtime, golden time. We go over, you get paid."

"Meal penalties?"

"If we owe you a meal, you'll get a meal. We're bringing in a catering company, one of the best. Your guys are gonna eat prime rib until their arteries explode."

Joe and Ed exchanged puzzled looks. "You're not using Sid?"

Francis looked at them. "Who's Sid?"

"Everybody uses Sid. There's only one caterer on the island."

Francis adjusted his sunglasses. "Well, now there's two."

Joe and Ed frowned. "Our guys like to eat local."

"Local? What do you mean?"

"Spam an' eggs, *loco moco,* poi. You know? Local."

Francis shrugged. "He'll cook whatever you want."

Yuki looked at the men. "Excuse me for interrupting, but wouldn't it be better if your men ate a healthier diet? I mean, really, who knows what's in Spam?"

Ed looked at her. "Belly buttons and assholes."

Yuki made a face and went back to minding her own business.

Joe turned to Francis. "What's the name of this outfit?"

"It's Jack Lucey out of Las Vegas."

Joe nodded soberly. "I've heard of him."

The half papaya arrived. Francis squirted some lime juice on it, careful to shoot a little of it in Joe and Ed's direction. He scooped up a spoonful.

"I've worked with him before. He's quite a character."

Seven

Hannah sat in Joseph's kitchen and drank a cup of coffee. She was on her lunch break and still had time before she had to go back to work, so she relaxed, enjoying herself. She sat back and put her feet up on the table. Even though she was dressed in her school-teacher outfit, a pair of navy slacks and a buttoned pink and white striped blouse, she slouched in the chair, letting wrinkles grow like weeds on her freshly pressed clothes.

She was Hawaiian, with black hair and beautiful brown skin, her black eyes twinkling out of a delicate moon-shaped face. Her body was thin—her mother thought this to be evidence of some Japanese ancestry—and she had small, beautifully rounded breasts like the Tahitian women in paintings by Gauguin. Stuffed into professional clothes, she felt like a fraud, not like a native Hawaiian but like any Asian salary woman working for a big corporation in Tokyo or Singapore.

Hannah had always chafed under the school's dress code. This was supposed to be laid-back Hawaii, the Aloha State, where even the governor wore sandals and an aloha shirt to work. But the school administration wanted the faculty to appear crisp and professional. Perhaps there was some logic to it. If the teachers stood around chatting in Hawaiian dressed like hippies and surfers, it might give the wrong impression. They were under enough pressure as it was.

The No Child Left Behind law demanded English proficiency as a sign of a good school—as if speaking a native language somehow meant you weren't as smart as kids in Connecticut. It was a big bunch of mainland bullshit. But it meant they were constantly forced to test their kids, allow auditors to come and watch the classes, and put up with all kinds of bureaucratic indignities.

Hannah sipped her coffee and looked around the kitchen. She liked it when she stayed over at Joseph's house. It was immaculate, almost compulsively clean, compared to her house; there were no mounds of dirty laundry dotting the landscape like those termite hills in West Africa, no stacks of magazines, books, and newspapers covering every available inch of counter space. Joseph's house was antiseptically spotless, as if he expected the health department to arrive any minute for a surprise inspection.

Joseph would pick up after her. Put her laundry in the hamper, recycle the newspapers, and clean the dirty dishes that she stacked in the sink. He used to joke, as he put her sweatpants in the wash, that it was nice to have a woman's touch around the place. Hannah liked him to pick up after her. It showed he cared. He spoiled her that way.

Hannah's black eyes twinkled as she heard Joseph come into the house. "You want some coffee?"

Joseph shook his head and bent down to give her a kiss. "Sid just called. He's flipping out about something."

"Call me later."

Joseph looked at her, slouching in the chair with her feet up. "You're gonna wrinkle your clothes, sitting like that."

Hannah smiled. "I know."

...

Jack couldn't believe it. Didn't any white people live here? What was wrong with this place? Isn't this supposed to be America? Everywhere he looked there were Chinese-looking island people going about their business. Even some of the signs were in Chinese or Japanese or something. They might as well be in Hong Kong.

The white people, people like Jack, stuck out like the sunburned Hawaiian-shirt-wearing bumpkins they were. They weren't from around here. They were from Michigan and North Carolina, Kansas and Oregon, Ohio and Minnesota. They'd come all this way, to the middle of nowhere—the single most isolated group of islands in the massive Pacific Ocean— for some sun. They looked like they'd got it, too. Skin peeling off their noses, their foreheads and necks the color of boiled lobsters, Day-Glo gaudy shirts draped over beef-fed guts, and stick legs as white as a picket fence back home.

"We need to get some sunscreen."

"I got some. SPF thirty."

"Is that good?"

"Yeah. I think it is."

"I don't wanna look like these French-fried mother-fuckers."

"Wear a hat."

"Drive, will ya? I'm roasting in here."

Stanley cranked up the AC. "Better?"

"Just hurry up."

Stanley was driving. This meant they crawled along as slowly as possible; stopping for every little thing they could stop for. Jack wondered if Stanley had ever run a yellow light in his life. The car lurched to a stop the nanosecond the light turned yellow. Nope. But then Stanley had never had an accident, either.

The constant stopping and painstakingly glacial maneuvering was tedious; in fact, it bugged the shit out of Jack. If he'd watched *Oprah* or had any kind of psychological training, he would've recognized that Stanley's driving was passive-aggressive behavior designed to make him crazy. And it did; it drove him nuts.

"Drive. Please."

"Look at the traffic."

"I can see it. It's all going past us."

"You want to drive?"

That was a rhetorical question. In Las Vegas, Jack drove. He didn't even like to have Stanley ride in the same car. But the car rental agency wouldn't let Jack drive in Honolulu. Stroke survivors weren't allowed on the insurance plan. This was news to Jack, and it really pissed him off. The clerk—she looked Chinese but her name tag said GAYLE-ANNE—had stood there, not a drop of aloha in her manner, not even pretending to be friendly, and told them that only Stanley could drive. She said the word *liability* over and over again. Loud and slow. Like Jack was a retard. As if *he* was the liability.

Jack made sure to bang his walker against the side of the Lincoln a few times just to show them what kind of liability a cripple could be.

So Stanley was at the wheel, the demonically sluggish pace giving Jack plenty of time to check out the city.

Jack saw a sign that read: LA FEMME NU. It had all the graphic nuance of strip club signage. But what language was that? Maybe the D and E were burned out. Jack smiled to himself. Maybe this town will be all right after all. A strip club. Wonder what those Chinese chicks look like bangin' their pussies against a pole?

He'd come back later, after he'd dumped Stanley at the hotel, and find out. But first they had work to do.

...

Francis needed to lie down. He desperately needed an hour of sleep and perhaps a hit of Xanax just to take the edge off. His body shook and quivered; he looked and felt like a palsy-riddled octogenarian as he made his way down the corridor toward his room.

The stress of keeping it together while dealing with the Teamsters, coupled with the reek coming off the Asian girl, had been too much. He'd thought that having a good hearty breakfast might turn the tide against the relentless pounding of his hangover, but all he'd really accomplished was to give himself a barbaric case of indigestion and greasy pork-product burps. There was actually one point where he thought he might lose it and launch a Technicolor yawn all over the table. But he was a grown-up. He maintained.

He carefully opened the door to his room and crept in. He was hoping the lifeguard was still there; instead, it looked like a grenade had gone off. Not only was there broken glass, apparently a bottle of Barbancourt rum, and splinters from the smashed ukulele, but all the dresser drawers had been pulled out and overturned and their contents strewn around in a frenzy of looting. Francis saw that his suitcase had been upended on the bed and then tossed out onto the balcony.

He walked into the bathroom and noticed that his prescriptions of Xanax and Valium were missing, as well as some extremely expensive vitamins Chad had given him. The vitamins had been custom-mixed by his nutritionist to help him cope with the stress of his job. Had Chad fucked the nutritionist, too?

Francis saw his carry-on bag sitting in the bathtub, its guts dumped out and rifled through. His digital camera was gone, as well as his cell phone and Palm Pilot. For the first time it occurred to Francis that perhaps the young man was not an actual lifeguard. Good thing he'd stuffed his laptop, a wad of per diem, and a few hits of really good E in the little safe tucked in the closet. At least it wasn't a total loss.

Francis was suddenly desperate for a cocktail, so he opened the minibar—miraculously untouched—and searched for some vodka and orange juice. He found something called POG that looked like orange juice, and after reading the ingredients, learned that it contained some orange juice among the papaya and guava, and mixed it with a little bottle of Absolut.

It tasted pretty good, actually. He washed four Advils down with it, draining it completely, before slumping backward onto the semidemolished bed and cracking his head on the coconut-shell bra that had been hiding in the mess.

He felt a lump growing on the back of his head. He knew he should put some ice on it but couldn't find the energy to move. Instead, he felt a certain jolt of satisfaction fill him. Here he was, wasted and fucked, ripped off and robbed, feeling like death warmed over. It hurt. But he was partying. Getting down and dirty and having fun. All the things Chad said he couldn't do. That was always the reason Chad gave for his infidelities. Francis was just an old stick-in-the-mud. He didn't know how to have a good time.

Francis was determined to prove him wrong. Here he was in Honolulu giving as good as he got. And he was just getting started.

...

Joseph arrived at the office, an immaculately clean yet ramshackle kind of warehouse filled with stacks of equipment, much of it nonfunctional and piling up in the far corners. There was an industrial kitchen with boxes of canned goods stacked on huge tables, all arranged around a massive stove salvaged from the old Canlis restaurant in Waikiki. Joseph found the Teamsters, Joe and Ed, standing around the coffeepot with his uncle. The Teamsters nodded sympathetically while Sid fumed.

"Fuckin' haole motherfucker."

Joe picked at his Styrofoam coffee cup while Ed looked at his feet and shrugged. "He's paying full freight."

Sid shot Joe a murderous look. "All de times I fix you pineapple fried rice —"

"What the fuck you want me to do, tell the membership they can't take the job?"

"Yes."

Ed cleared his throat and tried to reason with Sid.

"Our people are starvin'. They're livin' on food stamps, for chrissakes. What do you think they're gonna say if they find out we turned down a fat job like this? You gotta be reasonable, Sid."

Sid didn't feel like being reasonable. "Dey're gonna eat haole food. Mainland food. It's gonna kill 'em. Why fo' you wanna poison everybody?"

Ed and Joe shrugged. "You're the best. We know that. That's not the issue."

"Wot's the issue den?"

"We signed the contract."

Sid glared at them. "I never work a nonunion show. Never. You know dat."

Joe and Ed didn't have much to say to that. It was true that Sid never worked nonunion shows. It had been that way for years. If a nonunion show came to Oahu, they'd soon find that there was no way to feed their crews except making takeout runs from some nearby *okazu* or mom-and-pop puka. It was expensive, and not every crew member wanted a lunch of *musubi,* squid *laulau,* barbecue meat stick, or fried butterfish collars with rice.

The nonunion producers would whine; they would moan. They would talk about how Steven Spielberg was asking him, Sid, for a personal favor. But Sid didn't care, and since Steven Spielberg himself never called and asked for the favor—well, they could go fuck themselves.

The smart producers knew that if they wanted to film on the island it was cheaper and easier to go with the flow: unionize, pay the fee, get the food, and everybody's happy. You did whatever it took not to piss off the locals.

Sid wasn't the only one with a monopoly. It was one of the ways to survive, and each person in the little economic ecosystem helped the other. During boom times when there was plenty of work, Sid made sure that films and TV shows coming to the island used union employees, and the union made sure they ate only from Sid's trucks. Like the shark and the pilot fish, *mano* and *nenue,* it was a classic symbiotic relationship. Everybody worked; everybody prospered.

Besides, people on the mainland could afford it.

Joseph poured himself a cup of coffee and added a splash of condensed milk. The heavy white liquid swirled languidly, like pond scum, slowly turning the black coffee brown. Sid turned to Joseph.

"What you think den?"

Joseph sipped his coffee. "Let's go talk to them. They might need us."

Sid grimaced. "I don' wanna work wid dat fuckin' guy."

Joseph shrugged. He tried to be philosophical about these things. "He's got the job, we don't. Better to try and make something out of it."

"Better to burn dey trucks."

Joe and Ed recoiled. "We didn't hear that."

Ed seconded him. "We were never here."

And with that the two Teamsters set down their coffees and moved quickly out of the warehouse.

Joseph turned and looked at Sid. "You're not going to burn their trucks."

Sid looked at Joseph. "Wot you learn fo' in college den?"

"I'm just saying we go talk to the guy."

"Jack Lucey's a fuckin' scumbag. Dis is what he do. He moves inna territory and shoves da little guy out."

"We're not little. We're well established."

"He killed dat guy in Vegas."

"That's just a rumor. You don't know for sure. Let's talk to the producer. Maybe we can work something out."

Sid grumbled; he didn't like what was happening. Not at all. "Okay. We talk. Den we burn dey trucks."

...

The smell of failed deodorant filled the gym. Wilson, his body glistening with sweat, his veins roaring with blood, his lungs heaving, his muscles pumped up and expanded like a king cobra ready to strike, lay back on the bench press and rested. He listened to the rhythmic clank of metal on metal as the other men continued to lift.

Wilson was upset. He'd been hoping that a good work-out would calm him down, but it had only made him tired and angry. He didn't understand it. How come his dad made him leave when Joe and Ed showed up? What was so top se-cret that he couldn't hear? If there was a problem, he could fix it. That's what he did when he wasn't keeping the coffee hot on set or slicing bagels for the stand-ins.

In the nightclubs and discothèques he was the expert, the fixer. He made sure it was safe for the rich and beautiful, the hot and hunky. Wilson put the guys with the biggest bankroll with the babes with the hottest bods. He kept the dorks and retards outside, behind the rope. And if someone got drunk or caused trouble, he'd bash their face in.

These guys from Las Vegas were trouble, right? Why not just bash their faces in?

Wilson sat up and mopped his face with a towel. He felt his biceps, hard as stone. He smiled. These arms might come in handy.

He realized that he resented his cousin, Joseph. Joseph was always at the '*ahas,* the all-important powwows and big business meetings, while Wilson was excluded. He didn't know much about finance and loans and paperwork things, and he couldn't cook for shit, but that didn't mean he was stupid. He was supposed to be part of the family, the *ohana,* and part of the business. They should include him.

Wilson went into the locker room and bought a couple vials of anabolic steroids from a bodybuilder he knew. He went into a toilet stall and sat down. Wilson figured he might need the boost if he was forced to practice the ancient Hawaiian art of *lua* and break some poor fucker's bones. It's good to be prepared.

He carefully—and it was slippery because he was still sweaty—filled a new syringe with a double dip of the stuff and injected it into the muscles on his left calf. It burned going in. Although he liked the muscle mass he got from taking steroids, he didn't like the way it altered his mood, making him short-tempered and cranky. Normally he was pretty laid back.

...

Francis spread his new purchases, courtesy of an accommodating bellhop at the hotel, on top of his desk. A vial of Levitra, a six-pack of Viagra, and a gram of crystal meth; it was a good-time vacation party pack. He took a moment and surveyed the decrepit termite feeder of an office that served as production headquarters. A kind of fungus, the color of pureed iguana, grew freely from under the windowsill, slowly spreading across the dark brown paneling. The window was filmed with years of cigarette smoke residue, tinting the sunlight a carcinogenic hue, and the spattered brown carpet felt vaguely squishy underfoot. The brown-on-brown motif was carried further to include the curtains, ratty and scarred, and the cheap wood-grain Formica desk. Even the lamp was brown. It was like being inside a mushroom.

The place, however, had a Third World charm, and Francis liked it better than the soulless industrial parks he usually worked in. It was nothing like Chad's architectural marvel stuffed with expensive modern masterworks. There were no shoji-screen offices or modern concrete fountains in the foyer, no clever series of Ed Ruscha prints or massive Julian Schnabel paintings, no automatic espresso machine from Italy, and no handmade leather chairs from France. But hey, that's okay; look out the window, it's fucking Hawaii. He'd get some fresh orchids and it'd be fine.

That is, until Joseph and Sid came busting in.

Francis swept his treats into the desktop drawer and turned his attention to the two men. At first Francis didn't know what to make of them. There was the one who called himself Sid, standing there like a Sumo wrestler, huffing and puffing and all pissed off. Then there was the cute one, taking a step back, listening. Man, was he cute.

He ignored the big one, tuned him out. These guys are always the same: gimme, gimme, gimme. Francis was sick of hearing it. It was whining disguised as tough-guy talk. He'd heard it from the Teamsters in Miami. He'd heard it from the Gambino family when he did a movie in New York City. He'd heard it in San Francisco, Seattle, and Chicago. Every goddamn time he did a job it was some big fat tough guy telling him he owed it to them, to the locals, the union, the mafia, the fucking brotherhood-of-whatever. Pay up or else. Gimme, gimme, gimme. Who did they think he was, Santa Claus?

Francis kept his eye on the young one. He traced a line with his eyes from the handsome face to his articulated biceps to his firm pecs and down to the left-leaning bulge in the crotch of his pants. Francis felt a little tingle begin around his nipples. They stiffened.

As Francis continued to get aroused, Sid continued to rant and fume. Francis nodded, like he was listening, and then—this is what he always did—he passed the buck. It wasn't his decision. It came from the network. In fact, the deal had been done before he'd even been hired.

It was true, actually. Francis didn't know why he wasn't using the locals, but it wasn't his job to argue with his bosses; it was his job to do what they said.

He smiled at Joseph. "I understand how important this job is to you guys. Let me call my boss and see what I can do about it. How's that sound?"

The fat one seemed vaguely placated but couldn't resist a last little threat. "You don' want no trouble."

Francis nodded. No, he did not. He looked at the young one. "Maybe we can have a drink and talk about it. What do you think?"

Joseph nodded. "Anytime."

Joseph handed Francis his card. Very briefly Francis felt the young man's strong brown hand brush against his. His nipples got a tiny bit harder underneath his T-shirt, and his brain secreted a burst of hormone, giving his cock the green light to erectify.

"I'll be in touch."

Francis watched them as they left his office, his eyes locked on Joseph's ass as he walked away. Nice.

Francis smiled to himself. The day was looking up.

...

She'd spent her entire life surrounded by Caucasians. She spoke like a Caucasian, dressed like a Caucasian, lived like a Caucasian. She ate Caucasian food and dated Caucasian men. She may have been a resident of Caucasia, but Yuki Sugimoto wasn't Caucasian. She was a Japanese-American or, more accurately, an American of Japanese ancestry. Not that she felt that way. She didn't speak any Japanese, could hardly relate to her grandmother, who'd survived an internment camp in northern Utah, and didn't even like Japanese food. Sometimes she'd catch herself in the mirror, her Japanese face and black hair giving her a shock, a surprise, a momentary spark of something distinctly non-Caucasian. It was a feeling that there was more to her, something special, mysterious, and undefined, some exotic magic she hadn't discovered yet.

Occasionally she would meet people who were surprised that she was so Americanized. She always thought that strange. She was born and raised in California. Attended public high schools and UCLA. What could be more American? Was it just because her skin wasn't white? Her eyes weren't blue? Her hair wasn't blond?

It didn't take long for Yuki to understand why she felt so comfortable in Honolulu. From the moment she stepped off the plane she felt right at home. Everywhere she looked she saw echoes of herself. Almost everyone had some Asiatic features. Black hair, rice eyes. It was the Caucasians who stuck out in the crowd. For the first time in her life she was a member of the majority. Everyone looked like her, and she looked like everyone else. They were her age, they spoke English, watched lots of crappy television, and remembered the band Oasis. Only they didn't look like the majority on the mainland. Here she was the norm. How cool is that?

She had just pulled out her bundle of dried sage to purify the outer office of negative energy and bad spirits when a cute guy and a big guy came in demanding to see Francis. They didn't wait to be announced, they didn't want a cup of coffee or a bottle of mineral water, they just barged right in to Francis's office.

Yuki was worried that Francis would be mad at her, especially since the big guy was ranting and raving about some kind of betrayal of trust or something. She didn't know what he was talking about, really. She kept her eyes on the cute guy's back, just watching him. He wasn't like the big angry guy. In fact he wasn't like any guy she'd ever seen before. He was handsome, that's for sure, but also calm and thoughtful. A very cool guy, but with a kind of authority about him too. It reminded her of a movie she saw with Steve McQueen. He was a race-car driver or something. He didn't say much. He didn't have to. It was very attractive.

Yuki found herself watching Joseph's back and, for the first time in a long time, she let her mind ponder erotic possibilities.

...

Waikiki. This is it. Wall-to-wall tits and ass just layin' out there. Chicks in thong bikinis facedown on their beach towels, their bare ass cheeks oiled and glistening like fresh do-nuts coming off the line at Krispy Kreme. Girls jumping around in the waves, the cold water making their nipples pop underneath their bikini tops like some kind of come-fuck-me flare shot into the sky. Off to the side, Jack watched as statuesque young coeds played volleyball, their breasts arch-ing and heaving with each bump, set, spike.

Waikiki. No wonder it's famous.

Jack scuffled his walker to the edge of the patio; he didn't mind being in the sun if it gave him a better view of the action. He had a couple of hours to kill before his meet-ing with the line producer—some fairy that the network hired as a favor to some big shot. Not that it made any dif-ference to Jack. You want to have sex with another guy, cool; that just leaves more pussy for me. Besides, that was the way things worked in this business—in any business, really—friends hired friends and did favors for friends and friends of friends. You wanna make it in Hollywood? Make some fucking friends.

Stanley, who had gone horribly native in some kind of matching Hawaiian shirt-and-shorts ensemble, arrived at the table. He was carrying a couple of fruity-looking drinks with pineapple kebabs and paper umbrellas sticking out.

"I got you a mai tai."

Jack glared at his son. "I don't like fruity drinks."

Stanley shrugged and sat down. "C'mon, Dad. We're in Hawaii. We should at least try the local food."

"Smells like prune juice. And what in God's name are you wearing? You look like a fucking retard."

Stanley ignored his father and took a sip. He recoiled. "Wow. These are strong."

"How could anything with a fucking piece of fruit sticking out of it be strong?"

Jack figured that 7-Up might be too strong for Stanley, but he was curious and took a sip. He was surprised—in a good way—to feel the several different varieties of rum burning their way down his gullet. Maybe there was something to these local dishes after all. Jack put the glass down and took the pineapple kebab out, setting it in the ashtray. He flicked the paper umbrella onto the floor.

"Now it looks like a drink."

"You like it?"

Jack nodded as he knocked back half the mai tai in one long greedy gulp. "Get me another one. But without all the bells and whistles."

"You can have mine."

"I don't want yours. I want my own."

"I'm not going to drink it."

Jack wasn't going to argue. He signaled for the waitress. "You should, because if you're gonna dress like that you oughta at least be loaded."

...

Joseph pushed the scoop of macaroni salad to the far side of his plate. He nibbled at the grilled chicken and rice and listened as Sid continued to fume.

"No way! Dey not doin' it."

Wilson leaned over and looked at Joseph's plate. "You don't want your macaroni?"

"Help yourself."

"You sure?"

"Please. Take it."

Joseph treated macaroni salad as if it were laced with strontium 90. He couldn't understand how it had become a staple foodstuff of the Hawaiian Islands. Pasta and mayonnaise mixed with pickles, frozen peas, and potatoes: hardly indigenous food. High fat, low fiber; he avoided it at all costs. Yet it was everywhere you went in Honolulu. Joseph found himself ordering Vietnamese spring rolls and finding macaroni salad mounded alongside the spicy fish sauce. He'd get Korean bulgogi and there it was, nestled next to the rice. Somehow it had insinuated itself into Hawaiian life. Omnipresent macaroni salad. It was a mystery.

Joseph watched as Wilson forked a glistening mound of macaroni into his mouth.

"I love dis shit."

Sid looked at the two younger men. "You listenin'? Huh? Dis not important?"

"I just wanted his macaroni."

"We're listening, Uncle Sid."

Sid picked up his plate and shoved his scoop of macaroni onto his son's plate. "Dere. Happy? Now leave your cousin alone."

Joseph tried to calm Sid down. "It's okay, Uncle, I wasn't going to eat mine."

"Yeah? Good."

Sid grabbed Joseph's plate and scraped his macaroni onto Wilson's, right on top of the fried Spam and egg.

"Hey, watch da egg. I don' like fo' da yolk gettin' on da macaroni."

"Everybody happy? We all got wot we want fo' to eat on our plates den?"

Joseph and Wilson nodded. They weren't about to interrupt. Sid leaned in, talking in a tough conspiratorial voice. "I'm plannin' things."

Wilson forked a piece of Spam into his mouth as he tried to speak.

"We know, Dad. Break dey fuckin' legs. Torch dey fuckin' trucks."

Joseph watched as bright yellow yolk dripped off the vibrant-pink processed meat product onto Wilson's T-shirt. Sid leaned across the table and smacked Wilson on the forehead.

"Don't talk like dat. Dat's not how you do nothing."

"Wot den?"

"It start small. Little dings and dents in da doors. Let 'em make a couple insurance claims. Den some driver hits your second cousin's new car. Den dey's a lawsuit. Always late. Never on time. Little things. Drive 'em fuckin' nuts dat way."

Joseph didn't like the sound of that. "That'll make the union guys look bad."

"Da union owes me."

"I know they do, Uncle, but we're not going to get their help if we ask them to do things that make them look unprofessional. Then the next production that comes in will go nonunion. It's not a good idea."

Sid glared at Joseph. "You gotta better one den?"

Joseph didn't respond. The truth was, he didn't. "Let me think about it."

...

Francis crunched a small mound of crystal meth with his credit card. The tappy-tap-tap of credit card against glass reverberated through the room. That, he mused, is the sound of the eighties. Francis scraped the powder into a line, rolled up a ten-dollar bill, and snorted half the line into his right nostril. It burned, like stuffing a chunk of dry ice up his nose, but it felt good too, like some kind of adventure was beginning. He hoovered the other half of the line into his left nostril, stood up, and stretched.

What a day. Nothing but an unbroken chain of migraine-inducing minutiae layered with bullshit and stacked on top of the general incompetence of his underlings. Frost it with a hangover and decorate with gastrointestinal distress, and it was the cake of all clusterfucks. The shit everyone with a job eats every goddamn day.

He would've gone ballistic if the smelly girl hadn't managed to handle a couple of fuckups on her own. Francis appreciated that. Maybe she was going to work out after all. He made a mental note to learn her name.

He felt the amphetamines slowly creep into his system. His heartbeat picked up. His blood pressure rose. The fatigue that had hung around his neck all day like a gigantic cartoon anvil suddenly filled with helium and drifted off into the sky. The party lights in his brain popped on and the mirror ball began to spin. He felt alive.

The day hadn't been a total loss. He'd gotten a lot of the groundwork done, all the administrative crap required when you're preparing to land an invading army for a few months. He'd met a really cute guy. Obviously straight, but hey, like they say, every man has his price. And, as Francis recalled from his college days, it was usually just a couple of margaritas that got most straight men bent.

Francis remembered he still had a little bit of work to do: a business drink with the guys from Las Vegas. Some political smiling and glad-handing with the below-the-liners before he went out. Still, it was no reason not to get started with his evening.

He pulled on some freshly pressed slacks and checked his reflection in the mirror. He looked pretty good. Fit. Handsome. A roguish sunburn gracing his nose. He ran his fingers through his hair, just to make it look like he didn't care, and threw on a Hawaiian-style shirt he'd bought in the hotel gift shop. He studied himself again, turning sideways to check his profile, and realized something was missing.

He took the bottle of pills off the dresser and shook them out into his hand. He decided on a Levitra first, because they work twice as fast as Viagra, and popped one in his mouth. Then he realized he was planning for a long night and didn't want the Levitra to wear off, so he popped a Viagra as backup.

By the time the elevator doors opened and the sweet sound of Hawaiian music welcomed him to the patio bar, the vardenafil/sildenafil citrate/methamphetamine cocktail had kicked in like a mofo. His cock stood upright in his pants, huge and throbbing, like a missile ready to launch. If he hadn't had the Hawaiian shirt hanging untucked in front, he was sure his penis would've been peeking out, taking in the scene. He was having difficulty walking, and his brain was firing signals at hyper-speed, making him feel hot and itchy and aroused.

At the far end of the patio, Francis saw the guys from Las Vegas waving to him. He'd worked with them before—not that he really remembered them, but he recognized them.

They were the guys who handled the production catering. Slopping up bad greasy food to complement the long hours and bowel-stirring anxiety that were the stock-in-trade of film-making. These were the guys the locals had their panties in a twist about.

Francis walked toward them, his cock rubbing against his pants with every step, getting harder and harder, the friction exciting the nerves, the nerves sending a signal to the brain, the neurotransmitters and neuropeptides in the brain telling his heart to beat faster and faster, sending oxygenated blood to his genitals and releasing serotonin. Francis smiled, he couldn't help himself; it was too funny. He was just trying to walk and he was about to erupt. He wasn't sure he could hold it back if it came. He hoped no innocent bystander would get sticky.

But Francis's arousal was short-lived. He was shocked back to his senses when Jack pulled himself to his feet to greet him. Maybe he shouldn't have looked, but it was a force of habit. Francis couldn't help but see the unmistakable outline of a big stiff water snake bulging out of Jack's pants.

The two men stood shaking hands, their erections straining toward each other like twin fingers of God.

...

Hannah sat on the sofa, grading her students' responses to a pop quiz she'd given that afternoon, as Joseph cooked in the kitchen. Occasionally he would peek out and see the piles of papers slowly spreading across his floor like an oil slick in an Alaskan bay. Although he was used to her wanton organizational habits, the way she took over the living room—really, the only room of his small wood-frame house except for the kitchen and bedroom—alarmed him. How could they ever live together?

Joseph liked his place neat, clean, and uncluttered. His home was sparsely decorated; he didn't have a lot of stuff. Just a nice modern couch with a kind of fake-bamboo looking wood trim around it, a rattan coffee table made in Thailand, two mismatched wooden chairs, and some funky lamps shaped like angry tiki gods that he'd found in a trash heap of set-dressing debris after a movie shoot. A battered old restaurant sign hung on the wall. Hand-painted, chipped, and faded, dating back to sometime around the attack on Pearl Harbor, it read: FAMILY STYLE—PLATE LUNCH—COCONUT SHRIMP. Amateurish doodles of dancing shrimp were festooned around the sign, dotting the edges.

He watched uneasily as the pop-quiz answer sheets spread across the room, covering every available surface. Even the brand-new television in the corner had become a repository for the blizzard of paperwork.

Hannah concentrated on her work, unaware that the grimy soles of her feet were smack against an ecru pillow and an open pen was resting dangerously close to the cushions.

"Watch the pen."

"What?"

"The pen. If the tip touches the fabric, it'll make a big spot."

Hannah capped the pen. His compulsions annoyed her. "I'm trying to finish up."

She turned back to her work as Joseph looked around his living room. The house wasn't much, he had to admit, but he'd been lucky to buy it a few years back before the boom in housing prices would've made this tiny, 800-square-foot cottage unaffordable. Located in a narrow valley on the other side of the freeway from a part of Honolulu called Kaimuki, it was a pretty part of the city, quiet and friendly, and he was in walking distance to the university on the off chance something interesting might be going on there. Now it was worth almost three times what he'd paid.

Joseph went back into the kitchen and took the taro greens out of the steamer. He divided them between two plates next to thick slabs of *hamachi* he'd seared quickly in a skillet so it would be blackened on the outside, sashimi-raw in the middle. He hated overcooked fish and didn't understand why people would ruin something by grilling the life out of it. When he cooked for mainlanders, which happened frequently in his line of work, they were always sending the fish back to be cooked a little more, turning something tender and sensual and moist into a dried-up, chewy thing. It was bizarre. What were they afraid of?

He dribbled soy sauce on the taro, put the plates on the table, and called out to Hannah. "Dinner's ready. You want a glass of wine?"

"Sure."

She tossed a stack of ungraded tests onto the coffee table and came in to join him.

"Smells great."

Joseph uncorked the wine, a pinot blanc from Australia, and poured two glasses. "Thanks."

She pulled out a chair and sat down. "Someday you'll make someone a great little wife."

She liked to tease him about his homemaking skills. As if being able to cook and keep your house clean was somehow anti-male. He'd been to her house. He'd seen the heaps of dirty laundry and the cardboard box filled with empty beer cans. Did he tease her when she liked to spend her Saturdays watching the University of Hawaii football team? Was that unfeminine? Of course, she could live like a frat boy and then squeeze into a bikini, and there was no mistaking the fact that she was a woman.

"You're just jealous."

Hannah gave him a wry smile. "I am."

She tore into the fish with her chopsticks, picking up chunks and popping them in her mouth. Joseph watched her eat. He liked that she had a big appetite. He believed you could learn a lot about people from watching them eat. How a woman eats can tell you a lot about what she's like in bed. For example, someone who is super picky about her food, someone who eats slowly and makes sure to trim off all the fat, would probably be prim and controlling in bed. Too rigid, lacking imagination. While someone who bolts down their food in a big, gluttonous frenzy might be fun in the short term, but they are usually selfish lovers, only interested in instant gratification.

Joseph liked the way Hannah ate. She was messy, but it was because she was enjoying her food. She wasn't afraid to eat with her fingers, get her face and hands sticky, and revel in the whole sensual experience. Watching her eat turned him on.

Although lately they hadn't been getting very messy together. Hannah was burned out from the demands of her job, at least that's what she told him, and had been spending more and more time at her own apartment on the other side of town. Joseph knew it was his fault. He'd become preoccupied with leaving Honolulu and had stopped making an effort. Not that he'd stopped caring for her. But he had ambitions, and she'd made it clear that she never wanted to live anywhere but right here. Joseph told himself that was why he hadn't proposed to her. He didn't want to spend the rest of his life trapped on this tiny island. But that wasn't all of it. He wondered if there was something more, something deeper. Hannah was the only woman he'd ever been in love with, but what did that mean?

She looked up from her plate and smiled. "You want me to sleep over?"

Joseph grinned at her, but before he could respond, he heard a bang on the front door and his uncle's voice as he came tromping into the little house.

"The fuckin' *mahu* isn't gonna help us den."

Joseph rose to greet his uncle. "What are you talking about?"

Sid stopped when he saw Hannah sitting there.

"Hi, Sid."

Sid broke into a big smile and rushed to put his arms around her. "How's it, girl?"

"Good. You?"

Sid took a step back and shook his head.

"Bad. Everything's goin' fo' shit." Sid could see from her expression that it was news to Hannah. "Don' dis boy talk to you den?"

Joseph tried to explain. "It's not that big a deal."

"Why you say dat den? We just sit around wid our thumbs up our butts, it'll be da end."

"The end of what?"

"Da end fo' da business."

Joseph tried to explain. "Don't be so dramatic, Uncle. It's just some competition."

Sid glowered at him. "He want fo' dis to happen. He forget about his *ohana*. He want fo' to go cook in some fancy place on the mainland."

Joseph's jaw dropped. "How do you know about that?"

"I know lots den."

Hannah looked at Joseph. "Did you get an offer from someone?"

Joseph flushed, embarrassed. "In New York City."

"When were you going to tell me about it?"

"I just got an offer. I haven't decided anything."

Sid looked at Hannah and Joseph and shook his head. "You two shoulda been married long ago."

"You came by to tell us that?"

"I'm gonna talk to Jack Lucey. Tell him wot fo' he can do." Sid turned and started for the door.

Joseph looked at Hannah. "I gotta go with him. I don't want him killing anyone."

Hannah nodded. "I'll be at my place."

...

Yuki had watched the well-toned Hawaiian warrior stand in his grass skirt and blow the conch shell to signal sunset and the ceremonial lighting of the tiki torches at the hotel. She had sat alone and sipped pineapple juice as the fire dancers came out and performed some flaming baton twirling while drummers pounded out a beat and hula dancers, with eye makeup like streetwalkers, chanted and shook their asses for the tourists. It was not the island experience she was looking for.

Yuki had asked the concierge at the hotel to recommend a place where the locals went for dinner. He'd looked at her like she was nuts and recommended Duke's Canoe Club, Sam Choy's, Benihana, and a couple of other places that reeked of the tourist trade. Frustrated, Yuki hit the streets, figuring she'd find something if she just started walking away from the beach.

She passed several department stores and fancy boutiques selling Hawaiian clothes. She walked past kiosks offering leis, stalls selling oysters with real pearls inside, and a woman in a bikini advertising a stage show starring Charo, the original coochi-coochi girl.

All along the way she saw people, her people, populating the background, forming a vast canvas underneath the Caucasian tourists that popped to the foreground like fluorescent daisies on a black velvet painting.

It didn't take long for her to walk into what looked like a convention of hookers on Kuhio Avenue. There were dozens if not hundreds of them. Yuki stared at a muscular black woman wearing micromini hot pants and a loose diaphanous halter top. The woman turned to Yuki.

"Don't be shy. I do girls. I do it all, sugar."

Yuki could only blush and stammer. "No, thank you."

She saw another hooker, a buxom Caucasian girl, wearing a silver catsuit with cutout circles up and down the side. It was the closest thing to a space suit she had ever seen on a human being. Yuki couldn't help herself.

"Excuse me, but, what are you wearing?"

The woman looked at Yuki and then said, "Money."

A black SUV drove by and slowed as it passed Yuki. The car pulled over to the curb, stopped, and a large Hawaiian man, wearing baggy cargo shorts and a tank top, climbed out and approached her.

"I can help you make a lot more money."

"Excuse me?"

"You shouldn't be out here. This isn't your scene. You can't compete with these girls."

He swept his arms dramatically to indicate the other women on the street. Yuki looked around. It was true; she couldn't compete, if the competition was to see who had the biggest tits and gave the best blow jobs.

"I'm not—"

"Of course you're not. Anybody can see that."

Yuki nodded, unsure whether she should feel insulted or not, and began to walk.

"Wait. I'm not finished."

"I am."

The man fell into step beside her. Yuki couldn't help but notice the Polynesian tribal bands tattooed on his biceps.

"I said you could make a lot of money."

"I heard you. I'm not interested. I'm not a . . . prostitute."

"I know."

That sounded condescending to Yuki. "Really. I'm not."

"A thousand dollars a night. Only one trick. How's that sound?"

"You're out of your mind. Nobody would pay that for me."

"They would if you specialized."

Yuki didn't want to hear about whips, chains, leather, rubber, gizmos, gadgets, dildos, butt plugs, or any other specialization. She kept walking.

"Cut your hair. Wear boy's clothes. You'd be surprised how many people want to be with a girl who looks like a boy."

Yuki turned and looked at the man. He was a pimp, a really large Hawaiian pimp. By all rights she should be terrified. But she wasn't. There was something about him that was more comforting than scary. He was being sincere. Honest and heartfelt and genuine. Yuki had never heard of a sincere pimp. But here he was, and he really believed what he was saying. He really thought she could be a sex object, that people would actually pay money to have sex with her. This idea was so alien and random that Yuki didn't know what to think of it. Was it exciting? Scary? Ridiculous?

Yuki's lips began to tremble; she thought she might burst into tears.

"Please leave me alone. I'm just trying to find a place to eat."

The pimp looked at her for a beat, deciding.

"Two blocks that way; turn left. You'll see a little place kitty-corner. They make good noodles."

"Thank you."

The pimp watched her go, shaking his head sadly at the lost business opportunity. "You could make a lot of money."

...

The muffled beat of technomusic pounded against the walls of the bathroom. Occasionally someone would throw open the door, and the full force of the sound would shake the stalls. But Francis wasn't paying much attention to the music; he was busy sucking cock. A handsome Australian's cock, at that. Uncut. Chad would be jealous.

Francis knew he should've slid a condom over the guy's dick before he put it in his mouth, but wedged into the stall of the bathroom, kissing and stroking each other, the crystal meth and Viagra propelling him forward, urging him to just rip off his clothes and start fucking—well, he just didn't care. He couldn't be bothered. In fact, he wouldn't mind catching some minor venereal disease, a little gift for Chad when he got home. That would show him.

The Australian had a big cock, much bigger than Chad's. Francis could feel it getting bigger, stiffer, as he sucked and stroked it, letting it drive deep into his mouth. Francis cupped the Australian's balls with one hand, the base of his cock with the other. He felt the balls tighten and rise, and then a surprisingly large amount of come began shooting down Francis's throat in hot little pulses.

Francis swallowed.

Eight

It wasn't difficult for Joseph and his uncle to find Jack. The concierge at the hotel was more than happy to tell them where the cranky old haole with the walker went. The concierge had loaded the walker into the trunk of the cab and everything. And had the gimpy old bastard given him a tip? Fuck, no.

So Joseph and Sid were on their way to La Femme Nu.

Joseph didn't like strip clubs. They weren't his scene. He liked to say that the ritual objectification of women was a soulless and sad pursuit that offended his sense of aesthetics. But really, the one time he'd been, he'd just found the whole thing depressing. The leering men, the prancing women with their shiny oiled skin, superinflated tits, and absurd costumes—they were almost cartoons, manga-stylized yet alive, simulating intimacy or, perhaps more accurately, simulating a fantasy version of simulated intimacy.

Joseph wasn't sure whose fantasy it was. Not his. The uptight nurse or librarian or schoolteacher, checking pulses or wearing big black glasses and holding a book, suddenly letting her hair down, unleashing her massive boobs, and banging her crotch against a large metal pole while men cheered and stuck money in her underwear—what planet did that come from?

Sid and Joseph passed through the neon portal of La Femme Nu. They found Jack scrunched up against the stage, his face staring up at the bulging rubber-wrapped vulva of a young Korean woman with gigantic pylon-shaped silicone-injected breasts. Jack had an astonished look on his face. Apparently he was experiencing something profound and life-altering, a real eureka moment. He turned to a Caucasian guy sitting next to him.

"Did you know Chinese chicks had such big tits? I can't fuckin' believe it!" Then, turning to the platform: "Come here, Tiger Lily!"

She swiveled her vacuum-packed ass over toward him, bobbin' it up and down to the beat as Jack lurched and wobbled to his feet. He stuffed a couple of bucks in her rubber panties, pulling the waistband out like a rubber band and then letting it go. Hearing the satisfying smack of rubber hitting flesh, he gave a feral howl.

"Oh, my God! You got the sweetest ass I've ever seen!"

Sid and Joseph watched Jack reel around, arms wheeling in the air as he fought for balance, and collapse back into his chair.

"You're so fuckin' hot, baby!"

Joseph couldn't help but notice that Jack was—well, highly aroused. He nudged his uncle.

"Uncle, look."

You couldn't miss it. Neither could the stripper. She bent down close, staring right at the apex of Jack's triangulated crotch.

"You want a private dance? I can make you happy."

"Oh, yeah, baby."

"Ten minutes, okay? I'll come for you. Maybe you come for me?"

Jack's eyes rolled in his head. "Oh, yeah!"

The woman turned and began abusing the pole with her ass. Jack watched in awe.

Sid leaned in to Joseph and shouted in his ear, "Lemme handle dis."

Before Joseph could argue, Sid had bulled his way past him and was taking the seat next to Jack. Jack continued to proclaim his new discovery.

"Oh, my God. No wonder there's ten billion of 'em! Look at the Chinese chick! Oh, my God! Look at those Chinese hooters! Who knew about this? Who?"

"She's Korean."

Jack turned and looked at Sid. "Korean? You sure?"

"Fo' sure."

Jack nodded, processing the new information, rethinking his trip to Hong Kong. "Is all Korean pussy like that?"

"I don' know."

Jack poured half a beer into his mouth and shook his head. "Here's to Pyongyang poontang!"

Sid had heard enough. He picked Jack up by the collar and lifted him out of his chair. Jack sputtered a little tough-guy talk, but Sid had him moving toward a room in the back. Joseph intercepted the bouncer.

"It's cool. Our friend needs to puke."

The bouncer nodded and went back to grinding his teeth and watching the crowd, waiting for someone to slip up so he could vent some of his cocaine-fueled tension.

Joseph hurriedly followed Sid, hoping his uncle wouldn't do anything he'd regret.

He found them in a semiquiet spot in back. Sid had squashed Jack into a vinyl banquette and was looming over him. Jack wasn't intimidated; he was bouncing off the seat, yelling at Sid, spit flying out of his mouth.

"I know who you are! You don't fucking scare me."

Sid, surprisingly, remained cool. "I'm not tryin' fo' to scare you. I'm tellin' you wot it is."

"Fuck you!"

Sid nodded, like a good parent waiting for a teenager to stop raging. "I'm only gonna say dis one time den."

"And I'm gonna say this until you go away. Fuck you! Fuck you! Fuck you!"

Sid just crossed his arms over his chest and looked down at Jack. He didn't say anything.

"If you don't mind, I'm going back to the Korean chick. I got some unfinished business."

Jack tried to stand, but without his walker he wasn't going anywhere. He flopped around, struggling and thrashing for a few minutes, and then gave up and glared.

"What? What the fuck do you want?"

"You gonna listen?"

Jack nodded. Sid leaned in.

"Here's the deal. You got the job. Good fo' you. You brought some trucks over. Good fo' you. The union is gonna drive your trucks, they gonna take real good care of 'em. They're gonna make you look good."

Jack nodded, waiting for the other shoe to drop.

"When the job's over, you leave da trucks where dey are and you go back to Las Vegas."

"In your fucking dreams, King Kamehameha."

"You don't want no problems den. You understand dat?"

Jack's face flushed red.

"I understand. Now you wanna know what I think?"

"Sure."

"You want a war, you got one."

"You don't wanna go there. Not with us."

Jack took that in.

"Oh really?"

Sid nodded.

"Dis is our island."

Jack pulled himself up, struggling to maintain his balance, and leaned as close as he could to Sid. Then he started yelling.

"Yeah, well listen to me, Honolulu tough guy, I'm from Las-fuckin'-Vegas. Do you know what I'm sayin' here? Do you have any idea what that means?"

Jack couldn't hold himself up. He crashed back into the banquette.

"Go blow your fuckin' conch shell or pick coconuts or whatever the fuck it is you people do. But don't tell me how to run my fuckin' business, because you are out of your league."

Joseph was sure that last outburst would put Sid over the edge, but Sid just shook his head.

"You been warned."

"And you're a dead man."

...

Yuki was exhausted. It had been a long day. On top of the constant demands of her job, her secret mission to cleanse her boss of his negative energy was the killer. Francis, she realized, was a force to be reckoned with, a one-man H-bomb capable of unleashing supercharged diva-destruction in all directions. Yuki, the staff, and any local hires would just be collateral damage, set decoration and props for the shock-and-awe campaign of self-annihilation that Francis was bringing with him.

She climbed into bed and turned off the light. As she was drifting off, she thought about the big Hawaiian pimp who'd approached her on the street. Although the idea of selling her body for money was creepy, she was excited that someone actually thought that, with a little retooling, she might be sexually attractive. When was the last time anyone had shown an interest in her? When was the last time she'd had sex? She realized, somewhat grimly, that she hadn't had intimate contact with another human being in almost four years. No hand holding, no hugs, no kissing, no touching, no getting laid, nothing.

It was depressing.

She'd distracted herself. Filled her days with classes, lessons, chanting, and volunteer work. But she realized that she would trade all the belly-dancing lessons, conga classes, feng shui seminars, and yoga retreats for a night between the sheets with someone. Anyone. They didn't have to be hot or hunky, they didn't even have to be male; at this point she just wanted contact. And along comes a pimp, a real live pimp who knows what he's talking about, who says, "Dress like a boy and people will want you."

How do you like that?

Yuki drifted off into a deep sleep and, as her REM kicked in, began to dream. In her dream, Yuki had short hair, cropped in the back and on the sides with a long, flowing lock that fell down over her eyes. She looked sultry, seductive. She wore a white cotton tank top underneath an unbuttoned Hawaiian shirt, her small dark nipples clearly visible through the thin fabric. She had on ankle-length khakis that were baggy and made her hips look boyish. She wore pink canvas high-tops and had a baseball cap perched on the back of her head. She wasn't sure what she looked like: a cool teenage boy, a dyke, or a superfashionable young woman who was hip, happening, and ready for anything.

Because it was a dream, she suddenly found herself on a tropical beach, maybe Ipanema. It was hot. The sand was littered with sunbathers laid out on towels, raw and pink and exposed, like sushi. The sun beat down, and the smell of broiling cocoa-buttered flesh mixed with the salt of the sea breeze. It made her stomach growl with a hard, deeply erotic hunger.

Yuki wasn't like the other women on the beach. She didn't have huge tits packed into a teeny bikini. She wasn't wearing a thong. Yet everywhere she looked men were lusting after her, beckoning, waving, offering drinks, cash, jewelry, even a new skateboard.

She had never felt so desired.

She heard them breathing: hot, heavy, panting. She stopped walking and stood there, trembling with excitement. The breeze from the surf sprayed across her skin and caused a tingling electromagnetic surge that shot through her body, connecting her lips to her nipples to her suddenly wet pussy.

The men could sense her desire; they could smell it, feel it whipping through the wind, stirring them like a sex cyclone. They came for her, running, walking, some crawling through the sand on their hands and knees; one was doing cartwheels and flips as he approached. Some of them wore business suits, others hotel robes, swim trunks, and baggy surf shorts. A few had bulging Speedos, skimpy racing swimsuits that barely covered their privates.

They came for her. They closed in, an anemone of strong, sleek arms wrapping around her, stroking her body, touching her all over. Her body began to drip and melt like a Popsicle on a very hot day. And then, as she felt their hot breath on her skin, they began licking her. Starting with her toes and ankles and neck and shoulders, slowly working their way toward . . .

Yuki woke up. She was disoriented and sweating profusely. Suddenly desperate for some fresh air, she jumped out of bed, opened the sliding glass door, and walked out on the balcony. The night air was cool and she shivered as her skin goose-bumped up and down her body. She hadn't had a dream so vivid or intense in years. She was annoyed that she'd woken up. It wasn't fair. If she couldn't get laid in real life, at least she should be allowed to get some in her dreams.

She felt her crotch. It was soaked.

. . .

Sid's knuckles were white as he gripped his beer bottle. "You hear wot dat haole motherfucker say to me?"

Joseph nodded, noncommittal, and sipped his beer while Sid continued to fume.

"I shoulda pound him right den."

"Beat up a cripple? They'd throw you in jail."

"He a gimp, but he fo' sure dangerous."

Joseph turned to Sid. "Uncle, why'd you give him an ultimatum?"

"You wanna give him a lei? Say 'Aloha haole mother-fucker'? Is dat wot you want den?"

Joseph shook his head. "I just don't know what we gain by threatening him."

"He threaten me."

Joseph couldn't look at Sid. He wanted to tell him to be reasonable, to stop behaving like a two-year-old who didn't know how to share his sandbox. What was happening was inevitable. Business as usual. They'd had a monopoly for years; it had given them the security to invest, to build something really good. But they'd been living in a bubble. Now that the bubble was popped, they'd have to adjust. Joseph wasn't afraid of it. They could handle the competition. It wasn't going to kill them.

But Joseph knew his uncle wouldn't believe him, so he didn't say anything. He looked around the bar. It was dark and wooden with neon signs advertising Mexican beer and filled with a mix of locals and tourists.

Sid waved to the bartender for another round. "We at war now."

"What are you talking about?"

"He bringin' war to da island. Dat fo' sure den."

...

Stanley heard the banging on his door, but he didn't want to answer it. What if it was some kind of criminal? Then he heard a voice he recognized.

"Open the door, ya putz."

Stanley wrapped himself in a terry-cloth robe provided by the hotel and looked out the peephole. Jack was in the hallway, his features distorted and deformed by the fish-eye lens, glaring at the door like he could open it telepathically.

"Stanley! Wake up!"

"Hang on." Stanley unlocked the door and opened it a crack. "It's late."

"Quit fuckin' around."

Jack shoved his walker against the door, making a loud scrape, pushed his way in, and scuttled into the room.

"You got someone here?"

"Of course not."

"You should. This town's full of hookers."

Stanley sighed. "I don't want a hooker, Dad."

Jack shot him a perplexed and disappointed look. "Why not?"

Stanley sighed again. "What can I do for you?"

"Listen to your old man for a minute. There ain't nothin' wrong with a whore. Don't let those Bible-thumping hypocrites tell you different. They all talk one way, but as soon as no one's lookin' they got a tranny bobbin' for dollars by the dashboard light."

"What're you talking about?"

"I'm just sayin', you have a need, don't be ashamed to get it treated by a professional."

Stanley put his hand up to his head. "I don't have a need."

Jack snorted. "Of course you do."

"No, I don't. I'm fine."

"You're in denial."

"Okay. I'll go see a psychiatrist. They're professional."

"A professional cocksucker will straighten you out faster than any kind of shrinky-dinky do-gooder."

"Thanks, Dad. You woke me up to tell me this?"

Stanley was tired. He took a bottle of water out of the minibar.

"Hand me a beer, will ya?"

Stanley twisted the top off a bottle of Heineken and handed it to his father. He sat back on the bed and sipped his water as Jack drained two-thirds of the beer in one long gulpy swallow.

"The fuckers are declaring war on us."

"Who?"

"The local fuckers. The Sumo and his kid."

"Samoan."

"Whatever. They braced me in the strip club."

Stanley was shocked. "What?"

"Have you ever seen the tits on a Korean girl?" Then Jack realized what he'd said. "Forget it. Of course you haven't. Only tits you see are in *National Geographic*."

Stanley was growing agitated. "What did they say?"

"What do you think they said? They want us out."

"What did you say?"

"I told 'em to go fuck themselves." Jack finished the beer and tossed the bottle on the floor.

"What did they say to that?"

Jack shot his son an annoyed look. "What do you think they said; 'Okay, we'll just go fuck ourselves, thank you very much for suggesting it'?"

"No . . . I—"

"They declared fuckin' war. I'm takin' the first flight back to Vegas. I'm gonna have a little chat with some of our AFL-CIO friends. Maybe they can apply some pressure, straighten this out."

"For a piece of the action."

Jack hoisted himself to his feet, grabbed his walker, and began to hobble toward the door.

"The cost of doing business."

...

If you didn't know better, you might open the door to this ratty little dive tucked away in a dank Chinatown alley, take one look at the thugs, junkies, and hired killers inside, and slink away as quickly as possible. But if you knew the truth, you'd know that the tough-looking customers drinking beer and eating questionable sashimi were all off-duty police officers, most of them undercover detectives from the narcotics and organized crime units. Despite appearances to the contrary, this was actually the safest place in Honolulu.

A detective, chronic-looking with a greasy ponytail, Fu Manchu mustache, and pirate earrings, was singing karaoke. He was drunk, as were the other off-duty law enforcement types in the bar, but his heartfelt and slightly raunchy rendition of "You Light Up My Life" was bringing down the house.

Joseph entered the bar and nodded to a couple of detectives he knew. That was the thing about growing up in Honolulu: You knew everybody and everybody knew you. Joseph knew a few policemen. He even knew a criminal. One of his best friends from high school had become a high-class pimp. Not that they ever talked about it. Joseph didn't ask and his friend never mentioned it. Sometimes, with friends, it's better not to know.

Joseph sat down at the bar and ordered a beer. An inebriated brunette—Joseph recognized her as one of the

Chinatown bicycle-patrol officers—pushed the karaoke song list over to him and ordered him to pick a song. In a bar where everyone's packing heat, it's best to do as you're told. Joseph nodded and scanned the list until his drink arrived.

The beer came with a glass of ice and a plastic bowl filled with little red globes of *li hing mui.* Following the local custom, Joseph plucked two of the *li hing mui,* sour pickled plums coated in a carcinogenic-red powder, and dropped them in the glass of ice. He then slowly poured the beer over the fruit. He did it carefully, because something in the plums causes the beer to foam up.

Across the room, Sid sat in deep conversation with the assistant district attorney. Sid was trying to figure out if there was a way to implicate Jack Lucey and his Las Vegas business in price-fixing, bid rigging, or extortion: basically, all things that Sid routinely did with the union's blessing. Sid was looking for allies or, better, someone to go to war for him. Joseph watched as the ADA, a friendly red-haired man with a perpetually sunburned nose, shook his head. Sid took a swig from his beer, nodded like he understood, and tried another tack. Joseph heard his uncle's voice rise above the karaoke clatter.

"But dis is *our* island!"

The ADA mumbled something in response. Judging from the way Sid shot a sideways glance and clenched his teeth, Joseph could tell it wasn't the answer he was looking for.

Joseph took a long drink of the ice-cold, sweet-plum-flavored beer and shook his head. As far as he was concerned, it was a little late to start shouting *This is our island* when it'd been stolen from them over a hundred years ago. The British and the French had both tried and failed to overthrow the

Kingdom of Hawaii and take control of the islands. They'd been repelled by a stubborn monarchy and a ferocious people. Only fat-cat robber barons from the United States had managed to pull it off, and they didn't bother with warships or a battalion; they had someone on the inside.

In 1875, King David Kalakaua, a boozer and womanizer—the real incarnation of Kamapua'a, the Hog God—signed the Reciprocity Treaty with the United States, allowing sugar and pineapple barons to sell Hawaiian goods to the mainland without a tax or tariff. The fat cats from San Francisco and beyond had anticipated this and gobbled up vast tracts of land, much of it purchased directly from the king himself.

A few years later Kalakaua extended the treaty and, in exchange, let the U.S. government build a naval base at Pearl Harbor. That was the beginning of the end for the Kingdom of Hawaii. Ten years after that the agribarons, Claus Spreckels, Sanford B. Dole, and C&H, the self-made kings of pineapple and sugar, sponsored a revolt against the monarchy and had the U.S. Marines land to "protect American interests."

On January 17, 1893, Queen Liliuokalani surrendered her crown under protest to avoid a bloody battle between native Hawaiians and the U.S. Marines. The islands were annexed as a territory and Dole was installed as territorial governor. American interests had been protected in perpetuity ever since. If you asked Joseph, they'd been protected at the expense of the Hawaiians.

The inebriated brunette handed Joseph the microphone and told him it was his turn to sing. Because he spoke Hawaiian, he had picked a native song. But he was not a natural singer and he held the microphone tentatively, hoping no one in the bar would pay much attention to him.

The music started, images of natural rainforests and waterfalls appeared on the screen along with the words, and Joseph began to sing in a high, lonesome falsetto the classic island song, "Hiʻilawe."

He might not have the best voice in the bar, but the song, with its hauntingly sweet melody and beautiful words about a magical waterfall, moved him and he found himself singing louder and with more confidence than he intended. The melody rose up through the clatter and silenced the bar. Even Sid, who was just beginning to offer his support, union connections, and cold cash to any political ambitions the ADA might have, shut up and listened.

Suddenly, in a little bar on a small island in the middle of the largest body of water in the world, Joseph felt a connection to this time and this place. He became filled with a kind of soulful nostalgia that he could only describe as profound.

It came out in his singing, and it moved everyone in the bar. He could see it on their faces as he sang. Even Karate Mike, the giant detective who never sang, closed his eyes and mouthed the words.

When Joseph reached the end of the song, the bar erupted, whooping and cheering. Harry the bartender took the microphone from Joseph and told him he had sounded almost as good as the great Israel Kamakawiwoʻole himself. Joseph smiled and nodded and even blushed a little as he sat back down, stuffed a few more *li hing mui* into his glass of ice, and slowly poured a beer over it.

He had never felt more Hawaiian.

Nine

His given name was Walter, but on the street everyone called him Lono. That's because if there was some news or a rumor, Lono would know it. If he told you that someone was poaching your whores or gunning for your little corner of the drug world, or that the police were gearing up to drop some damage your way, it was usually true.

His network of girls reported back to him almost hourly, bits of gossip picked up here or there, people seen in certain places at certain times. Little things. Information that a normal person would discard as useless or irrelevant. But to Lono they were all tiny pieces of a large and multilayered jigsaw puzzle. He was able to take all the tidbits of information and hearsay and piece together an extremely accurate picture of what was going down on the mean streets of Honolulu.

This ability—some would say *gift*—was very useful. It kept Lono and his girls out of trouble with the competition and out of jail, one step ahead of what was about to go down. He was like the warning towers for incoming tsunamis that dot the North Shore. He gave you just enough time to reach high ground before the wave hit.

But Lono was selective. He traded information, using it to keep his business running smoothly. He didn't help everyone, just special people. For example, the Japanese Yakuza and White Ghost Triad from Hong Kong held him in high esteem and, in fact, owed him many favors. In exchange for his information, they allowed his girls to work in many of the fancier hotels that were off limits to other pimps, and they never bothered to sweat him for a percentage of his earnings.

But it wasn't just the organized crime syndicates that Lono traded information with; there was a methamphetamine importer from Seoul who treated Lono like a brother, a high-flying money launderer who traded stock tips and investment advice for Lono's information, a couple of counterfeit artists who specialized in 10,000 yen notes, a certain high-ranking government official, and a retired hitman from New Jersey. They all prospered through their connection with Lono. It was, as Martha Stewart likes to say, a good thing.

So Lono knew it was only a matter of time before he found out who the boyishly thin Japanese-American woman was, where she was staying, and what she was up to. He had put the word out. Lono could tell from looking at her that she wasn't a doper, a local, or a tourist. That meant she was either newly arrived or here on business.

He knew she wasn't in the game; that much was obvious by the way she carried herself. She was much too open, not cagey or circumspect like a working girl would be. Her reactions and comments had seemed completely honest and unguarded.

Lono found himself replaying their conversation in his mind over and over again. He didn't know why he was suddenly obsessed with her. He could have any woman he wanted. Beautiful women were the currency he dealt, and it was common for pimps to dip into the till from time to time—if not for their personal pleasure, at least for quality control, making sure the product that was delivered to the consumer was the finest available. But Lono had never been tempted by any of his girls, even the exotics like Alice, the six-foot-four beauty from Tanzania, or Wachara, the hermaphrodite from Bali. He should've done both of them just to satisfy his curiosity. But the fact was that, unlike his customers, Lono wasn't looking to get off. To tell the truth, he wasn't sure what he was looking for. But he thought he'd seen a glimmer of it in that woman lost and wandering through the prowl district.

Lono had to see her again. But he didn't stress about it. He'd find her. It was only a matter of time.

Ten

Yuki looked like she'd just stepped out of a salon. That's because she had. Her hair was cropped super-short on the back and sides and left long, lanky, and shot through with streaks of red on the top. Her hair swooped along one side of her head and flopped over her face like a crazy cantilevered Mohawk.

It was the coolest thing she'd ever done, and just knowing she'd had the courage to change her appearance so radically energized her. Why hadn't her life coach ever suggested a haircut? Why waste all that time and money on aromatherapy workshops, Reiki classes, and *vipassana* meditation retreats when a new haircut totally changed everything? What if magazines like *Vogue* and *Glamour* were right? Maybe a makeover was more than just a makeover. Maybe a little color in your hair and some new eyeliner could do more than change your appearance; maybe it could change your outlook on life. Maybe it could even change your luck.

She walked across the street and into the Ala Moana mall. She thought it was strange to find a mall in Honolulu that was just like any mall you'd find in Omaha or Sacramento. McDonald's, Burger King, and the Gap might have an imperial stretch from Orlando to Rome to Kuala Lumpur, but Baskin Robbins and Hickory Farms were definitely made in the U.S.A. It was jarring to see all these Asian people surrounded by orchids and palm trees carrying shopping bags filled with cheese balls and smoked sausage while lapping at a double dip of Here Comes the Fudge.

Yuki scoured several boutiques, searching for the exact right outfit to go with her new look. She tried some slinky miniskirts, floppy sundresses, pegged black jeans, and even super-casual flat-front khakis. But nothing was exactly right, although she was pleased to see that she looked kind of sexy in the miniskirt.

Eventually she found what she was looking for in a clothing store for surfers and surfer wannabes. She found the loose-fitting calf-length pants, the thin cotton tank top, the Hawaiian shirts, the high-top canvas sneakers, even a black baseball cap with the words "Strong Current" embroidered on it. Strong Current. That kind of said it all. That was what she was feeling.

She stood in the dressing room looking at her new image in the mirror. A chill of recognition ran up her spine, and she felt as if her dream and this new reality had somehow managed to merge. For a brief exhilarating moment, Yuki was unsure if she was dreaming or awake. She felt the same surge of erotic energy crackle through her body that she had felt in the dream. The sensation made her gasp.

She paid for her purchases and wore them out into the mall. Everywhere she went, heads turned to appraise her. Men looked her up and down, trying to figure out if she was a hip teenage boy or the DJ of a lesbian disco. Either way, there was something sexually dangerous and alluring about her.

Being an object of sexual desire, or at least curiosity, was a new experience for Yuki, and she found it uplifting and slightly creepy. Being androgynous was going to take some getting used to.

...

"These motherfuckers think they can get away with whatever the fuck they want just because they live here. Just because it's some fuckin' island." Jack was seething.

"Calm down. You'll have another stroke."

"Calm down? You want me to calm the fuck down? What do you want me to do, huh? Grab my ankles and say 'Aloha, please fuck me up the ass'? Fuck that. I'm not sayin' that."

Stanley tried to be reasonable. "Look at it from their point of view. They're just trying to protect their business. We'd do the same if they came to Vegas."

"If they came to Vegas we'd plant their corpses in the fuckin' desert." Jack's expression changed. "Which isn't a bad idea."

"They aren't coming to Vegas, Dad. Don't get any ideas."

"Nothing says *stay out of my way* like a fuckin' bullet in the head."

Stanley turned and gave his father a stern look. "No."

"No?"

"Yeah, no. Okay? No. I can't make it any clearer than that."

"Pussy."

"Fine. I'm a pussy."

Jack looked out the window. He thought about telling Stanley to go fuck himself but then thought better of it. Chucking the fucking Sumo in a volcano was a good idea, no doubt about it. Nothing announces your business plan and puts you on the map like that. It had worked when that putz in Vegas had tried an end-around and called his Hollywood friends. Death is an effective business tool. It'd been proven over and over again—by dictators, tyrants, despots, and corporate CEOs. People get in your way, you disappear them. Make an example out of them. Suddenly there's no competition, and everyone else gets real cooperative.

Jack realized he'd have to make a corporate decision, exercise some leadership, without consulting Stanley. If he couldn't get the union to help, he'd take care of it himself. That is, if he made it to the airport in time for his flight.

"Could you drive faster? It's the fucking pedal on the right. You have to press it down with your foot."

"Relax, Dad."

"I don't want to miss my flight."

Stanley didn't reply; he just stared ahead as the car slowly crawled along Ala Moana Boulevard.

"There must be a faster way."

"I checked the map."

"That doesn't mean there's not a faster way."

"I guess I just take after Mom."

Jack laughed. "Your mother could kick my ass, drink me under the table, suck my cock raw, and then go out and party until it was time to wake you up for school. Trust me, you don't take after her."

Stanley couldn't help himself; he pouted. "That's not how I remember her."

Jack smiled. "Don't take this the wrong way. But once she'd served up her famous meat loaf and put you to bed— well, I couldn't keep up with her."

"She went out? After she tucked me in?" Stanley sounded slightly distressed.

"She had a standing poker game at Binion's."

"Mom gambled?"

"Texas hold 'em. She loved that game."

"You're lying. I don't believe you."

Jack could see the conversation was making Stanley uncomfortable, so he shut up and turned to look out the window. As the car crept along at a geriatric pace, Jack could see the ocean, the beach, palm trees, and the outline of Pearl Harbor off in the distance.

"Don't talk about Mom that way."

"Fine."

Jack was glad Stanley didn't want to talk about her. Jack didn't like talking about his wife that much either. She had died of pancreatic cancer long before he had the stroke or the air bags inserted in his penis. His memories of her and their life together were fading, receding into the ether, until Jack could hardly remember the man he'd been before. All he had were some photos and a few random memories. It was so long ago, it really did seem like a different life. Maybe that was a side effect of the stroke; maybe it was just self-preservation. Jack knew it was better to deal with the reality of now than memories of what you could do when you were healthy. He had seen other stroke victims in the rehab place grow despondent and then, ultimately, suicidal. Suicide wasn't for him. It was a loser's move, quitters who fold their hands and walk away. Nobody cares about the gambler who gives up. Winners might have to bluff sometimes, but at least they're still in the game.

They rode in silence, inching down the street as frustrated drivers honked and shook their fists at them. Jack watched a couple of young men on bicycles race by. He looked over at Stanley. He didn't say a word.

...

Joseph sat near the beach in the shade of a banyan tree. He watched as a group of New Age tourists practiced yoga in the shade of a group of coconut palms. A young woman, her body lean and rippling with muscles, led the group in a professionally mellow voice. Plank position, up dog, down dog, jump forward. Repeat.

Joseph looked up as the wind whipped the palms. Pods of bright green coconuts hung from the swaying trees, a good thirty feet above the class. Down dog meets falling coconut. He had never been conked, but he had a native's natural distrust of gravity, so he stayed under the banyans when he had the choice.

While he waited for Wilson, Joseph tied his running shoes. He didn't like to have company on his daily run, preferring to let his mind wander and relax as his body worked, but his cousin said it was urgent. It took a lot to upset Wilson, so Joseph told him to meet him here.

Wilson was late, as usual. Joseph couldn't really remember when his cousin had been on time for anything. There was island time, usually a good fifteen to twenty minutes slow; then there was Wilson time. That was whenever he got around to it or felt like it. But today he was glad Wilson was late.

He needed to think. He'd watched Sid stomp and yell

at the producer. That had failed. They'd braced Jack Lucey in the strip club, and all it'd done was piss him off. The union couldn't help, the local politicians couldn't help, and the sabotage angle was too risky. In other words, unless Joseph thought up a new approach or convinced Sid to back off, something bad was going to happen.

He watched as the yoga class went through a series of painful-looking back bends. He heard the crunch of tires on gravel and turned to see Wilson's van pull into a space. Wilson saw him and waved, sauntering over like a man who had all the time in the world.

"Hey, cousin."

"Joseph, how's it?"

"I'm waiting for you."

"Sorry, brah. I had things."

Wilson sat down next to him and looked over at the yoga class. He watched as the yoga teacher bent forward into a triangle pose.

"Look at her ass. It's a rock."

Joseph smiled and nodded. He'd noticed.

"Chick like dat can hurt you, man. Hurt you inna good way."

"I thought you said it was urgent."

Wilson continued to stare at the yoga teacher. "Yeah, brah. It is."

The breeze off the ocean picked up. A set of waves rolled in to shore. A formation of pelicans flew by. Wilson continued to watch the yoga class.

"You want to tell me about it?"

"Man, maybe I should take yoga fo' meet some girls like dat. I bet chicks get hot fo' a dude who can yoga."

Joseph turned and looked at the beach. "I wouldn't know."

"Shit, look at dat."

Joseph looked back at the yoga class and watched as the instructor did a pose where she balanced herself on her hands and placed her knees on her elbows. The overall effort highlighted her finely toned ass and brought it into clear view.

"I am definitely takin' me some yoga."

Joseph stood up. "I'm going for a jog. You want to come?"

Wilson looked deeply hurt. "Wot?"

"I don't have all day."

"Wot's your problem, man? Can't we just sit and enjoy da view?"

Joseph sat back down. "What's so urgent?"

Wilson glanced over at the yoga class and then turned to Joseph. "It's Dad. He's gone Vietnam."

"What?"

"Like last night I come home—you know, late like—an' he was at da kitchen table cleanin' his guns."

"I didn't know he had guns."

"Yeah. From the Marine Corps. He's got like a M-16 and a pistol."

"What was he doing cleaning them?"

"Dat's wot I ask. He say he was getting ready."

"Ready for what?"

"Fo' dem Vegas fuckers."

"Sid needs to calm down."

"He say it's war, brah. He's fo' real serious."

"Keep an eye on your dad. I'm going to go talk to the producer again. Maybe we can work something out. Do the overtime meals or something."

"I hear dat guy's a fag."
"Yeah. He probably is."

...

Francis had spent an uncomfortable night. He'd had fun, at first. Disco dancing, picking up a Russian sailor, and partying at his hotel. Who knew vodka could taste so good? But when he was done partying, when his body cried out for a rest, Francis had been unable to sleep. He'd done a little too much meth. So he'd spent a few hours sitting in his hotel room watching patterns emerge and dissolve on his ceiling. Oddly enough his erection, which the Levitra and Viagra had kept loud and proud all night long, wouldn't quit. It just kept throbbing.

Like a lot of things in life, it had been fun for a little while, but now it was annoying.

When Francis got to his office he almost had a heart attack. For a brief second he thought he might've called the phone number that the bartender at the disco had given him, a phone number that delivered teenage male prostitutes to your home, hotel, and—apparently—office.

But the hot young hooker turned around and smiled at him, and to his relief Francis saw that it was Yoko or Yukon or whatever her name was, his erstwhile assistant.

"Good morning."

"Wow. What happened to you?"

She appeared to blush a little. "I just wanted a change."

Francis nodded. Any change from the dowdy New Age nobody would've been good, but to transform herself into a kind of punky early David Bowie creature? Genius.

She ran her hand through her hair, pulling it away from her eyes. "Not too much?"

"It's very stylish."

"Really?

"Absolutely. You look great."

She beamed. "You want some coffee?"

"Please."

Francis walked into his office. He felt vaguely weird, slightly nauseated. Kind of like he felt when he came home early one day and found Chad in bed with Geoffrey the real estate agent. They were supposed to be looking for a new house, an investment Chad wanted to make, and from the looks of it they had spent the better part of the afternoon inspecting properties, just nothing to do with land or houses. When he found them lying in each other's arms, Francis felt as if about ten feet of intestines had just been yanked out of his body through his belly button. He became dizzy, disoriented. Like he'd turned on his favorite television show and found it recast with all new actors. Some of it was familiar; the names and dialogue seemed to fit with what he knew. The set looked the same. It was the same couch, the same painting on the wall. But at the same time, it was different. It made his stomach feel funny.

Francis couldn't understand why the same flood of peculiar feelings was hitting him at this moment. It wasn't Chad; Chad could go fuck a goat for all Francis cared. Why was he feeling so strange? Was it his assistant?

Francis couldn't remember if he'd ever been attracted to a woman. He recalled dating girls in high school. He French-kissed them and slipped his hand under their bras. He humped them on the couch when they were babysitting some neighbor's brats. In college he even had sex with one. It's not like he didn't try it. But he never felt turned on. Whatever it was about women that men were supposed to get, the attraction that caused all the divorces and overpopulation of the planet, he never felt it. But with this new style she'd assumed, his assistant had somehow managed to merge the masculine and the feminine and become something new. Something that made his stomach feel funny.

Yuki came into the office with his coffee. "You take milk, right?"

"Thanks. That's really nice of you."

"No problem."

She noticed a stack of contracts on his desk. "You want me to proofread those for you?"

Francis looked at her. "That'd be great. I have to admit I'm burning it at both ends lately."

"No problem."

She scooped up the contracts and walked out the door. He watched her ass, flat and boyish, as she left the room. He realized he needed to remember her name.

...

Sid needed ammo. He had a couple of clips for the M-16 that should be enough, he thought; he didn't really expect to shoot anyone with it. The gun had a severe-looking profile; it scared people, said you were serious. It was for show. If he had to do any real shooting he'd use the handguns. They were more practical.

He heard his son enter the house. "Wilson? You wanna go wid me fo' da sports store?"

Wilson entered the kitchen and took a beer out of the fridge. "We goin' fishing?"

"I need ammo."

Wilson's expression betrayed his nervousness. "Wot you need ammo for?"

"Why you look like you need da bathroom?"

"You don't need ammo."

"If I'm gonna kill dem haoles, I'm gonna need more. Look at dis. I only got six rounds." Sid ejected a clip from one of the handguns.

"You don' need more. You already got too much."

Sid looked at Wilson. "Why you so stupid?"

"Why you always say I'm stupid?" Wilson sat down at the table next to his father. "I don' wanna see you in prison."

Sid slid the clip back into the gun. "I'd die before lettin' dem take our work."

"Joseph says there'll be more work."

Sid sighed. "He don' know. You young ones don' know."

Wilson didn't feel like drinking his beer anymore. He left it sitting on the table. He watched as his father sadly shook his head and fingered the pistol.

"You gonna tell me wot I don't know?"

"When Captain Cook land here he feel like a god. He wants us to bow down an' kiss his feet. An' you know wot we did? We killed him. We clubbed him an' speared him like a little *moana* fish. Haoles keep comin' here actin' like dey King Shit. You know what I say? I say we should club all dem too."

With that Sid stood up and tucked one of the pistols into the elastic waistband of his tracksuit.

"Now I'm gonna get some ammo."

...

The visit with Francis changed everything. Joseph left the production offices in shock, reeling from the conversation, feeling like he'd just been the guest star on a *Twilight Zone* episode. Even though he didn't have an appointment, the producer had seemed happy to see him. Glad he'd stopped by. Joseph had been relaxed and friendly in his approach. He wanted it to feel off the record. A man-to-man kind of talk. No threats. No undercurrent of retaliation.

Joseph had explained to the producer about the community living here, how tough it was to scrape by in one of the most expensive cities in the world, how local ownership was really important to them, especially given the number of Japanese, Chinese, and Dutch interests buying up large swaths of real estate and swallowing businesses whole. He had even tried to appeal to the producer's spiritual side—after all, he was from California—and told him how an all-Hawaiian production crew got a special blessing from the island gods.

The producer—Francis was his name—had listened. He'd looked into Joseph's eyes, paid attention, nodded when he agreed or understood. It seemed to Joseph that it was all going really well.

The producer told Joseph he preferred using locals. It helped get shooting permits, locations, and police cooperation if they knew their fellow townspeople were getting paid. The producer said he could call the network and make up some story about civic unrest or political pressure and maybe get the other guys knocked out of the picture. But it wouldn't be easy. He'd have to lay his ass on the line.

The producer, Francis, looked Joseph in the eye and asked if he'd lay *his* ass on the line. He said, "If I lay my ass on the line, I expect you to do the same."

Joseph didn't know what he meant. Did he want a reduced rate? A kickback? That's when it all started to get weird.

The producer stood up and came around from behind his desk. Joseph noticed the erection right away; the front of Francis's pants poked out like a pup tent.

He sat down next to Joseph and said, "I really want to fuck you."

Joseph resisted his flight-or-fight response. He reminded himself to breathe deeply and keep his cool. It wasn't the gay sex that bothered him—Hawaii was a very liberal state—it was the quid pro quo. It was the way it made him feel like a prostitute. If all it took was sleeping with the producer to solve all these problems, why weren't the real reasons good enough? Why did it have to come down to sex?

The producer pressed his case. It would be so easy. He'd throw in a nice sushi dinner, a few drinks, some ecstasy if he'd like. All Joseph had to do was say yes. Joseph didn't know what to do, so he decided to buy some time. He told the producer that maybe this was the way things were done in Los Angeles but it wasn't the way business was done in Hawaii. Still, in the interest of the community and to preserve the local economy, he'd think about it. He really didn't know what else to say.

...

Francis danced around his office. All his adult life he'd watched directors pull the old casting-couch trick on young actors and actresses. He'd seen studio execs fucking agents. He'd seen bright young D-boys and D-girls, the people who do the grunt work of tracking and developing screenplays, fuck their way into a vice presidency. And Chad? If he kept fucking the way he was fucking, he was going to be a studio head in a few years.

But Francis had never done it. He'd never traded sex for favors. He'd never traded sex for anything but sex. But now . . . why not? It felt good. He was on top of the world, and if things went his way he'd be under that cute Hawaiian hunk in no time.

Francis sang the chorus from "Kung Fu Fighting" and bumped his ass against his desk like he was doing the Hustle. He shifted his legs and did the Electric Slide to the door before reaching for the knob and breaking into the Robot.

It was a little bit frightening.

Francis threw open the door and looked out at his assistant. For a brief second he thought it was just his lucky day. She was bent over, retrieving a folder from the bottom drawer of the filing cabinet. It took a superhuman amount of willpower and restraint to keep himself from walking up behind her and just thrusting his boner against her ass. Francis found himself standing in the doorway, a disco song in his head, an erection pounding in his khakis, and a bit of drool coming out of his mouth. God, he wanted her. More and more, she was becoming his fantasy cabin boy. Perhaps a three-way with her and the gorgeous Hawaiian was in order? This seemed like a particularly brilliant idea to Francis. Maybe inviting a bona fide female into the mix would seal the deal with the obviously heterosexual Joseph.

He saw how she'd looked at Joseph when he came in. The same way he did. Hungrily.

...

Hannah sat at the kitchen table looking over a stack of essays that her students had turned in. She concentrated, whipping out her red pen and scribbling comments in the margin, as Joseph rinsed a fillet of *opakapaka* and dried it with a paper towel. He held it in the light.

"What do you think?"

Hannah looked up. "About?"

"This *opakapaka*."

She shrugged. "You're the cook. I'm sure it'll be great. Everything you cook's great." She said it matter-of-factly.

"You sure about that?"

Hannah nodded. "You don't need compliments from me. You know you're good. One of these days you'll be famous. Maybe you'll even have your own TV show."

"Not if I stay here."

Hannah grimaced and turned back to her papers. "I don't want to talk about it right now."

Joseph nodded and turned his attention back to the fish. He expertly dredged the *opakapaka* in a pile of freshly grated ginger, coating both sides, before dropping it into a hot pan. The ginger and fish snapped and sizzled as it hit the hot oil.

"Would you like some more wine?"

"Please."

Joseph pulled a bottle of sauvignon blanc from New Zealand out of the fridge and drizzled a little of the wine on the cooking fish.

"Don't waste it."

"Just a drop. To keep the fish moist."

He poured her a glass. She took a sip and smiled. "Cheers."

"Cheers."

They clinked their glasses together. Hannah leaned forward, the top of her dress falling open to reveal her breasts, and gave him a soft kiss on the lips. She'd only meant to give him a small kiss and go back to work, but he reached around and held her face in his hands and continued kissing her.

Joseph was surprised at how quickly he became aroused. Once he tasted her tongue as it slid into his mouth—sharp with the citrusy bite, hint of summer melons, ripe apricots, and a slight mineral aftertaste—he felt his body jolt awake. His toes curled in his flip-flops as she lifted one of her legs and gently slid it up and down his torso.

Joseph kissed her ears, running his tongue along the outside of them, and then began to suck on her neck, gently. He felt her head drop back as she relaxed, letting the sensations take over her body. The red pen fell to the floor in a hail of graded papers.

Joseph slid his hand up her torso and down the front of her dress, brushing her nipples with his fingers. Hannah began moaning and wrapped one of her legs around him, pulling him toward her. Their kissing intensified, as if neither one of them wanted to breathe air, hungrily sucking and slurping, feasting on each other's mouths.

Joseph felt her hands grapple briefly with his pants and then his cock was free, throbbing with an intensity and sense of purpose that he hadn't felt in a long time.

As Hannah stroked his cock, he moved his hand down her perfectly smooth inner thighs until he reached her crotch. He had expected to find a pair of her signature thong panties, but instead a slightly furry, very warm and wet vagina greeted him. He spread her labia lips with his fingers and gently inserted his thumb into her. Hannah moaned and tugged on his cock, pulling it toward her.

He lifted her from the chair, easing them both down onto the floor. She straddled him, spreading her legs wide, her knees skidding on the linoleum, and slowly slid down until she had him all the way inside her.

As they moaned and pushed and thrust against each other, a few facts became clear to Joseph. He was having sex with a woman, which meant he was probably not gay, and the *opakapaka* was burning.

Eleven

The air conditioning at the Steak House was blasting, icy cold and scented with the aroma of fire, butter, and burning animal flesh. Just smelling it restored your faith in civilization.

Jack hobbled behind the hostess as fast as he could. Through the maze of tables and chairs, his walker legs catching on the plush carpet, his body lurching left, then right, juking like Emmitt-fucking-Smith to avoid busboys and waiters and platters of sizzling meat, as if the restaurant had been designed as his own personal obstacle course. The hostess zoomed ahead of him, not even looking back to see how he was doing. Didn't these people realize you could only move so fast with a walker?

The hostess had offered him a booth near the front door, but Jack had turned it down. Partly out of pride—he didn't mind walking to the back of the restaurant, he just couldn't sprint there—and partly because he was meeting someone and didn't want anyone to overhear his conversation.

The hostess was standing by a table, patiently waiting for him to creak and clomp and eventually shuffle over and park his butt in the booth. He noticed her glancing at her watch and lightly tapping one of her feet. It made him want to slow down. What does she think this is, an Olympic-fucking-time trial?

After he lurched himself over and settled in, she dropped the menus, spun on her heel, and walked off. Jack glared at her as she zipped back to her hostess station. Her officiousness and energy, the way she buzzed around the place, probably caught the eye of her boss and earned her praise. She was probably the employee-of-the-fucking-month. But she annoyed Jack. She was the kind of woman he disliked intensely. All the hustle, the hurry-up, the bustle, the drive. Where did she have to get to? What was so important she couldn't wait a minute? Sure she was cute, but in a bony, blond, hurry-up-and-come-I've-got-a-hair-appointment kind of way. Women like that might rule the world someday, but Jack would take a voluptuous redhead with a hangover any day of the week.

Jack sank back in the booth and let the frosty breeze cool him down. A Mexican man with a thick mustache brought him a glass of ice water; he took a sip and began to feel better.

Jack saw Paul Rossi enter the restaurant, take off his sunglasses, and wait for his eyes to adjust before he finally recognized Jack and headed toward him. Jack watched him walk. He didn't waddle or lurch like most of the union guys; he had no hitch in his get-along; he moved with an athlete's slow and confident gait. That's because he wasn't like the other guys; he wasn't an old-school Teamster. Paul Rossi was one of the new breed of union leaders. Despite the apparent ethnicity of his name, he was actually a blue-eyed, blond-haired executive with an MBA from Pepperdine. Paul had surfed as much as studied when he was in college, and he retained that sun-blasted, wind-whipped, casual appearance even now, as head of the Teamsters local in Las Vegas.

Paul slid into the booth with Jack and flashed his bleached white teeth in the approximation of a smile.

"Jack."

Jack looked across at Paul and rose up a little to shake his hand. He didn't understand how the AFL-CIO brain trust could put this wonder boy with his jeans, pink polo shirts, and slip-on loafers in charge of Las Vegas. But then, Jack was a traditionalist. He'd been close to Paul's predecessor, a huge man named George Noriega who died of a massive coronary about six months ago. Jack and George went way back, and if he were alive George would be the man Jack would entrust with his dilemma. Instead, he had to turn to the young buck from Malibu.

"Paul. How's it goin'?"

"The membership's working. As long as my guys are collecting a paycheck, life is good."

"Yeah. Work is good."

The waitress arrived. "Ready to order?"

Jack looked over at Paul. "What're you gonna have?"

Paul flashed his gleaming teeth at the waitress. "Just some iced tea." He turned to Jack, apologetic. "I already ate."

Jack nodded. "Well, I'm starving. Give me the New York, medium rare, baked potato with everything, ranch dressing on the salad, and a bottle of Bud."

Paul looked at Jack. "Watching your cholesterol, I see."

Jack shrugged. "I been eating fucking mahi-mahi for a week, I need something real."

"Hawaii's beautiful."

"If you like scenery and uncooked fish."

The iced tea and beer arrived, and both men took sips before returning to their conversation.

"How's that going? Hawaii and all?"

Jack shook his head. "Not so good. That's why I wanted to talk to you. I'm hoping maybe you can help."

Paul nodded, squeezing the lemon section into his tea. "What can I do for you?"

"Well, there's another company there and—well, I don't know how else to say it, but they threatened me."

"Threatened you?"

"Yeah."

"How?"

"Gave me the old get-out-of-town-by-sundown speech."

Paul nodded. "Some things never change."

"I was hoping that with my relationship with the union and all . . . you might be able to do something."

Paul blinked. "How can I help?"

Christ, this guy was clueless. George Noriega would already be on his cell phone putting the fix in. Jack reminded himself to be patient. He didn't want to say anything that could be held against him later in a court of law, or whatever it is they're always saying on TV.

"I don't know. Maybe talk to the guys at the office over there."

"Sure. I could put in a call. I don't know what good it'll do, but I'm happy to try."

"I'd make a donation."

Paul shook his head. "That's not necessary."

This was news to Jack. How many times had he been asked to make donations or keep phantom workers on his books? Lots. And now it's not necessary?

"It's no big deal."

"Look, Jack, I'll level with you. Things are different now. Really. The union is being run like a business. We're trying to develop what they call a corporate culture. I'm afraid I'm not going to have much influence over the local in Hawaii."

Jack felt the anger rising in him. He tried to push it back, but the more he resisted the more pressure he felt. "He threatened my life."

Jack almost gagged as the words came out of his mouth. It sounded like he was whining and he hated himself for that. Paul was taken aback. "What?"

"He said he'd kill me if we didn't leave."

Paul's expression changed. "Did you go to the police?"

"And say what, I'm a punk-ass bitch? I don't have any proof. It's his word against mine, and he's local."

"It sounds serious."

Jack lost his temper. He almost shouted. "You better believe it's serious."

Jack tried to drink some beer and calm down, but he ended up choking and coughing and spluttering foam all over his shirt. When he finally caught his breath he turned to Paul.

"I'm embarrassed, okay? Some island cocksucker tries to shove me out. It's embarrassing."

Paul nodded.

"I got a lotta dough tied up in this. Even mortgaged my house."

Paul looked away and finished his iced tea. It was instantly refilled. After a long pause, he turned to Jack and spoke in his most comforting voice.

"There's nothing the union can do, okay?"

Jack was humiliated. Here he was whining like a baby to some sprout who didn't know the first thing about who he was or what he'd done. He'd bared his soul, put his cards on the table, and all he got was turned down.

"But . . ."

Paul interrupted him.

"I know you've done a lot to help us. Believe me, George Noriega told me all about you."

Jack nodded. "George would know what to do."

Paul took out a piece of paper and wrote seven digits on it. He slid the paper across the table to Jack. "This guy's a problem solver."

Jack looked at the numbers and then looked at Paul. Maybe he'd underestimated him.

"Thanks."

"Enjoy your steak." Paul stood and left without shaking Jack's hand.

...

After he'd put out the fire, thrown the burned fish in the sink, and got the smoke alarms to stop their ear-bleeding beeping, they'd moved to the bedroom. They lay curled together, the sheets whipped around them in a crazy twist. Hannah studied his face, trying to figure out what he was thinking.

"I'm sorry about the fish."

Hannah smiled. "I'm not. That was the best bad meal I ever had."

Joseph laughed. "Yeah? You liked it?"

"You should cook like that more often."

Hannah sat up in bed, her breasts bobbing and settling as she leaned against the headboard and turned to him.

"Joseph? Are you all right?"

"I'm fine."

"It seemed like you had something to prove."

Joseph stretched, raising his arms over his head and flexing his legs to reach out as far as he could, and released with a sigh.

"I've just had a lot on my mind lately."

"You really want to go to New York."

It wasn't a question. Joseph started to make some noise but she cut him off.

"I understand. If I were you I might feel the same way."

Hannah stood up and pulled on a T-shirt before grabbing her hair and yanking it back into a sloppy ponytail.

"I have to finish grading those papers."

Joseph sat up and grabbed her, pulling her back into his arms. He held her for a long moment, feeling her warmth, enjoying her smell, letting her imprint on his body. He kissed her neck.

"I have to run over to Sid's. I could pick up a pizza."

. . .

Driving to his uncle's house gave Joseph time to think about Francis's offer. It would be easy just to say yes, spend a couple of hours being uncomfortable, and then it'd be over. Kind of like going to the dentist. But it wasn't that simple for Joseph. The who, what, why, where, and how of sex were defining qualities. Sex was the one thing Joseph had, that anyone has, that was uniquely his. Sex can be a simple pleasure, consumed and enjoyed and forgotten like a vanilla ice-cream cone, or it can be a conduit for love, passion, and desire. It could be all those things together. But it was his choice, to share or not to share.

As he drove, Joseph suddenly realized a fundamental truth. Everything comes down to sex. Everything. The need to stick it in is the mover, the shaker, and the prime motivator driving humankind. It is the center of human endeavor, the beating heart of history. Even the drive and desire for money, prestige, and power were just ways for ugly guys to get beautiful willing partners. You make enough money, you can purchase sex, an intimate act reduced to a commercial transaction. And how many times had he heard the cliché, Power is an aphrodisiac?

It was an epiphany. He realized that the history of mankind, all the great and stupid wars—the Trojan War an obvious example—all the scientific discoveries and inventions, everything from the cure for smallpox to the pocket fisherman and Swiss Army knife; all the books, poems, and plays ever written; all the songs ever sung, the art ever made; everything ever done by any human anywhere: It was all for one deep overpowering reason.

To get laid.

It's not a strange concept. It makes sense. We are animals. We are, at our essence, biological. And the biological urge is to reproduce. Propagate. Keep the species from going the way of the dodo.

Joseph thought about the history of Hawaii. In the early days, tribal conflict was simple and clear-cut: kill the men, take the women, stick it in. Then the Europeans arrived, but did things really change? Did Captain Cook come to these

islands in search of spices and gold or to get off with some
dark-skinned honeys? Did Columbus leave Spain searching
for a quicker route to India, or was it just a kind of Old World
booty call?

The more Joseph thought about Francis's offer, the
angrier he became. He didn't want to be bought. He didn't
want to be subjugated. He didn't want to personify the history of Hawaii and let some conquering white man plant his
pole in him. No fucking way. That's how we got like this.

It was dark when he arrived at his uncle's house. Joseph
let himself in through the screen door on the back porch. He
heard the television murmuring from the family room, saw a
light on in the kitchen.

"Uncle?"

"In here."

Joseph followed the sound of his uncle's voice, through
the kitchen and into the family room. Sid was sitting on the
couch, a handgun resting on his lap. He was watching figure
skating on the TV.

"What're you doing?"

"Watchin' TV."

"Ice skating?"

"I like it." Sid pointed to a young man in a pirate costume doing some kind of elaborate spinning moves in the air.
"Triple toe loop."

Joseph watched as the young man landed smoothly on
the ice and then began to do some kind of crazy tap dance
steps to Dixieland music. Sid was delighted.

"He Russian. Dey got all da good ones in Russia."

Joseph sat down on the couch next to Sid. "I talked to
the producer."

Sid arched an eyebrow. "Wot he say?"

"He's willing to hire us."

Sid turned to Joseph. He was beaming. "Yeah?"

"He wants me to have sex with him."

Sid sat back, thinking. He turned and gave Joseph a searching look. "He say dat den?"

Joseph nodded. "Yeah."

"Wot you say den?"

"I said I'd think about it."

"Wot's to think about?"

Joseph shrugged. "I don't know. I didn't want to say no right away. I thought I'd go back and talk to him some more."

"You should fuck 'im."

Joseph looked at his uncle. His jaw dropped. "I'm sorry. What?"

"Fuck 'im. Give 'im wot he want. It would be good for da family."

"But Uncle, I'm not gay."

"I'm not Italian, I eat pizza."

"Uncle Sid. I don't want to have sex with him."

"Lot of people gotta do wot dey don' wanna do. Fact of life."

"This is different."

"I'm not Jewish, I like bagels."

"It's not the same thing."

Sid shrugged. "Wot's so different den? Still two people wit' dey clothes off goin' at it."

Joseph had heard enough. "I gotta go." He stood up to leave.

"Rent some gay porn. You see. Not dat different."

Joseph turned to his uncle. "I thought you'd be outraged."

Sid looked at Joseph. "I'm a businessman. Seem like a good deal to me."

...

Lono sat at a table eating a plate of *zaru soba,* scooping up the cold buckwheat noodles with his chopsticks, dunking them in sauce, and slurping them down as he kept one eye on the door, casually watching the customers, mostly Japanese tourists hungry for a taste of home, as they entered. It was the same quaint restaurant, kind of like a rustic country lodge in Japan, that he'd recommended to the woman he was looking for. The food was good. The location, on a quiet side street between Kalakaua and Kuhio avenues, was prime for anyone staying at one of the big hotels in Waikiki who wanted to get away from the tourist glitz and catch a little peace and *udon.*

He'd been coming here about the same time for the past couple of days, hoping to bump into her. Lono knew it was a long shot—for all he knew she'd gone back home or moved on—but he also understood that people are creatures of habit; when they find something or someplace they like, they return again and again. If she were still in Honolulu, she'd eventually make it back to this restaurant. She was the type.

He was on his second cup of hot green tea when he finally realized that she'd been sitting at the bar for almost half an hour. When she entered, Lono had thought it was a teenage boy from Tokyo. But when he heard her ask the waitress for extra tofu, he recognized her voice. She looked fantastic, even better than he'd imagined. She had, for whatever reason, taken his advice and changed her appearance completely.

But while Lono the pimp might've dressed her in a more urban style, a clean white tracksuit from Adidas and a Sacramento Kings jersey, he had to admit that her new look was very good. Very sexy. Like some androgynous Brazilian skateboarder hipster. New York street-cool but with a kind of Rio de Janeiro samba style. If he had been attracted to her before when she was all mousy and New Agey, now he could hardly look away.

But something troubled him. He had thought she was out of the game, yet here she was, a few blocks from the prowl, dressing the way he'd suggested.

Lono resisted the urge to approach her. Instead he decided to be smart. He'd follow her, see what her sport was, and then make his move.

Lono signaled for the check, slapped some cash on the table, and slipped out the door.

...

Jack had called the number Paul Rossi had given him. He'd been surprised when a woman answered the phone. At first he thought he'd dialed it wrong, but she asked him what he wanted and he said, "I have a problem." She told him she didn't know what he meant, but if he went to the Paris Hotel on the Strip and played the third slot machine from the end in the last row of slot machines on the southwest side of the casino between ten and eleven, someone might talk to him about his problem.

So here he was. Jack plugged another quarter into the slot and punched the button. He watched the wheels spin around and around, annoyed with himself for even caring if he won or lost. He checked his watch. He'd been there fifty minutes already and figured he'd won five or six bucks. But he was getting aggravated. He wasn't used to waiting around for people.

"*Bonsoir.* Would you like another beer, monsieur?"

Jack turned and saw a cocktail waitress, a full-figured Latina with a thick Sinaloan accent, bending over him, dressed like a French maid. Ordinarily her deep cleavage and full round ass would've given him pause and on a normal night he might even flirt with her, try to get in her pants. But not tonight.

"Sure."

She handed him a fresh beer off the tray she was carrying. Jack pulled a crumpled wad of cash out of his pants pocket and dropped a well-worn five on her tray.

"*Merci.*"

Jack didn't even watch her as she walked away. Instead he turned back to the stupid slot machine, something called Moolah Galaxy, and plugged in another quarter.

He played a few more times and then checked his watch. It was eleven, straight up. Jack sat there. He was tired of playing the slots and sick of waiting. He wondered if Paul Rossi was just fucking with him. He didn't know what was going on, but he knew one thing. Fuck this. He was out of here.

Jack grabbed his walker and started to hoist himself up to standing.

"You giving up?"

Jack turned and saw a serious-looking young man standing behind him.

"Yeah. I'm played out."

"The next one is the winner. That's the way it works. You pump the machine for hours and then you give up. The next guy comes and *bam,* first time he's got the jackpot."

Jack studied the man for some kind of clue. He was obviously powerfully built, with the thick muscles of a boxer and the square jaw of a marine; he had a kind of nondescript sandy brown hair and pale blue eyes. But he wasn't dressed like a hitman, at least not Jack's idea of a hitman. The man was wearing faded blue jeans and some kind of simple gray pullover sweater. Hired killers don't wear sweaters.

"Be my guest."

Without saying a word the man leaned over, dropped a quarter in, and hit the button. They both watched as he hit three cherries and the machine began regurgitating coins at an alarming rate.

"Heard you have a problem."

...

Hannah sat on the bed trying to finish grading her students' papers before Joseph came back with the pizza. Her stomach had been growling for about an hour and the handful of stale peanuts she found languishing in the back of a cupboard hadn't done much to quiet it down. She stuffed a piece of gum into her mouth and turned her attention back to her work.

As part of their requirements for accreditation, her students had been asked to write an essay in English. Each paper offered up a different set of challenges. The kids had, to say the least, their own unique understanding of grammar and sentence structure. But unlike most of her colleagues, she didn't take off points when some of her more creative students dropped a few words of pidgin in their essays and reports. Why shouldn't they? It was the language they spoke at home and on the streets. It was what they grew up with. It was what she grew up with too. It was authentic Hawaiian flavor. She wasn't going to punish the kids for that. She wasn't going to tell them it was bad grammar. As far as she was concerned, it wasn't. Why were people always trying to squash the uniqueness out of Hawaiian life? Why try to make it bland and homogeneous like the mainland? It's not Disneyland with pineapples.

It amused her that Joseph refused to speak much pidgin. He'd use some words, like *pau,* when he was finished eating. But he never spoke in the slangy patois of his uncle. Perhaps he was too well read. Or maybe he was embarrassed to be so Hawaiian. Maybe that's why he wanted to leave.

Hannah was still trying to wrap her brain around that. They both had nice places to live, and if they pooled their resources they could have an even nicer place. They had good jobs. They had the weather, the beach, their friends and family. They had each other. Now Joseph wanted to give all that up.

Most people work their whole lives in boring jobs to make enough money to move to Hawaii and spend their golden years chilling out in the tropics. Here they were, already a big step ahead, and what does Joseph want to do? Go to the mainland and work his ass off. She wondered if he knew how cold it got in New York. How crowded and expensive and stinky it was.

She wondered if she could be happy without him.

He entered the bedroom carrying the pizza one-handed, doing a bad imitation of the little Italian guy printed in red on the takeout box. Hannah was hungry, so it took her a minute to notice that Joseph wasn't wearing any clothes. He'd somehow managed to undress between the front door and the bedroom while still balancing a large sausage-and-pepper pizza with one hand.

He stood there, like a waiter in a nudist colony, a full-blown erection saluting her. Hannah burst out laughing.

"What are you doing?"

Joseph smiled. "You ordered sausage."

And with that he tossed the pizza on the bed and dove on top of her. He pulled her legs up in the air and plunged into her as she giggled. Hannah tossed her head back and groaned as Joseph began thrusting. She threw her arms around his shoulders, feeling his strong muscles flexing, and sucked on his neck. She began to twist his nipples. He moaned.

"You're gonna make me come."

Hannah smiled. "I don't want the pizza to get cold."

...

Francis sat on his hotel bed and looked at his cock. It was still mighty erect, hard and throbbing, ready for action. Only before it had been pink and healthy as a newborn with a perfect Apgar score, and now it had developed a slightly bluish tinge around the edges. Francis was worried. Sure, some of it could be wear and tear; he'd abused his penis like a madman ever since he arrived. But it was also unsettling, like wrapping a rubber band around your thumb and leaving it on for too long. It was turning that kind of blue.

Tomorrow would be two days since he'd popped the Viagra cocktail, and his dick was showing no sign of taking a rest. Francis, on the other hand, was exhausted; the constant boner had become more of an albatross than a joy. He needed to rest and hoped that if he took the night off, had a quiet meal and a hot bath, laid off the booze and speed, it might help his cock deflate.

The hotel room had its own Jacuzzi tub in the bathroom and he'd spent the last half hour soaking in it, letting the steaming water and bubbling jets unwind his speed-freaked muscles. It worked, too. He felt all the chemical tension and fatigue begin to melt away. But the Jacuzzi hadn't had much effect on his cock. It stood out of the water like a buoy bobbing in the harbor.

Periscope up!

After the bath, Francis sat in his terry-cloth robe and calmly ate a green salad and grilled skinless chicken breast while he watched an old movie, a clumsy drama about some straight guy who falls in love with a woman who doesn't believe in love because she's a successful something-or-other. He drank Evian. He was being good.

Then the phone rang.

"I figured you'd be sitting alone in front of the TV eating room service, so I thought I'd call."

It was Chad.

"Good timing. I was just getting ready to go out."

"Isn't it past your bedtime?"

"This is paradise. Who has time to sleep?"

"Really?"

Chad sounded skeptical. Frances tried to sound blasé.

"Really."

"Maybe I should come over and you could show me a good time."

Francis looked at his cock. He really wished it would go down. "I don't think that's a good idea."

"Why not?"

"You know, I'm working all day. You'd be bored."

"I could hang out by the pool."

And fuck everyone who came within a ten-foot radius.

"I'll think about it."

"You're still mad at me."

"Yeah, Chad, I am."

"I said I was sorry."

Francis didn't say anything. He looked at the movie playing on the TV and saw the two leads throw their arms around each other in what looked like the Delta Airlines terminal at LAX.

"I *am* sorry."

"I'm sure you are."

"I'm trying to change."

"Don't do it on my account."

Francis was agitated. Whatever vestige of relaxation he'd had was shot. He opened the drawer by his bed and pulled out the little plastic Baggie of crystal meth. He dumped some on the table.

"Goddammit, Francis, cut me a break here."

"I'm tired of the lies, Chad. I'm sick to death of them."

Francis hated himself for being so melodramatic, for sounding like a fucking soap opera. He bent over, stuck a rolled-up bill in his nose, and hoovered up a line of speed. Chad didn't say anything.

"I've got to go."

Francis started to hang up the phone. But he could hear Chad trying to say something before he did. It sounded like he was apologizing. Apologizing for the ten thousandth time.

...

Lono walked slowly down the street. He stopped casually and window-shopped. Sometimes he'd nod a quick greeting to one of the streetwalkers cruising for tourists. He kept one eye fixed on the young woman across the street. He could tell by her stride that she wasn't cruising. She was on her way somewhere. So Lono played it cool and kept his distance.

He followed her through the Kuhio Mall and the International Market. He waited as she stopped and looked at tie-dyed sarongs at one kiosk, handmade raffia beach bags at another. Lono had never liked the International Market. It was like a low-rent Disneyland: no rides or attractions, just a place for tourists to come and buy earrings made out of coconut shells, T-shirts with stupid slogans like I GOT LEI'D IN HONOLULU, or plastic trinkets with the word ALOHA imprinted on them. Little souvenirs of Hawaii made in China and Malaysia. He was glad to see she didn't buy anything.

She crossed Kalakaua Avenue and headed down the drive toward the Royal Hawaiian Hotel. This was where Lono had to close the gap between them. He had to see if she was a guest of the hotel or if she was a working girl on her way to meet a client. It was dark on the grounds of the hotel, tiki torches lighting the path at night, and he was able to get within about ten feet of her.

He was relieved to see her take a room key out of her pocket and go directly to the elevator. She nodded at the doorman as she passed.

Lono stopped. He didn't need to follow her anymore. In a few minutes he'd learn everything he needed to know about her from the front desk.

...

Yuki got into the elevator and waited for the doors to close. A sharp tingle, a kind of heebie-jeebie feeling, crept up her spine and gave her a delicate spasm. She thought her aura must've picked up someone else's energy and that energy had bounced from chakra to chakra up her spine like a pinball until it hit the top lotus in her third eye and sent it pinging. Someone was watching her, sending her sexual energy. It felt good.

When the elevator doors opened on her floor, Yuki saw Francis standing there. She could tell right away that he was amped up on something. He was tapping his feet and chewing on the skin around his thumbnail.

"Going out?"

Francis stopped chewing his nail and looked at her.

"Yeah." He started to get into the elevator but suddenly stopped, holding the door with his hand. "Say, would you like to join me for a drink?"

"I don't drink alcohol."

"How sensible." He made that sound like a put-down.

"Not very often anyway."

"Have you tried a mai tai? They make really good ones downstairs. And they have nice music."

Yuki was going to decline his offer. She wanted to go to her room and get into bed. She wanted privacy so she could relish the residual effects of whatever had happened to her. But then she remembered her promise to herself. She'd promised to help Francis get over his negativity. It was supposed to be her mission.

"Okay. But just one."

Francis grinned at her as he ground his teeth. "You won't be disappointed. They're yummy."

...

The hitman's name was Keith. He'd been with the 31st Marine Expeditionary Unit and was well trained in urban assault, sabotage, infiltration, extraction, and assassination, an education provided by the government, his tuition paid by the taxpayers. He had learned the art of the kill, spent time in Afghanistan perfecting it, and gone on to relish it during black ops in the Philippines and Colombia. Now discharged, he was offering his services, the only thing he knew how to do, to the general public.

He gave Jack the creeps.

Keith had wanted to talk in a more private location, so now he and Jack stood in front of the Bellagio, watching the water fountains boom and swing through the air, as patriotic music blared from loudspeakers.

"Do you want to know why?"

"Just the target's name and location."

"He's Samoan. Last name's Tanumafili—something like that."

"I'll need you to be precise."

Jack reached for his wallet and pulled out one of Sid's business cards. "Here."

Keith looked at the card and then handed it back to Jack. "You can keep it, I don't need it."

Jack nodded. He didn't know why Keith couldn't keep it, but he wasn't about to argue with him.

"Honolulu?"

"Yes."

Keith nodded. He turned and watched as the fountain sent multiple sprays up in the air, the water swaying and dancing like a giant octopus in an animated musical.

"It's amazing."

Jack looked at the professional killer. "What is?"

Keith pointed to the fountain. "That. I don't know how they do it."

Keith's eyes glistened in the light as he watched the fountain perform its water ballet to Aaron Copland's *Appalachian Spring*.

Jack shook his head. He didn't give a flying fuck about the Bellagio's water fountain. He wanted to get back to business: find out how much this was going to cost him, when it would happen, how it would go down. He had questions. He needed answers. But Keith didn't even look at him; he watched the fountain like a little boy watching the trapeze act at Barnum and Bailey's.

Jack sat on a bench and turned his attention to the tourists walking by. They were couples mostly, men and women out for a fun time in Las Vegas. They were going to see a show, maybe something with an avant-garde circus act from Budapest and contortionists from Bangkok or a spectacular where effeminate magicians risked their leather-clad asses teasing tigers through flaming hoops. Some of them were on their way to see saggy-boobed showgirls in campy productions that only a drag queen could love. If they weren't going to any show, they were getting plastered and emptying their wallets in the casinos. Las Vegas. You gotta love it.

Jack noticed a middle-aged man sitting in a car near them. He didn't look like a tourist. Jack studied him. He looked like a cop. Jack sat up straighter. He turned and looked at Keith, but Keith wasn't paying any attention; he was mesmerized by the dancing fountain.

It suddenly occurred to Jack that this could be a setup. What if Keith was an undercover cop? What if Paul Rossi had betrayed him? Jack began to regret the whole thing.

"Maybe we should just forget it."

That got Keith's attention. "It's almost over."

"I'm just having second thoughts."

The fountain display ended with a booming crescendo of sound, lights, and spray.

Keith turned his attention to Jack. "Did you ever see anything like that?"

Jack shook his head. "I don't think so."

Keith looked at the now dark and quiet pond in awe. "Amazing. Really amazing."

"Yeah, it's real nice."

Jack watched as the man sitting in the car opened his passenger door and a young woman, still in her dealer's costume, jumped in. The man started the car and then merged with traffic, driving off down the street. Jack turned back to Keith.

"How much is this gonna cost?"

"Twenty grand."

"Twenty?" For some reason that seemed like a lot of money to have a fat Samoan killed.

"I can't take my guns on the plane. Have to work by hand. Price goes up."

Jack nodded. It made sense. "Okay."

Keith smiled. "We have a deal?"

Jack nodded and extended his hand. "We got a deal."

The two men shook hands.

"You'll get a call about where to wire the money."

Jack dragged his walker over and clambered to his feet. "Thanks."

He began walking away. Keith grabbed his shoulder. The killer's touch sent an icy shiver through Jack's body.

"Don't you want to stay for the next show?"

Jack winced a little smile in the killer's direction. "I've seen it."

...

Lono knew everything he needed to know. He sat at the bar and nursed a beer while he took in the scene on the patio. Yuki—that was her name—sat at a table with another guy. Her body language told him the guy wasn't her boyfriend. He was probably a colleague, maybe her boss.

He watched as she sipped a mai tai, not really drinking it. The guy, on the other hand, was already on his third. He'd ordered for her with each of his rounds, and now she had cocktails stacking up in front of her like planes circling O'Hare the day before Christmas.

Lono watched as a trio under a little cabana began to play a kind of watered-down Hawaiian elevator music for the tourists. Lono didn't recognize the two older men play-ing guitar and ukulele, but the middle-aged woman singing softly and swaying her hips in a grass skirt was a former em-ployee. She saw him sitting at the bar and gave him a wink. Lono nodded back and shot her a smile. It was nice to see people move on and find gainful employment doing some-thing they like. How many times had he seen prostitutes grow ungracefully into middle age? Cutting their prices until they were the Costco of blow jobs, the Pic-N-Save of fucking.

She had a sultry voice, slightly husky from years of Marlboro Lights, and Lono wondered if she didn't run a little business on the side. She still had her figure and, judging from the leering old men in their brand-new Hawaiian shirts who stared at her coconut-shell-covered breasts, she could still work the magic. It made Lono laugh. Maybe this is what happens when we get old. We do the same tricks, only slower.

He turned his head, casually eyeballing Yuki. He saw the guy was now working his way through Yuki's collection of watery mai tais. From the look of it, the way he was leaning in close and pawing at her, he was trying to come on to her. He could see her resisting. But the more she resisted, the more she pulled back, the more pressure he applied.

The trio began playing a nauseatingly slow version of "Tiny Bubbles"; it was dirge-paced, more lethargic than Don Ho at a funeral. Lono wondered how such a song could be-come a Hawaiian classic. We don't drink too much cham-pagne around here. He looked over and saw Yuki get up from the table and walk off the patio toward the beach. Outside the soft tiki glow of the patio, she was immediately swallowed by the blackness of the beach at night. Lono watched the guy stumble to his feet and run after her, calling her Yoko.

Perhaps they were lovers. Lono wasn't interested in getting in the middle of a domestic dispute. That's where the well-meaning Good Samaritan gets killed and the couple bond over the disposing of the body. But they didn't act like lovers, not even lovers having a fight.

Lono stood and paid his bill. He walked up to where the trio was playing and dropped a twenty into their tip jar. The singer blew him a kiss. Lono walked off the patio along the sidewalk until he was out of sight and then discreetly stepped off the path into the night.

It took a couple of minutes for his eyes to adjust as he strolled cautiously toward the sound of the crashing surf. He couldn't see anything for a while, couldn't hear anything over the sound of the waves but the faint murmur of music coming from the patio and a car alarm going off somewhere. But as he moved deeper into the night, his eyes adjusted, and eventually he could see two figures silhouetted against the dull silver ocean.

Lono went into a crouch and circled around, trying to be casual, trying not to be seen. As he got closer he could hear them. The woman was agitated, angry, almost in tears; the man's voice sounded breathy and threatening.

Lono moved closer and froze. It was an unmistakable image, like some kind of Balinese shadow-puppet porno show. The man was standing in the sand, his pants crumpled around his ankles, his erect cock pointing up toward the big dipper, his right hand whacking away as fast as he could.

Lono could hear them.

"You want it, don't you?"

"I told you. No."

"You want to touch it. You want to serve me."

"I should sue you for sexual harassment."

"Watch me do it. Look at it."

"No."

She turned her back on him.

Lono saw the man shuffle a couple of steps toward the woman, his pants hobbling him, the sand dune-ing up in front of them as he dragged them toward her. Lono watched as the man reached out with his free hand and grabbed her. She struggled to get away from him, but he had a maniac's grip.

That's when Lono fucked the guy up.

...

Although she was a pacifist and didn't approve of violence for any reason, Yuki had to admit she was relieved when the big Hawaiian saved her from Francis's drunken dementia. She just wasn't equipped to talk him down off his speed- and rum-fueled psychosexual high-wire walk.

It had gotten weird fast. He began referring to her as his cabin boy and complaining that she wasn't reporting to the deck for her nightly watch. He was going to have to strap her to the mast or rope her to the plank or some kind of bizarre nonsense. At first she'd laughed. She thought he was just drunk and joking, like he was flirting with her. But soon it became clear that he believed what he was saying. He had slipped into some kind of method-acting role as captain of the ship and believed it was his obligation to sodomize her for her various lapses of duty and assorted transgressions.

That's when she left the table.

He'd followed her, of course. But she hadn't expected him to start masturbating in front of her and demanding that she worship his hard-on. That was just too much. Although she didn't believe that Francis would rape her, or even hurt her really, she was relieved when the big Hawaiian entered the picture.

She had seen fights in movies, those slow-motion kung fu ballets with people doing back flips and walking on walls, but had never seen one in real life. In real life they don't last too long. An explosion of violence. A winner. A loser. Just a couple of seconds, no more, and Francis was knocked out on the beach.

Yuki recognized the Hawaiian. He was the pimp who had started her transformation. The one man who saw her potential. She had secretly hoped they'd meet again, and now here he was, like a shining prince, saving her from the weirdness.

As he led her away to the relative safety of the streets, he introduced himself. He had a cool Hawaiian name, Lono, and—could this be right?—he asked her if she'd like to go out with him. Yuki couldn't remember the last time anyone had asked her out on a date. Actually, that was a lie. She could remember quite clearly because it had been four and a half years ago.

"Would you like to get a drink? Are you hungry?"

"I don't want to go to a bar."

She watched as Lono thought for a moment, his handsome face scrunched in contemplation, his dark, intelligent eyes searching her face for clues.

"How about a shave ice?"

"What's that?"

"Kind of like a Japanese snow cone."

Yuki shrugged. "Okay."

He extended his arm for her to hold. She was still trembling a little and gladly took it. He was very strong, his arm soft and hard and smooth and firm. Holding on to him made her feel light, like she could float. For a brief, fleeting moment, she thought about Francis. She hoped he wasn't dead.

...

Hannah and Joseph sat naked in bed, eating pizza and sucking on longneck bottles of Kona. Hannah smiled at him.

"Cold pizza and warm beer. My favorite."

Joseph smiled apologetically. "Dinner's been a disaster. Sorry."

"Don't apologize. Unless something's going on that you need to apologize for."

"What do you mean?"

Hannah put down her slice of pizza. "You're acting kind of . . ."—she searched her mind for the word—"amorous."

"Is that a bad thing?"

"Not at all. But it's a different thing. I'm wondering what's up."

Joseph thought about telling her it was nothing. But she was someone he'd shared a large chunk of his life with. She was someone who'd stuck by his side through good times and bad. She had heard him complain about his growing claustrophobia from living on the island, and she'd heard him rant about the plight of the natives. She didn't judge him. She didn't push him or try to change him. She accepted him as he was. If anyone would understand his fears and frustrations, it was Hannah.

So Joseph told her about Francis's offer and Sid's belief that he should actually go through with it for the good of the family. He laid it out for her. Told her everything.

When he was done, she was laughing.

"What's so funny?"

"You."

"Me? What's so funny about me?"

"That's why you kept jumping me. You wanted to make sure you weren't gay."

"I'm not gay. Not that there's anything wrong with being gay. But I'm not."

She laughed some more. "Oh, honey. You are a goof."

"I'm not gay."

"No one ever said you were."

"So why does Sid want me to sleep with that guy?"

Hannah looked at him. "You should. It would help everybody if you did."

...

Sitting at a little table just outside the shaved ice store on a small side street, Lono watched Yuki dig in to a massive bowl of the stuff. She'd gotten the kind he'd recommended, sweet red azuki beans and *lilikoi* syrup.

"You like?"

Yuki nodded, her mouth full of melting ice. "I'm getting brain freeze."

"That's a common side effect."

She scooped up a big mound of the ice and held her spoon out to him. "Have a bite."

"You sure?"

"You've earned a reward."

Lono smiled. "What did I do?"

"Saved me."

"You could've taken him."

Yuki smiled; she locked eyes with him and pushed the spoon up to his lips. "C'mon."

Lono knew resistance was futile; he wanted her to feed him, to put something cool and refreshing and sweet in his mouth. He parted his lips.

"I thought this was your favorite."

"Mmm. It is. It is."

Lono had eaten this exact same dessert from this exact same shave ice stand hundreds of times. He'd had it at least once a week for as long as he could remember. But this was the first time it tasted so sweet it almost brought tears to his eyes. The ice she put in his mouth was crunchier, more crystalline. The *lilikoi* syrup was brighter somehow, not just the color but also the flavor. And the azuki beans? Had anyone ever tasted such earthy sweetness and depth of flavor in a shave ice before?

"Do you want another bite?"

"Please."

She playfully spooned another helping into his mouth. He could tell she was having fun feeding him. She was looser than when he met her before. Sexier. Confident.

He tasted the shave ice, and the second bite was even better than the first. That's how Lono knew he was in love.

...

When the beach patrol finally found Francis, sometime after midnight, he was curled up in a fetal position, his pants around his ankles, his right hand still clamped on his erection. He had two cracked ribs and a bruised kidney, but his face was what scared them. At first they thought he'd been in an accident or fire, but after they shined a flashlight on him they realized that it was just sand sticking to the blood that was smeared all over.

One of the patrolman noted—he actually wrote it down in his evidence report pad—that the badly beaten man had muttered one word over and over.

"Chad."

Twelve

When they got back to her hotel room, there was no awkward pause, no small talk, no hesitation whatsoever. They got right to it. Yuki hadn't even gotten the door closed when Lono leaned into her, putting his lips gently on hers and sending his soft warm tongue gliding into her mouth. She returned his kiss, only she wasn't gentle; she kissed back ferociously, wrapping her arms around him, holding on to his strong shoulders, using them for leverage to drive her tongue deep into his mouth. Her tongue wrestled with his, slipping back and forth in their mouths as she pressed her crotch against him.

She could feel him getting stiff. She could feel his hardness, his length. It was a big one, and she wasn't going to let it get away. She unbuttoned his shorts—they fell to the floor with a *thunk*—and reached into his underwear, fishing for his cock. He kicked his shorts across the room without ever breaking from the kiss as he slid his hand up her shirt, feeling for her breasts.

He started lightly, just brushing the tender ends of her nipples with his thumb. But the sensation caused Yuki to emit a loud moan. Somehow holding on to his cock, stroking the head of it, somehow that connected with his twisting of her nipples, like two ends of an electrical current, positive and negative, alternating and direct. It sent a shock through her body. A heart-skipping, hair-raising, eyes-rolling-up-to-the-ceiling blast of current.

And then she had to have him inside her. She pulled his underwear down and then her own, ripping her panties when they snagged on the doorknob. He hoisted her up as she lifted her legs, wrapping them around his waist. She gasped when she felt the head of his cock press against her labia lips. She pulled hard with her legs, wanting him to plunge into her, but he resisted. He let his cock slide in only an inch or so and then he stopped. He held it there. Not in and not out.

Yuki felt herself expanding. A vibrant and moist electromagnetic charge rolled through her. It started right there at the entrance to her pussy and radiated outward through her body in strong rolling waves of sensation. If she'd had her eyes open, she might've seen her aura crackle for a brief blue flash.

As he held her there, not entering and not exiting, loitering at the door, her vagina became like a snake, pulsating, undulating, gripping and pulling, expanding and contracting until it had slowly enveloped his cock like an anaconda that swallows its prey whole.

When he had fully penetrated her and was thrust in as far as she thought he could possibly go, Yuki gasped. Lono's cock was touching her in places she'd never been touched before, reaching deep into her body and making her tremble.

He used his strength to hold her up, pressing her against the door, gently driving his cock into her. It seemed to Yuki that it went deeper with each thrust. But she didn't really know for sure. She just pulled him hard with her legs and squeezed him with her pussy, locking them together in a groove, a rhythm punctuated by moans, grunts, and the chain lock on the door whacking gently against the wood.

Yuki had always been a big believer in the school of self-pleasure. She unabashedly masturbated with abandon on a regular basis. She believed that having orgasms was like eating vegetables and getting regular exercise; it was good for you. Like a bowl of Cheerios, it was part of a healthy lifestyle. But all the orgasms she'd had, even the ones with her battery-powered, multispeed, latex dildo, hadn't prepared her for this.

As Lono thrust into her, picking up the pace and the intensity, her body got hot. A tingling at the base of her spine soon turned into a burning, uncontrollable, almost painful sensation. The heat spread and expanded, rippling through her body. She threw her head back, banging it sharply into the door, but didn't notice. Weird gurgly sounds began rising up out of her throat, and her breathing became shallow, staccato.

Yuki closed her eyes. In her mind's eye she saw her clitoris suddenly light up like a roman candle. Burning white-hot phosphorus. And then the convulsions came. Her back arched and her body shook with strong pulsating spasms. The orgasm rocketed up her spine, exploding in her head like a bottle rocket, and for the briefest possible moment Yuki lost consciousness. She stopped breathing.

She died a little death.

...

Lono felt her melt against the door and then fall into his arms like a deflated pool toy. He stopped thrusting into her and held on. Even though her body was still, he could feel her vagina contracting and jumping in wild spasms around his cock. He watched her eyes flicker open and try to focus, like she was coming back from some kind of trance.

Lono lifted her up and slowly pulled himself out of her. He then gently carried her over to the bed and put her down. She sighed and reached down, touching herself, giving her clitoris a last little tingle. Lono watched her groan and wriggle and then he began stroking his cock. She looked up at him and watched as he stood over her and jacked off.

When he came, she couldn't help herself; she squealed with delight as hot arching gobs of come rained down on her.

Thirteen

Jack thought it was a done deal. He'd spent twenty minutes on the phone with the young woman at the bank, giving her detailed instructions on the whys and wherefores of transferring cash. He'd sent it in four installments of four thousand nine hundred ninety-nine dollars and ninety-nine cents. That way the bank wouldn't be required to report the moves to the IRS. He figured the hitman would be happy to pay a nickel to keep it all under the radar. The wire transfers were small enough to be lost in the paperwork shuffle of day-to-day business transactions. And sent to the hitman's numbered account, they were virtually untraceable.

Jack poured himself a cup of coffee and sat back. He was feeling pretty good about the world. Sometimes, Jack realized, the best-laid plans of mice and men really work out just fine. His business was expanding into a lucrative new market and he was about to show the Sumo just who was a punk-ass bitch.

It was Stanley, of course, who stuck a wrench in the deal. He called from Honolulu.

"Dad? What are these transfers for?"

Jack didn't like to be questioned or second-guessed. "None of your fucking business."

There was a long silence on the phone. He heard Stanley clear his throat.

"Okay. Well, the bank called because I need to approve the transfers."

"What the fuck're you talking about? I just made 'em."

"They need my approval."

"Since when?"

"Since you had the stroke."

Jack's coffee had suddenly gone ice cold; it left a bad taste in his mouth. Suddenly struck with vertigo, he felt dizzy and grabbed the table for balance. He didn't say anything for a long time.

"I've been signing checks."

"You're approved for that."

"So why can't I transfer money?"

Stanley avoided the question. "What are they for?"

Jack erupted, shouting into the phone. "I told you, it's none of your fucking business. Now call the bank and tell them to release the money."

"Not until you tell me what they're for."

"I can't."

"Then write nineteen thousand nine hundred ninety-nine dollars and ninety-six cents' worth of checks."

"It has to get there today."

"Why?"

Jack calmed down. He tried to be reasonable. He tried to sound like a father.

"Son. Just approve the transfers."

But Stanley had the upper hand, one of the few times

in his life he ever did, and he wasn't about to relinquish his power.

"Sorry, Dad. I'm not going to do it until you tell me what it's for."

Jack looked at the phone. He looked at his coffee. He looked out the kitchen window at the swimming pool sparkling in the backyard. He looked at his walker. He heard some squeaking from the phone and turned his attention back to it. And then, like Mount Saint Helens, he blew his top, unleashing a furious diatribe of profanities, bile, and rage into the phone. All the anger-management classes in the world couldn't have calmed him down; at one point he screamed and shouted so much so fast that he forgot to take a breath and almost passed out.

But despite all his rage, there was nothing he could do. Stanley had the last word.

"No."

And that's when Jack realized that he was fucked. He hung up on Stanley and dialed a number. A woman answered.

"Hello?"

"Forget it."

"I'm sorry?"

"I met the guy. Yesterday. At the Paris casino."

"I'm sorry, I don't know what you're talking about."

Jack hung his head. Of course she's not going to say anything on the phone.

"Could you give a message to someone for me?"

"This is not a message service. I'm sorry."

"I want to call it off."

"I don't know what you're referring to."

"Just tell the guy, okay?"

"Perhaps you have the wrong number?"

Jack couldn't take it. He lost his temper. "I can't pay."

There was a long pause. "We do not accept cancellations at this number."

"Okay. Tell me who to call. I'll cancel with them."

"We do not accept cancellations."

Jack smacked his palm against his forehead. What is with this chick? "I can't pay. Okay? I'm broke. It was all a big mistake. End of story."

"If you ordered the product, it will be delivered."

"Tell him to fuckin' stop. Why can't you do that?"

"I'm afraid I can't help you. Good-bye."

And she was gone.

Jack tried another number. He dialed Paul Rossi at the Teamsters local. It took some finagling; Jack had to tell the assistant that it was an emergency, a life-and-death situation. Which, he realized, it was.

After sitting there stewing for a good five minutes, listening to Bachman Turner Overdrive's classic "Takin' Care of Business" and half of a song by Foreigner or Journey or Boston—he couldn't tell them apart—on the classic rock station they played when you were on hold, Jack was patched through to Paul's cell phone.

"This is Paul."

"Jack Lucey. I got a situation."

"How can I help you, Jack?"

Jack bristled at the obsequious tone. "I called that number you gave me and worked something out with the guy. Now I want to cancel, but he won't let me."

Jack listened as there was a long staticky pause on the other end of the phone.

"I don't know what you're talking about, Jack."

"The number you gave me. In the Steak House."

Another pause. More white noise drifted down the line.

"Sorry, Jack. I don't remember giving you any number. Perhaps you have me confused with someone else?"

Jack didn't want to be bullshitted. "Fuck that, Paul. The guy's a nut. I want to cancel the deal. Fucking call him and tell him it's off."

"I'm sorry. I'm in a bad cell zone. I can't hear you."

"I said to call him and cancel the fucking deal."

"You're breaking up."

Jack screamed into the receiver. "Cancel the fucking job!"

"Look. I'll call you back next week."

And then he was gone.

Jack looked at his phone for a beat, then hurled it against the wall. "Fuck!"

...

They stuck a tube in him. He could feel it. Sticking some kind of needle into his arm like he was oblivious to the pain, jabbing it in a few times until they were satisfied.

"Ouch."

"Doctor, he's coming around."

Francis wanted to ask the nurse if she was good at spearfishing, because that's what it felt like to him. Standing motionless out on the reef, watching little black-and-yellow striped angelfish darting under the water, waiting, adjusting for parallax, and then—*bam!*—shooting the spear right through the wriggling little thing. That's what it felt like. But he couldn't say that—he wasn't feeling so well—so he did the best he could.

"Bitch."

"He's awake."

"Sir? Can you look at me?"

Francis tried to open his eyes, but it was difficult. Then someone opened his eyes for him and shined a searing bright light in them. You might as well throw his retinas in a microwave.

"Aahh! Fuck!"

"How much Thorazine did they give him?"

The nurse held up two fingers, indicating that they'd given Francis a solid dose.

"Sir? Can you hear me?"

Francis tried to nod. Weird. His head wasn't moving. Had he broken his neck? Was his head still attached to his body?

"Yeah?"

"Sir? Your penis. How long have you had the priapism?"

Even if Francis had been completely lucid he'd have had no idea what the doctor was talking about. He searched his brain for some kind of response that might make sense.

"It's a rental car."

The doctor nodded. "That's nice, sir. Do you remember what kind of drugs you were taking?"

"Sure."

Francis was tired, and whatever had happened to him or whatever they were doing to him, whatever it was, it was beginning to hurt like hell. Why weren't they giving him something for the pain? Wasn't he in a hospital?

"Did you take cocaine? Amphetamines?"

Francis nodded. "A little."

"How much did you drink?"

"I wasn't driving."

"We know that, sir. Did you drink any alcohol?"

"Mai tai. I had mai tai."

Francis wanted to go to sleep. Couldn't he answer all this in the morning? What was the emergency?

"Did you take any sildenafil citrate?"

Francis was starting to get annoyed. What was with these questions? He wasn't a doctor.

"Speak . . . fucking . . . English."

That took some effort. He was exhausted. He hoped that would be the end of the questioning.

"Viagra. Did you take any Viagra?"

Francis nodded.

"Okay, good. That's what I wanted to know."

The doctor leaned close, talking directly to Francis's face.

"Francis. Can I call you Frank?"

Francis was too weak to tell the guy that his name was not Frank, had never been Frank. No Frank. But he didn't say anything. At least he didn't say anything that resembled language.

"Frank? We need to do something about this priapism. Your penis."

Francis batted his eyes, blinking up at the doctor, who he now noticed was a fairly handsome young Asian man.

"We need to deal with your erection."

Although he'd been drugged and beaten and drugged again, Francis smiled.

. . .

Joseph stood in the kitchen doorway, drinking a cup of coffee and looking around his little house. He saw a design magazine on the coffee table in the living room and moved quickly to pick it up and throw it in the trash. He stopped himself, because he hadn't finished reading the article about gourmet kitchens, and because everyone knows that one design magazine does not make a person homosexual.

...

She couldn't help herself. She hadn't been this close to any male anatomy in years and she wasn't going to let it get away without an encore. She wasn't about to go another four years without this. No way. You can keep your crystals and Pilates classes and clothes made out of hemp. Yuki had no use for those anymore. What she wanted was right here. She remembered what her life coach had told her: When you find something you want, grab hold and don't let go. So as Lono lay next to her, breathing deeply, all snuggled and relaxed, she began stroking his cock.

It responded. Like she had trained it herself.

...

The stripper with the gorgeous blue-black skin and giant tits with nipples like Hershey's kisses turned around. She lowered her G-stringed ass right onto Jack's crotch and ground into him in hard, slow, circular movements. She was tired, he could tell. Sweat flew off her forehead as she danced and humped and did the slip 'n' grind. Her body was shiny and slick with moisture. She'd been at it for almost forty-five minutes, and still Jack couldn't come. She twisted her head back and looked at him, gasping, like she needed oxygen.

"You get your nut yet, baby?"

It's not like he didn't want to. He'd been tense all day. He needed this.

"Not yet."

She slipped into overdrive. Moving to the beat, letting her body slap against his in big, moist thrusts.

"You close? Are you gonna do it for me, baby? You gonna make Momma proud?"

Suddenly Jack had heard enough. He pushed her off of him. "I guess I'm not in the mood."

The stripper stood there, hands on hips, her extra-jumbo, man-made breasts heaving as she tried to catch her breath, and looked at him.

"You're what?"

Jack felt a little sheepish. He handed her two hundred-dollar bills.

"I'm pooped. I've been traveling."

He noticed a river of sweat running down her head, collecting around her neck, and waterfalling between her breasts.

"Pooped?"

"Sorry."

For a brief second it occurred to Jack that she might just kick the living shit out of him. He handed her another hundred-dollar bill.

"Maybe next time?"

She snatched the bill from his hand and walked off. "I'm gonna take a shower."

Jack hung his head. He'd never had a failure like this before. Well, he'd come up short a few times in his life, once or twice, almost always due to massive scotch intake. But he hadn't had that problem since the air bags had been installed. Normally he was an ejaculating machine. But tonight, even with his permanent boner, he just couldn't get it up. This whole hitman thing was weighing on him.

Leaning heavily on his walker, Jack raised himself up and slowly started toward the door. Today, for some reason, he felt old.

Baxter was there and, as always, he opened the door for Jack.

"Thanks, Baxter."

"Mr. Lucey. Hold up a sec. You gotta thing on your— um, on your pants."

Baxter was coming around, trying to help. Jack looked down and saw what he was talking about. The front of his khakis were wet. Soaked. A big sweaty butt print smack dab in the middle of his crotch.

"Shit. Looks like I pissed myself."

"Come on."

Baxter helped him and led Jack off to a little side office by the front door.

"Here you go. I keep some towels in here."

Jack sat down and looked around the tiny little room. It must've been a coat check before the building had been converted into a strip club. Baxter reached into a cubbyhole and pulled out a towel.

"What a fuckin' day."

Jack began drying himself. Baxter smiled.

"Happens to the best of us."

Jack looked at Baxter and realized he didn't have the energy to explain what really happened. That he'd made the poor girl work so hard. It was easier just to let it slide. If the doorman thinks I pissed myself, big fucking deal.

"I must be gettin' old."

"Don't sweat it, Mr. Lucey. You wouldn't believe some of the stuff I've seen."

"Yeah?"

Baxter swelled with self-importance. He ran his fingers over his bushy mustache, smoothing it out.

"Oh, yeah. We get all kinds in here: drug dealers, Mafia guys, regular joes, frat boys—you name it."

Jack thought about that for a minute.

"Listen, maybe you know something about this kind of thing."

Baxter leaned in. "What's up?"

"I've got a friend who may have got himself into some trouble."

"What kind of trouble?"

"Well, he—" Jack stopped. He changed his mind. "I shouldn't be talking about this. If he found out I'd told you we'd both be in the fuckin' soup."

"It's cool. Just you an' me. Doorman–client privilege."

Jack nodded. He looked Baxter in the eye. "Promise?"

"Absolutely."

Jack finished wiping his pants and threw the towel in the corner.

"My friend had a problem, so he hired a hitman."

Baxter couldn't help himself; he grinned. "Cool."

"Not so cool. Because he realized he couldn't pay the guy and the hitman doesn't know that yet because he's undercover or whatever."

"So he's gonna do the job and then find out he's not getting paid?"

"Yeah."

Baxter shook his head in amazement. "Wow. Your friend is dumb. He's gonna have a pissed-off hitman coming after him."

Jack nodded, though the pissed-off hitman should really go after Stanley. "So what would you do?"

Baxter was obviously enjoying himself. "You wanna stop the guy?"

"My *friend* wants to stop the guy."

Baxter scratched his head. Jack was beginning to think that confiding in a hulking doorman at a skanky strip club was yet another really stupid thing he'd done in what was becoming a parade of stupid things. This, he realized, is how you end up behind bars.

Baxter snapped his fingers. "I got it. What if you get someone to do the hit before the hitman?"

"I don't follow."

"If another shooter gets the victim before the guy who's been hired, then he can't be mad about not getting paid because he didn't do the job. You see?"

Jack thought about it while Baxter continued to expound on his idea.

"It's better than whackin' the first shooter, 'cause those guys are usually connected. And this is the beauty part—" Baxter was beaming—"it still solves your friend's problem."

Jack suddenly understood. "You wouldn't know where I could hire a shooter, do you?"

"It's you? You're the friend?"

Jack nodded.

"I'll tell you what, Mr. Lucey. I'll do the job for you."

"You're a hitman?"

"Not really. But it's, like—it's my dream job. It's something I've always wanted to do but, you know, nobody ever gave me the opportunity." And then, as an afterthought, "I'll give you a good price."

Jack played it cool. "Can I count on you?"

"You want me to demonstrate? I could whack somebody as, like, a sample."

Jack shook his head. "That won't be necessary. Just the one."

Baxter grabbed Jack's gimpy hand and shook it enthusiastically. "Thank you, Mr. Lucey. Thank you. You won't be sorry."

...

Joseph opened his closet and stared at his clothes. He had a closet full of colorful clothes, but then Hawaiian shirts are colorful by definition. Hawaii's a colorful place, and Hawaiian shirts are a Hawaiian thing. Of course there were gay Hawaiians who wore them, but that was more about being Hawaiian than being gay. Wasn't it?

He closed his closet door and sat down on his bed. What was he worried about? Just because everybody he knew, including his longtime girlfriend, thought he should have sex with a guy didn't mean they thought he was gay. Right? Not that it would be a bad thing if he was. There's nothing wrong with being gay. But he wasn't. Right?

Fourteen

No one met him at the airport. No one said aloha. No one threw a lei around his neck. No one even noticed him. That was the way he liked it. He picked up his rental car and followed the Xeroxed map they'd given him at the counter to the Ala Moana Hotel just on the edge of Waikiki. It was a nice hotel, the kind of place a businessman might stay, upscale but not too fancy. The kind of place where an innocuous young man could blend right in, get in, and get out, without arousing any suspicion at all.

After he checked in, Keith went for a walk. He strolled down Kalakaua Avenue, stopping in a menswear store to pick up some khaki-colored shorts and a few Hawaiian shirts with big hibiscus blossoms speckled on them. He wore one of the shirts out of the store and down the street. Although he thought the shirt with its pale orange background and splotchy white floral pattern looked like he'd fallen asleep under a flock of seagulls, Keith knew he needed to wear it; he needed to acclimate. Besides, it was better than sweltering under a bright blue burka in Afghanistan.

Keith walked into the Surfrider hotel, strolled through the beautiful old lobby, and came out to the cocktail bar under a massive banyan tree. He sat with his back to the hotel, admiring the handsome people on the beach, watching a couple of young men take a surfing lesson, and thought about what he needed to do. He ordered a beer.

What he'd learned in the military—Assassination 101—had been pounded into his head in drill after drill and then tested and reinforced in hostile environments. The operational protocols had become second nature to him: infiltration, execution, extraction. Easy. Effective. Like shampooing your hair: wash, rinse, repeat.

Keith checked his list off in his head. He was here, he'd infiltrated. As far as anyone knew, he was a businessman on vacation. He'd already gone through the phone book and located Sid Tanumafili; that wasn't difficult, that's the easy part. Now he had to plan the execution and extraction. These were linked. The last thing you want to do is take out your target and not have a clue how to get your ass out of the area. That, he realized, was the main problem with being on an island. All they had to do was close the airport and he'd be trapped. It's not like doing a hit in Denver; you can't just get in your car and drive to Phoenix. You can't pop somebody and then stroll down to the corner and catch a bus. Nope. Here the rules were different. The extraction had to be part of the execution. It had to be airtight.

Keith ordered a second beer. Everyone else was drinking, and he didn't want to stick out. Besides, he was enjoying himself. He watched as a large catamaran sounded its horn and drifted slowly to shore. Dozens of tourists, burned a crispy pre-melanoma red from being out on the water all day, clambered off the boat and waddled back to their various hotels. A family from Seattle walked by. Where they had once been as pale as uncooked chicken, they were now scarlet and blistering. The wife was complaining to the husband, bitching and whining, her voice getting higher and higher as she got more and more upset. She was annoyed that the sun was so strong here. Keith had to chuckle. What did she think? That her husband could use the dimmer and take the UV index down a couple of notches? Keith heard the woman start in again. Why did they have to come here, was he trying to give her skin cancer? Why couldn't they go somewhere else? Keith shook his head and laughed.

...

Yuki knew Francis was in the hospital. She knew where he was and how he got there. But that didn't mean she was going to visit or send flowers. As far as she was concerned, he got what was coming to him.

She was at work. Someone had to keep things going. Someone had to push the paperwork through. So that's what she did. Although she had to admit that her heart wasn't in it.

All she could think about was Lono. The image of him on top of her, thrusting his cock into her, kept replaying in her mind. She could recall his taste, the salty raw flavor of his tongue thrusting into her mouth. She remembered how strong and solid his arms felt. She smiled when she thought about the sweet sweaty whacking sound of their bodies colliding.

Even though they'd made plans to get together tonight, Yuki couldn't help herself. She daydreamed. She felt her body getting warm, her pulse racing. She got up, locked herself in the bathroom, and masturbated. She let the phone ring.

...

Sid was mad. He and Wilson stood in front of Joseph; their body language—arms crossed, legs hip distance apart, heads cocked slightly—said it all. They weren't going to take no for an answer.

"After all I done for you?"

Joseph groaned. Nobody likes a guilt trip. "Uncle, I said no."

"You gonna make my house payment den?"

"I won't do it."

"Wot you scared of?"

Joseph glared at Sid. "You go fuck him."

Sid shrugged. "I be happy to. 'Cause it mean I got food fo' my family mouth."

Wilson chimed in. "We all gotta sacrifice, brah."

Joseph looked at his cousin. "You wouldn't do it."

"Sure I would, but he wants you, brah."

Sid came over and put his arm around Joseph. "People do it fo' all da time. All over da world men are fuckin' each other den. It's no big deal."

Wilson added his two cents. "It's okay wit' Hannah. She said so."

All his life Joseph had listened to his uncle, ever since his parents had decided to move to the mainland for the security of steady employment and a more affordable standard of living. Without his mother or father around, Joseph had gone to his uncle for guidance. He'd taken his advice about college, which kind of car to buy and how much to pay for it, how to get a mortgage for his house, and what to do when he grew up. They'd sat together and talked and drank and turned Sid's small fleet of lunch trucks into one of the best production catering companies in the business. Sid was his father figure, his business partner, and his friend. And now he was asking Joseph to whore for the family.

"Sorry. No can."

Sid shook his head violently. His face grew flushed and his eyes bugged out.

"Once dat guy move in we never get 'im out. Dey take food from our mouth fo' da rest of our life. You gotta stop 'em before dey get in. Dey just like da vines."

The vines were a pet peeve of Sid's. Some visionary brings a vine from the mainland over to Oahu to grow in his yard, a plant not native to the islands, and the next thing you know it's gone crazy, growing up telephone poles and down the lines until it finds a tree, then covering the tree and killing it, and on and on. The plants were insidious, unstoppable. They had altered the flora and fauna of the island forever. Another invader from the mainland.

"There's enough work to go around."

Sid spit on the ground. "Wot we doin' now den? Wot we doin'?"

It was true. There wasn't any work at the moment.

"Something will come up. I was talking to Ed the other day. He was getting all kinds of feelers from L.A."

Sid stared at him. "Look me in da eye den."

Joseph looked Sid in the eye.

"You gonna do it?"

"No."

"Fo' da family den?"

"The gay thing is *pau*."

"Even if it mean we hungry?"

"Even if it means we sell everything and open up a little *okazu* in Waialua."

Sid paused. He didn't say anything for a long time. Wilson stared at Joseph, trying to keep a determined expression on his face. Finally, Sid spoke.

"You not my blood. You not my partner."

"Uncle, what are you talking about?"

Sid exploded, shouting at Joseph. "You fired! I don' wanna see you no mo'."

With that he turned and walked out. Wilson followed. Joseph watched them leave. Saw the screen door smack into the wood and watched as their hulking figures slowly disappeared down the walk. He listened as car doors opened and closed, an engine started, and the car drove off, the tires making sticky sounds on the hot pavement.

...

Francis lay in bed in one of those ridiculous hospital gowns. That was humiliating enough. But the day was young, and Francis knew a fresh round of embarrassment and degradation was on the schedule for later. Already he'd had a parade of first-year residents standing around looking at his cock. They all had their chance, poking and prodding, squeezing and palpating. He'd learned to respond to their commands like a dog: Cough. Inhale. Exhale. They made him roll over and took turns snapping on rubber gloves, lubing up, and sticking their fingers up his ass to jab at his prostate. None of it felt particularly erotic. But the head doctor told him this was a valuable learning experience for his students. They didn't get to study examples of priapism that often.

Francis understood why. If he hadn't had the shit kicked out of him on the beach, these pimply med students wouldn't be standing around admiring his woody. No way. He could think of a million other uses for it.

When he wasn't being bombarded with inane questions like *When did you attain your last orgasm?*, Francis was on the phone to the mainland, telling the story of how he survived a brutal attack on the beach. He left out the part about exposing himself to his assistant.

A nurse came in with another bouquet of flowers. These were from the executive producers, and he had her set them right next to the ones from the network execs. Francis was a little disappointed that he hadn't gotten any flowers from Chad. Chad was the first person he'd tried to call when he woke up. But, typically, Chad wasn't home or in the office and, according to his assistant, was "unreachable." Francis had called Chad's cell phone and left a message informing him that he had been practically beaten to death. He figured he needed to exaggerate to get Chad's attention. But still no phone call, no flowers, no nothing.

It occurred to Francis that the only reason to be involved with someone was so they would come and be by your side when you needed a hand to hold or a shoulder to cry on. Francis remembered how he felt as he watched the attack on the World Trade Center on September eleventh. He worried about the people who had no loved ones to call. What if you were just standing there, knowing the end is near, everyone else is on their cell phone muttering *I love you* and saying good-bye to their families, and you've got no one to call? That would suck. That would be him.

The nurse opened the door and smiled. Francis couldn't tell if her expression was one of pity and empathy or bemusement and sadism. He guessed it was a bit of both as the brain trust trooped into his room and lifted the sheet.

Just when you think they've done the most horrible things they can do, they come up with something new. They came in to take measurements, a whole class of them. Gawking like a busload of tourists, making notes and nodding as the doctor in charge rattled off a string of arcane facts and unintelligible medical gibberish. After his little speech and demonstration, he held an impromptu Q&A session before letting each one take a turn molesting the patient.

The students, some of the women tittering and leering like Girl Scouts at a nudist camp, held fancy-looking calipers and other instruments of torture.

They measured from the tip to the base. They measured the circumference, the diameter, the density, and the weight. They took turns at this: snapping on rubber gloves and grabbing his dick like they actually knew what they were doing. He felt the cold touch of the instruments as they went about measuring and calling out numbers. Francis was relieved that they were all speaking metric. Centimeters and millimeters and grams. They might as well have been speaking Chinese. And then one of the pimply-faced little nerds with his white doctor jacket and his plastic pocket protector and stupid stethoscope dangling from his pencil neck piped up with "That's not even six inches."

Francis burned with embarrassment. He wanted to scream, to cry, to defend himself. *Not even six inches?* You wouldn't know it if I stuck it in your mouth.

And then someone brought some food. They rolled a little cart in front of the bed and left his meal under its clear plastic cover. Because he had six stitches in his lip, the doctor had put him on a liquid diet. Francis took the lid off the food and looked at it. He knew why comedians made fun of hospital food. It was easy. And it was unappetizing: a bowl of clear broth and a plastic cup of lukewarm pudding the color of camel's teeth. Francis lay back and closed his eyes. . . .

...

He woke up feeling like fried roadkill. His mouth hurt where his stitches were, his ribs ached, his head throbbed, and his cock was still hard.

"Well, well, well. Sleeping Beauty stirs."

Francis blinked a few times. He recognized the voice. He thought he might still be dreaming.

"I flew all this way. The least you could do is say aloha."

"Aloha, Chad."

Chad stood there in all his glory. Fit and well dressed, his hair layered and perfectly highlighted, his teeth bleached to a gleam, his tanning-booth tan making his skin glow with a healthy radiance. He took off his nine-hundred-dollar designer glasses and bent close to Francis.

"Can I see it?"

"What are you talking about?"

"You know."

"I'm hurt. I'm laying here with stitches in my mouth and bruised ribs, and all you want to do is look at my cock?"

"The doctor told me about your condition."

"I have an erection. It's not the first time."

"C'mon. Please. Maybe I'll do something nice for you."

"Fine. Just close the door."

Chad put his glasses back on, closed the door, and lifted up the sheet like an excited child unwrapping toys at Christmas. Then he froze.

"Oh, my God." Chad gasped, his left hand shooting up and covering his mouth. "Honey, what did you do to yourself?"

"It's the stupid doctors; they've been poking it every half hour."

"How long have you been like this?"

"Two days. I think. I haven't been keeping score, you know." Not like you, he thought. "Why? What's wrong?"

"Your dick is blue."

Francis lifted up the sheet and looked for himself. Sure enough, there it was, just under six inches long and the color of a Smurf.

...

Joseph sat under a tree and watched the waves wash in. The water was clear and green, like an old Coca-Cola bottle, and he could see bits of kelp and a few small jellyfish rolling around in the surge. On the far end of the beach, a couple of giant sea turtles lay sunning in the sand. Joseph thought he ought to be brooding, but he didn't really know what to brood about. He didn't even really know what to think of the last twenty-four hours. The best he could figure is that everyone he knew had gone insane.

"I thought I'd find you here."

He looked up to see Hannah standing there. She'd already changed out of her teacher clothes and was wearing a tank top and board shorts. She looked good. Strong and clean and sexy. Joseph couldn't help himself, he smiled at her even though he was perplexed by her decision to take Sid's side.

"Somebody's got to watch the turtles."

"Mind if I join you?"

"Just don't try and convince me to do anything I don't want to do."

Hannah smiled sheepishly and sat down, plopping her butt in the sand. Out of habit, she began to glide her hand across the sand, grading it, smoothing it out around her.

"What did he say?"

"He fired me."

Hannah was surprised. "What?"

Joseph looked at her and nodded.

"But it's half your company."

"Then he disowned me."

Hannah shook her head. "He's just mad. You know how he gets sometimes. Tomorrow he'll come back and ask why you weren't at the office cleaning the trucks or something."

"Tomorrow I might not be here."

Hannah looked at the sand. She began to draw wavy lines in it with her fingertips.

Joseph watched her. "I thought we were monogamous."

Hannah bit her lip. "We are."

"So why'd you want me to do it?"

She shrugged. "I don't know. I guess I thought it might shake things up."

Joseph squinted off down the beach and watched as one of the sea turtles slowly dragged itself back toward the water. It was a heavy, tortuous process as it scraped and pulled and dug into the sand with its flippers, fighting gravity with all its strength, until the first blast of ocean smacked into it and the turtle lifted off the beach, momentarily weightless, spinning like a top on the water, and was pulled out to sea, riding the wave like a reverse surfer.

...

"I don't want to do any more anal." She said it like she meant it.

Lono didn't have to ask why. He could imagine. He took a sip of hot green tea and smiled across the table at the two women. They were looking good. They had to. In the old days it was enough just to be willing to do the job. But this was the modern world, the market for pussy was glutted, and if you wanted to stand out from the crowd you had to offer something better than the skanky whore or strung-out runaway. Any old junkie can suck your dick, but the discriminating customer, the man with a significant bankroll who has come to the islands to relax and play a little golf—unless he's like that movie star who craved the jolt of frisson from sexual encounters with the gamier purveyors of cheap pussy and fast blow jobs in cars; unless he's like that—the discriminating customer is going to want a higher quality product. He's going to want this year's model, not some old jalopy. And even if you provide them with someone young and beautiful and exotic, the discriminating customer is going to want more than just a spin between the sheets; he's going to want something memorable. He's going to want a fantasy fulfilled. And he'll pay top dollar for it.

Some pimps think it's enough to keep the girls out on the street and working. They could be fifty-year-old glue sniffers with crabs and a wicked dose of the clap, it didn't matter, so long as they were out bringing home the Benjamins. But the smart pimp elevated his game. He stayed off the streets and under the radar.

Lono was a smart pimp. No skanky-ass dope fiends for him. His girls had to be fit and well groomed. Lono provided health club memberships, personal trainers, whatever they needed to get in shape and stay that way. He got girls who were young but not illegally so, and he trained them to be outgoing, personable, and in control. They may have dressed provocatively, letting nipples protrude or cleavage be revealed, but they were wholesome, classy, and clean.

Lono was a stylist. His girls were archetypes. They came dressed as hula girls, geishas, nurses, newscasters, Laker girls, teenage rock stars, cheerleaders, or the girl-next-door. They were memorable. They fulfilled fantasies. They were very expensive. Lono was often surprised how many men requested someone dressed in a smart suit with a briefcase. Like fucking your female boss could empower you.

The girls Lono employed were like actresses. They played their parts and said their lines, professional to the core. They preyed on the simple psychology of men. They were good girls who'd let their hair down and go wild because you were so sexy you drove them crazy. Or they were bad girls who just wanted to be good because you had saved them. And always because you, the paying customer, had the biggest cock they'd ever seen.

"I keep getting hemorrhoids."

"You try those medicated pads?"

"I need some time off the anal. That's all."

"The pads work."

"I don't want to do any more anal."

Lono nodded. Jessica, the beautiful Korean girl who didn't want to do any more anal, adjusted her silicone-enlarged breasts in her tight leather bikini top and licked her lips.

"I want to book more three-ways."

Lono nodded. Now she was thinking. He could charge more than twice for a threesome and it took almost the same amount of time. Besides, most times the clients just wanted to fuck each other but needed the prostitute there for reassurance.

"I'll see what I can do. Will you do anal in a three-way?"

Jessica nodded. "If I have to."

Lono looked over at Terika, a lithe young woman with hair dyed a honey blond.

"What about you?"

Terika squirmed in her seat. She was nervous. "I'll do anal. Three-way, fifty-fifty, whatever you want me to do."

"Thanks."

"But I was wondering if I could have Christmas off this year."

Lono stared at her. He didn't say anything. Normally he would've scolded her. Christmas was one of the busiest times of the year. He could have Terika bringing in three or four thousand dollars a night during the holiday crush.

"Why?"

"I want to go see my grandma in Detroit. She's ninety-two."

Jessica flashed her eyes at Terika. She gave her a look that said, You're wasting your time, girlfriend. But Lono surprised them.

"Go see your grandma. It'll be all right."

The women exchanged surprised expressions. Not that Lono was a hard ass or unreasonable, but he did maintain a level of professionalism that was unusual in the flesh-peddling biz.

"Thanks, Lono. Really. That's awesome."

Lono smiled. "Merry Christmas."

Jessica, sensing magnanimity in the air, leaned forward. "I don't like it when they pee on me."

Lono's expression changed. He didn't like opportunists.

"It washes off."

Terika elbowed Jessica. "We better go. Heavy schedule tonight."

Lono nodded and watched them as they got up and left. Although they were looking exceptionally good, especially Terika, with her round firm ass moving in her leather skirt like some kind of jungle cat, Lono couldn't get Yuki off his mind. His voice mail was full, normally something that would've made him smile, only now it seemed like an anchor strapped to his leg, keeping him from spending time with her. All he wanted to do was rip off his clothes and crawl into bed and make love.

It hadn't always been that way. You work in the sex trade too long and it can warp your mind. You become like any other merchant. Rugs, used cars, surfboards, jewelry, drugs, pussy: It's all merchandise. You stop thinking of women as people, as human beings. They become commodities, objects of supply and demand. And there is always a demand for sex.

Sometimes he thought of himself as a simple farmer selling pineapples along the roadside. You find the ripest, juiciest fruit and display it for the customers. If people like your product they pass the word along. You get repeat customers, regulars. Soon you carve out a share of the market and you're in business.

It wasn't that simple, of course, but it doesn't take a rocket scientist to be a successful pimp. The downside, if you don't get busted, was personal. Lono had begun to see sexual desire as a weakness. A character flaw. Something that must be resisted at all costs. How many good Christians had he seen commit adultery, hundreds? How many marriages had been destroyed by the siren call of his girls, dozens? How many bankruptcies had been declared because someone was spending all his money enslaved to a fantasy?

If whoring was the world's oldest profession, it was created by desire, the world's first impulse buy. You couldn't have one without the other.

Lono wasn't weak. He couldn't be. If he appeared fragile or indecisive or looked for a second like he didn't have his shit together big-time, someone would move in on him: take him out, put a bullet in his brain or a knife in his back, and start running his girls. It was, after all, a cutthroat business.

To cope with the pressures of pimping, Lono thought of himself as one of the Jedi knights in the *Star Wars* movies. He liked their loner rebel attitude. It inspired him. It wasn't like the nerdy do-gooders on *Star Trek*. The Jedi were unflappably cool. They could be surrounded by beautiful women or storm troopers from the Death Star; either way, they didn't break a sweat. They used their mental strength to defeat their enemies and stay on the path of righteousness. Lono believed his preservation lay on that path, so he became like a Jedi. A Jedi pimp.

And then Yuki entered his life.

...

Jack bumped his walker along the hallway until he reached a couple of steps.

"You couldn't find an office with a fucking ramp?"

"We'll put one in later."

Stanley held out his hand and Jack reluctantly took it. What else was he going to do, sit there?

"I don't ask for much."

Jack wanted to yell some more, but he had to concentrate on the stairs. He raised one leg and then leaned his body to drag the other one up. It took a long time to climb two little steps.

"There's a great view. You can see the ocean."

"We're on a fuckin' island. Any way you turn there's gonna be ocean. It's like tellin' me our office in Vegas is good 'cause we can see the desert."

"I like the ocean."

Stanley was defensive. Normally Jack would've gone on the attack, yelling at his son, trying to toughen him up for the day he'd be taking over the business and taking on the world, but today Jack wasn't feeling up to it. He was preoccupied with thoughts of a pissed-off renegade hitman coming for his money.

"Hand me my walker."

Even Stanley sensed a change. "Long flight, huh?"

"Yeah, it was long. I'm flyin' to the middle of fuckin' nowhere and they only had old bags for stewardesses."

By *old bags,* Jack meant women over the age of thirty-five.

"Did you talk to the union?"

Jack nodded. "Those cocksuckers are worthless."

"What'd they say?"

"The new guy, Paul Rossi, is a fucking fag."

"They told you that?"

Jack looked at his son. "Not in those words. You gotta read between the lines."

Stanley heaved a sigh. Why was his father so difficult? Why was it always nicer when he wasn't around?

"What did he say?"

"He said no."

"No?"

Jack nodded. "That's what the big man on campus said."

"So what're we gonna do?"

"I was trying to arrange an alternative. That's why I needed the money wired ASAP." Jack sounded tired.

"What kind of alternative?"

"The kind you don't want to know about."

Stanley crossed his arms and looked his father in the eye. "Dad, I want to help. But you've got to let me in on it."

"I can't."

"Why not?"

Jack realized that Stanley wasn't going to budge, so he changed the subject.

"You got the phones working?"

"Of course."

"I need to make a call."

Stanley led Jack past the large plate-glass window, with its magnificent view of downtown Honolulu, swaying palm trees and ocean glistening in the background, to a small office.

"Check out the view, Dad."

Jack stopped himself from snapping at Stanley. He paused to look at the view. "That's nice."

He meant it. Jack entered the office and turned to close the door after him. Stanley was surprised.

"I need to make the call in private."

Stanley was instantly suspicious. "Why? What did you do?"

Jack sighed. "Stanley. Trust me. You don't want to know."

And with that he closed the door.

...

Keith had been sitting in his rental car for four hours. In fact, he could've sat there for days. It didn't bother him. He was patient. Good hunters always are.

Keith rigged the dome light so it wouldn't turn on when he opened the door. He slipped out of the car and walked up toward Sid Tanumafili's house. Keith had been watching it since Sid came home at six o'clock. Since then, all he'd seen or heard was the flicker of a TV set and the occasional flushing of a toilet during the commercials.

He could've killed him. It would've been easy. Sid didn't keep his door locked, and it would've taken Keith only a minute to enter and exit. Sid would've been found lying on the couch with a broken neck. The neighbors wouldn't have heard a thing. They wouldn't have seen a thing. But Keith hadn't worked out his exit strategy. He didn't want surveillance cameras at the airport catching him trying to go standby back to the mainland. That would give the police too easy a time frame. What he wanted to do was disappear Sid's body. Let it wash up on the beach two weeks after he'd gone back to Vegas. Something like that. He still had to work out the details.

Keith crept along the outside of Sid's house and peered in the kitchen window. He noticed a few empty bottles of Kona beer in the sink, a dirty plate, a Zojirushi fuzzy logic rice cooker, and a handgun on the counter.

The handgun gave him pause. A Smith & Wesson nine-millimeter semiautomatic police issue is a fairly serious weapon, not something your average joe uses for home protection. It signaled to Keith that Sid had some experience.

Keith went back to his car. It had been a long day, and he realized that he'd have to spend the next few days running some intensive background checks. He wanted to know if Sid had been in the military or, worse, if he'd been a policeman. It meant a day of boring paperwork. That was the stuff Keith hated the most. To do it correctly without leaving a trail means creating a maze of information requests to mask the one you really want. It was dreary, tedious, and time-consuming. But if it turned out that Sid had been a cop or a marine, Keith would abort the mission. A murdered cop, even a retired one, would bring too much heat. And a marine? Forget about it. Keith was *semper fi* all the way.

...

Jack watched as Stanley ate some kind of weird-named fish. It was snapper, but they didn't call it that. They called it *uku* or *moi, onaga* or *opakapaka*. And when you said, "What the fuck is that?" they always told you it was some kind of snapper. Like the Eskimos with three hundred words for snow, the Hawaiians had three hundred words for snapper.

"You're not hungry?"

Jack looked down at his food. He'd ordered chicken and wasn't quite convinced that chicken was what they'd brought him. Maybe it was a kind of snapper.

"I ate on the plane." Jack drained his beer and signaled the waitress for another.

"You want to try some of this?"

"I'm sick of fuckin' fish. All they eat here is fish, fish, fuckin' fish. I eat any more fish I'm gonna vomit."

"It's an island in the middle of the ocean."

Jack shot Stanley a look. Stanley shrugged.

"At least it's fresh." He tried to change the subject. "So what do you think of the new office?"

"It needs a ramp."

"We'll get one."

"And rails in the bathroom. I had to claw my way up the wall after taking a shit."

"I already ordered 'em."

Jack nodded. His beer arrived, and he proceeded to drink it as quickly as possible.

"You okay?"

"I'm fine."

But the truth was, Jack wasn't fine. He was anxious, he'd lost his appetite, his palms were clammy, and he was constipated. He hardly responded to the signals being sent to his brain by his constant erection. He was obsessed with two distinct and unpleasant possibilities looming in his future. In scenario number one, the creepy fountain-obsessed hitman does the job and then kills Jack because he refuses to pay him. In scenario number two, Jack has to go to the fuzz and plea-bargain to save his life. He'd trade protection and life for a conviction of soliciting a murder-for-hire. He'd go to the slammer; he knew that. Wouldn't that be fun? How could he explain his hard-on in the prison showers? What kind of nickname would they give an old cripple with a boner in the big house?

It wasn't like he felt guilty about having Sid offed. That wasn't it. The fucking Sumo deserved it. But things were getting weird, and Jack didn't know what to do. His anxiety was amplified by the fact that he couldn't reach Keith. In fact, the number he'd been calling had mysteriously been discon-nected. Jack didn't know what that meant.

It was this combo of paranoia and desperation that had forced Jack to go proactive and hire Baxter. It was an auda-cious plan. He hoped the young man could pull it off.

...

Chad went back to his hotel. He'd had enough of Francis, his neediness, and his freaky-looking dick. He pulled his rental car around to the front and let the valet take it. Chad slung his black leather Prada carry-on bag over his shoulder and walked into the lobby of the Halekulani. He liked this hotel. Even though it was smack dab in the middle of Waikiki, it was first class all the way. He had stayed here during the film-ing of a historical epic a few years earlier and had requested the same room: a luxury suite on the corner with views of Diamond Head and the ocean.

After he dropped his bag on the bed and tipped the bellhop, Chad looked around his room for a minute, adjusted the thermostat, and headed downstairs to the bar.

The night was balmy, a humid breeze blowing in from the ocean, the tiki torches flickering and snapping. Chad found a table near the pool. He ordered a mai tai and relaxed. He'd done a quick scan of the relevant males in the bar and had located two possibles and one probable. Now came the easy part: Just sit back, sip your drink, and see who makes eye contact. Chad was a closer. He didn't play games or flirt. He wasn't a tease. Once he made eye contact, it was only a matter of time.

It didn't take long before Chad hooked one. Bingo. We have a winner. Chad smiled to himself as a young man with pale blue eyes and a fabulous physique joined him at his table.

"I'm Chad. What's your name?"

"Keith."

"Can I buy you a drink, Keith?"

"I could use another beer."

Chad signaled the waiter as Keith settled into a chair. "What brings you to the islands? Business or pleasure?"

Keith smiled at Chad. "I'm hoping a little bit of both."

Chad grinned, his perfectly bleached and veneered teeth gleaming in the flickering tiki light. "A man after my own cock." Chad was anything but subtle.

Keith grinned. "What about you?"

"I don't want to bore you."

"You're here to work on your tan."

The drinks arrived.

"I have a friend in the hospital. I came to cheer him up."

"Is he okay?"

Chad shrugged. "He got beat up. But like I said, it's boring."

Keith smiled. "I need to eat something. Do you mind if I grab a menu?"

"I could use some food myself."

"Be right back."

Keith got up and walked over to the bar to snag a couple of menus. Chad watched him go. He admired his tight muscular ass and the strong graceful strides. This, Chad realized, was going to be fun. In fact, he was going to ensure it. He took a small plastic bag filled with little pills out of his pocket. He plucked two hits of ecstasy out of the bag, popped one in his mouth, and dropped the other into Keith's beer. Made in Amsterdam, purchased by a young screenwriter, and smuggled into California on the studio's corporate jet, it was the very best money could buy.

Keith came back with a couple of menus. He handed one to Chad and then sat down.

"See anything you'd like to eat?"

...

At first he couldn't tell what was wrong. Everything looked the same, but it was somehow different. The air had been displaced, the atmosphere altered. Joseph looked around his house, his mouth dropping open in astonishment as the slow, burning realization that he'd been dumped crawled into his consciousness. While he was out, Hannah had come and taken all her stuff.

He went to the bedroom and opened the set of drawers she'd used for almost a decade. They were empty. He looked in the bathroom. Her shampoo and conditioner, even the empty bottles that somehow managed to stay stuck in soap scum for months on end, were gone. Her makeup—not that she wore much—and hairbrush, combs, hair product, tampons, eye drops, three dozen tubes of Dr. Pepper–flavored Lip Smackers lip balm—she was addicted to those—and a big bag of cotton balls . . . all gone.

With a rising sense of dread fomenting in his stomach, he went to the kitchen. Joseph threw open the refrigerator door to find that she'd removed all the containers of her favorite brand of yogurt and the Cholula Mexican hot sauce she liked to dump on almost everything.

Joseph picked up the phone, hit the speed dial, and got her message machine. He hung up without leaving a message and walked into the living room. He sat heavily on the couch and looked around. Even though she didn't have that many things in his house—the average visitor might not even notice any difference in the before and after of her leaving—to Joseph it seemed like his home had been stripped bare by bandits.

Tears welled up in his eyes. He tried to suppress them but failed, and the warm wet tears rolled down his face.

Fifteen

axter had kept his sunglasses on during the flight. Not like he needed to, but he thought that's what hitmen do. They keep their shades on. It didn't even occur to him that it looked strange until a friendly ophthalmologist in the next row asked him if his eyes were bothering him. Baxter was trying to look inconspicuous, like the guys in the movies. He glared at the ophthalmologist and tried to think of something tough and funny to say. But nothing came to mind, and after an uncomfortable pause the ophthalmologist went back to reading his in-flight magazine.

Movie depictions of contract killers were the only point of reference he had, and he'd seen every movie on the subject ever made. There were a lot of them, from samurai epics, to Westerns, to movies about La Cosa Nostra, to the Hong Kong gun-battle ballets, to the new breed of postmodern Derrida-influenced deconstructions of the hitman genre—he devoured them all and had built up an impressive DVD library.

His favorites were the new ones. The supercool team of hipster killers dressed in black, their hair slicked with product, driving vintage muscle cars, hanging out with icy-beautiful women and talking about cheeseburgers.

They were his heroes. He wanted to be like them. So he sat on the plane dressed in black jeans and a black shirt with his sunglasses on, acting cool and glaring at friendly ophthalmologists.

He was glad he had his sunglasses on when he walked out of baggage claim and into the broiling tropical sun.

Reggie, a slender man with a limited intelligence, stood smoking a cigarette by the curb. He was also dressed in black with sunglasses and stood like he was posing for the cover of *International Contract Killer* magazine. Baxter saw him and nodded. Reggie returned the nod and dramatically flicked his cigarette into the street.

"Nice flight?"

"Yeah. Nice."

They had agreed to arrive at the airport separately and take different seats on the flight. The plan was to travel incognito. Unconnected. No one's going to remember some guy sitting by himself. They'd be anonymous, covert, and deeply cool. The fact that they were both dressed from head to toe in black and on the same flight was a bit of a miscalculation, and twice the flight attendant had asked if they'd like to sit together.

"Did you reserve a car?"

Baxter nodded. "Mustang convertible."

Reggie smiled. "You rock."

Reggie was one of Baxter's oldest friends. They'd met in high school and hung out. Fifteen years later they were still hanging out. Reggie, who tended bar at the Hard Rock Hotel, shared Baxter's fascination with the criminal underworld and jumped at the chance to come along and be a real bad guy with Baxter. It was a career opportunity, and it sure beat tending bar.

They were about to walk over to the rental car agency when a police officer came up to them.

"Where do you think you're going?"

It was like a sucker punch in the gut; Baxter couldn't catch his breath. His heart skipped a couple of beats, and he burst out in a cool sticky sweat.

"I'm—uh, I'm . . . you know? On vacation?"

Baxter gagged. He turned and looked at Reggie. Reggie's face registered a mix of fear and flight, as if he couldn't decide whether to burst into tears and confess everything or just take off running.

The cop, a plump Hawaiian man in his early twenties, put his hands on his hips.

"You think you can get away with it?"

Baxter reminded himself to breathe, play it cool. They'd just arrived. They hadn't done anything wrong. This cop couldn't prove shit. A cool contract killer would just tell this guy to fuck off, but not in an aggressive way, in a clever Hollywood way. Baxter thought about it.

"I don't have SPF three hundred."

The cop looked at him. "What did you say?"

"What're you doin', man?" Reggie whispered.

But Baxter was starting to feel it. He had the look; now he had to cop the attitude. "I don't have SPF three hundred. I can't stand here all day. Get to the point."

It took Reggie a moment; then he picked up on the hard-guy act, although his voice quavered when he spoke. "Yeah. You wanna arrest us? Arrest us."

The cop shook his head. "I wanted you to pick up that cigarette butt you threw in the street. But now I'm going to write you a ticket."

Which is what he did.

...

Joseph got in his pickup truck and started driving. He didn't have a plan or a destination; he just wanted movement. He needed to get out of his house, away from the empty feeling he got when he was there. Driving helped. Just the simple act of going made him feel better. His stomach was knotted and felt like a block of ice, but the sun warmed his skin and took the edge off his pain. He rolled down the windows and let the wind blow through the cab. The air smelled sharp and fragrant, and after a while he began to feel slightly normal. Not happy, not sad.

After a few hours of aimless cruising, Joseph found himself near a farm where he got fresh papayas. He pulled over to the side of the road, climbed out of his truck, and stretched. His muscles were stiff from sitting, and it felt good to walk down the dirt path into the papaya grove.

Joseph's flip-flops slapped softly against the moist ground as he walked between the trees. Papaya trees are strange creatures, slender green trunks rising up to a frizzled top, fat papayas sprouting out of the trunk and dangling there like a supermodel's breasts. He spotted a ripe one, turning bright yellow against the green trunk, found a stick leaning against one of the trees, and used it to knock the papaya off. It hit the ground with a satisfyingly earthy thud. Joseph picked it up and carried it back to his truck.

He took a pocketknife out of his glove box—kept there for exactly this purpose—and expertly sliced the papaya lengthwise in half. Pinkish golden juice spilled out of the fruit as he separated the two halves to reveal a cluster of glistening black seeds nestled in the middle. Hawaiian caviar. Papaya pits. Joseph laughed. He realized that he was in the pits too.

But as he scraped the seeds out and let them fall to the ground, he suddenly began to feel better. What people call pits, the part of the fruit they worry about breaking their teeth on and discard, are really seeds. New life sprouts from seeds.

Joseph felt the tingle of liberation, the endless possibilities, that getting dumped can bring. It hurt, no question about that. But like the cliché says, every cloud has a silver lining. Like it or not, Joseph was now free of his *ohana*. He could do anything.

...

Love is funny. That's what Yuki was thinking as she lay on her side watching her lover—imagine that!—sleeping. Never in her wildest dreams would she have thought she'd fall in love with a pimp. Weren't pimps some kind of horrible urban monsters who preyed on innocent young women, got them addicted to smack, and then used and abused them until they were worn out or dead? That's what she'd heard anyway. She was sure some pimps were like that, but Lono wasn't. He seemed normal, not at all like Superfly.

Love is funny. It'll make you rationalize almost anything. Yuki could almost justify what Lono did for a living. If there weren't a demand for it, he wouldn't be doing it. Somebody's got to do it, right? Who would protect the girls, right?

But she wasn't stupid. She knew what he did was wrong. Maybe not morally wrong in the big picture of things, but it was illegal. He was a criminal.

Yuki thought about trying to change him. Ask him to go straight, do something different. But how many times had she read in books and magazines that you shouldn't go into a relationship thinking you can get your partner to change? It's disastrous. If Yuki really wanted to be involved with Lono, she'd have to accept him and love him for his true authentic pimp self.

Her life coach would've had a cow. He would've rattled off all the conventional reasons why the relationship wouldn't work, how it was actually a symptom of a self-destructive cycle of behavior that she needed to break out of if she really wanted to grow. He'd probably even hit below the belt and tell her it was just plain bad karma. He might ring bells and circle her with a burning clump of sage to cleanse her of negativity. He might prescribe a bath of mineral salts and fresh rosemary. He might light white candles and chant. He wouldn't be supportive, that's for sure.

But love is funny, and for the first time in her life Yuki didn't give a rat's ass about that kind of spirituality. She was finding the meaning of life, the ultimate answer to all the questions of the universe, and it was right here breathing warmly beside her in bed.

...

Keith was thirsty, really parched. His head was woozy from lack of sleep and residual amounts of N-methyl-3,4-methylene-dioxyamphetamine still coursing through his nervous system.

He slipped out of bed, feeling his kidneys creaking painfully when he stood up, and went to raid the honor bar. He fumbled with the key, trying to open the lock on the fridge, but managed not to wake Chad. He wondered why they kept the mini-bar locked. Does having a key make you more honorable?

The cool air from the fridge felt good on his hot feet. He sorted through the domestic and imported beers, sodas, and tropical juices and pulled out a bottle of Evian. He cracked it open and drained it. The water was painfully cold and made his teeth chime as it slid down his throat. But it made him feel better. He pulled out a second bottle and began sipping it, enjoying the sensation of being turned into a snowman from the inside out.

He turned and looked at Chad. In the half-light of the hotel room, Chad looked a lot older than he did in the drug light of last night. Not that Keith minded having his drink spiked or fucking a slightly older guy. He had no regrets. He'd had a good time. And he needed it. Stalking and planning a murder can make you tense, and it really helps to blow off some steam without blowing your cover.

One good thing about his stint in the marines was that Keith was exposed to all kinds of drugs: clinical-trial-quality amphetamines that his CO gave him to keep him awake for days on end when he was off on a covert op, and muscle-relaxing horror reducers to help him come down after he was extracted and debriefed. They were the finest pharmaceuticals the Pentagon could procure, but the best stuff he got was from his fellow soldiers—opium from Afghanistan, hashish from India and Morocco, LSD from Okinawa, mushrooms from the Costa Rican rain forest, ecstasy from some student scientists at Cal Tech.

A young man who puts his life on the line for his country should be allowed to party, and Keith and his fellow marines could party like the legendary Assassins of Alamut. They rode the line between psychosis and pleasure until they blurred and became one. And being die-hard marines, they never left anyone behind.

Keith had been impressed by the quality of the ecstasy that Chad had given him. Where did he get that stuff? There was none of the speedy teeth-grinding high he'd had with it before. This stuff was mellow, filling him with waves of euphoria. At one point, rolling around on the bed with Chad, feeling a hot wet tongue lighting his body up, he felt like he'd entered the pleasure dome of Xanadu. When he finally came, it was like an explosion of primordial life force being squeezed from every cell in his body and channeled out the end of his cock. He'd never felt anything quite like it.

Afterward, when he would normally throw on his clothes and depart, he lay in bed. He couldn't move. Didn't want to break the spell. He was feeling good. Good about himself. Good about the world.

Now that he'd come down, he wasn't feeling that good about anything. He was feeling downright cranky. He knew he had a tough day ahead of him, trying to dig up any and all information on Mr. Sidney Tanumafili without anyone suspecting that he was looking for information on Mr. Sidney Tanumafili. It was going to be boring. There was no way around that.

It occurred to Keith that perhaps he could take another hit or two of the ecstasy and still do his research. It might even make it fun.

Moving quickly, Keith searched Chad's jacket until he found the small plastic bag loaded with pills. There must've been thirty or forty of the little devils. He shook one out and popped it in his mouth. Breakfast of champions.

He started to put the bag back in Chad's jacket when it occurred to him that two is always better than one, so he took another one, letting it melt under his tongue.

Keith stood there for a long time, naked in the middle of the room, sipping his water and waiting for the drug to kick in. He watched Chad sleep and mused. Life must be all right in Chad's world. He slept like a man without a conscience. No nightmares, no guilt. Just sweet, heavy dreams.

Keith looked at the bag of ecstasy in his hand and decided that, fuck it, he'd just take them all with him. *You give me one without asking, I take them all without asking.* That seemed like a fair trade to him. He got dressed quietly, pocketed the bag of pills, and slipped out the door as the first tingling rush of sensation began to emanate from his heart and flash through his brain.

...

They came for him. A nurse jammed a spike into his hand and started dripping something that felt chilly and weird into his veins. The doctors and residents stood around him and looked at his penis. They came and took Polaroids. Front, left, right, straight ahead. They even held a little ruler next to it for reference, like a mug shot. Francis groaned to himself. Great. Just fucking great. Now there's photographic evidence that I'm not even six inches.

They continued to poke, prod, and measure. They asked questions.

"Does this hurt?"

And then they'd pinch or squeeze or twist his dick.

"A little."

But he was lying. The truth was he couldn't feel a thing. His cock was so numb it could've been dipped in liquid oxygen. Hit it with a hammer and it'd shatter into a million shards of frozen dick.

He heard the doctors conferring.

"I'm afraid if we don't act quickly, more tissue damage will occur and atrophy will set in."

Damage? Atrophy? Francis wasn't a doctor, but he knew enough to know that those aren't words you ever want to hear, especially when it concerns your penis.

"Can you feel this?"

"No."

"How about this?"

"Nothing."

"Now?"

"Those are my balls."

"Good. Just checking."

The doctor looked at Francis.

"I'm sorry, but we have to take action. The drugs didn't work."

"What are you going to do?"

The doctor smiled reassuringly. "We're going to insert a needle into your penis and drain the blood. It shouldn't hurt. We'll make sure we get the area good and numb."

He patted Francis on the shoulder.

"It's like tapping a maple tree."

Francis really didn't want a needle stuck in his cock. "Are there any side effects?"

"We won't know how much damage has already oc-curred until we get your penis back to normal."

Francis closed his eyes. Defeated. Humiliated. Disgusted with himself. Back to normal. Fuck that. That was the last place Francis wanted to be.

...

Baxter threw his bag in the back of the Jeep and opened the driver's side door. He looked over and saw Reggie standing in the middle of the parking lot with a disgusted look on his face. Baxter waved him over.

"C'mon."

"I thought we were gonna get a Mustang, man."

"This is all they had."

"You reserved a Mustang, you should get a fuckin' Mustang."

"They gave us a discount."

"Fuck that."

Baxter was exasperated. The rental car place had been fiasco enough, and now his partner was giving him shit. "Do you want to do this or not?"

"Not in that."

Baxter looked at the Jeep. "It's a convertible."

"It looks like Barbie's car."

Baxter had to agree. Bright fuchsia with a pink-and-white striped canvas top, it did look like Barbie's car.

"Honolulu Barbie's beach buggy."

"I'm sorry, man, I don't know what the fuck you want me to do. You got a better idea? I'm all ears."

Reggie, of course, didn't have a better idea. "We could get one of them little cars."

It was hot out in the rental car parking lot, standing in the midday sun, dressed in black. Sweat beaded up on Baxter's forehead until it gained a critical mass; then it would roll off to the side and plunge down his sideburns to his neck, where it would be absorbed by the collar of his hot black shirt. This isn't what they should be doing; they should be in the car, cruising, AC blasting, top down. But no. They were arguing in the parking lot. Broiling under the tropical sun. How could he be a cool hipster hitman with this shit going on?

It was too much for Baxter. He turned to Reggie and snapped, "Look at me. Just look at me, motherfucker!"

Reggie made a show of looking away and then slowly turning to face Baxter.

"How big am I?"

"You're pretty big."

"Pretty big?"

"Okay, dude, you're big. You're not Shaquille O'Neal, but you're big."

"So how am I gonna fit in one of those tiny cars?"

Reggie defended himself. "At least they're not pink, okay? That's all I'm trying to say. That's the point, okay? You don't have to go off on me, man."

Baxter could see that Reggie was getting obstinate; this was not how those cool guys in the movies behaved, so he changed tactics.

"I'm sorry, man. Let's go to the hotel and see about changing the car later. Okay?"

Reggie nodded. "Okay."

They climbed in the pink Jeep and Baxter started it up.

Reggie looked around. "Pretty comfortable once you're in it. You got enough leg room?"

Baxter nodded. "Yeah."

He backed the car out of the slot and headed out of the parking lot toward the freeway.

Reggie smiled. "You know, I always wanted a Jeep. Maybe after we pull off a couple of jobs I can get one. We could go boonie crashin'."

Baxter smiled. Now Reggie was getting into it. Planning for the future. That was how you became successful. You kept your goals in sight, eyes on the prize.

Baxter reached down and clicked on the radio. The sweet sound of Hawaiian slack-key guitar began drifting through the Jeep. It was slow, sublime, and beautiful. Baxter hated it. He turned the radio off.

"That sucks."

The car bounced up the on-ramp and joined the traffic on the freeway into town. The Honolulu skyline rose in front of them, more impressive and cosmopolitan than they'd expected. Baxter looked at Reggie. The two men exchanged a grin.

"Look at us! This is totally fuckin' cool, man."

Reggie nodded in agreement and flashed a thumbs-up. "Can we take the top down later?"

...

Jack wanted to make a show of it. He wanted to cover his ass. He'd done it this way before in Vegas. You plan to have someone bumped off, you'd better make it look like you didn't have a motive or else the cops would be crawling up your rectum with ten thousand different kinds of questions. So Jack was preparing to make a public attempt at reconciliation that would put to rest any suspicions when Sid's bullet-ridden carcass was discovered floating in the harbor.

Stanley drove him the two miles to Sid's warehouse. It only took about an hour. Jack made Stanley wait in the car. The last thing he wanted was for his namby-pamby offspring to go in there and start sucking up to the Sumo and his friends.

Jack shouldered the door open, jammed his walker into the gap, and entered the warehouse. It was surprisingly clean inside, not at all like the grimy cinder-block bacterial holding area they used to store their trucks and equipment in Nevada. But then maybe Honolulu health inspectors didn't accept bribes. Maybe they didn't have kids going to Dartmouth like the guy in Las Vegas.

He found Sid sitting on a chair drinking coffee from a Styrofoam cup with Joe and Ed from the Teamsters union. Sid was wearing a gigantic faded T-shirt commemorating some kind of surf contest, a pair of shorts that looked like they used to belong to a rhinoceros, and some well-worn flip-flops. Ed, the guy who looked like Oddjob from *Goldfinger,* was wearing baggy shorts with a floral pattern and a tank top with the word SEKIYA's written across it in script with a picture of a Japanese fan. On his grimy feet he had what looked like those shower shoes they give you at the health club so you don't get athlete's foot. Joe was equally outfitted, but with a Hawaiian shirt dotted with tiki mugs.

It was one thing about Hawaii that Jack didn't understand. How do these guys get away with dressing like that? Even in the heat and humidity—and the heat here was nothing like Vegas—Jack dressed like a proper businessman. Not in a suit, but at least a clean shirt, bolo tie, and freshly pressed slacks. How do you expect people to take you seriously if you're dressed like a beach bum?

Sid stood up and glowered.

"Wot fo' you come den?"

"I think we got off on the wrong foot."

"You gonna do wot I said?"

"You know I can't do that. I've got too much money invested."

Sid shook his head. "No can? Dat's too bad den."

Ed tried to lighten the mood with good news. "I hear from the mainland that there's gonna be a lot of work coming. Enough to go around for all of us."

Sid looked at Ed with disgust. "Wot about now den? Wot we doin' now? Am I workin'? Am I out dere feedin' your kine guys?"

Ed looked at the floor. "No."

"Dat's da problem den. Wot gonna happen when dere's only one job fo' two of us?"

Jack shrugged. "Lowest bid gets the job."

Sid nodded. "I don' wanna cut my prices. Dey too low now. You get da fuck offa my island."

Joe took his turn at being helpful. "There's a lot of work comin' in. Honest. Couple network shows and a movie."

Sid pointed to the catering trucks sitting idle in the warehouse.

"I got four trucks."

As if that explained it all. When Jack looked at Sid, he struggled to repress his burning desire to tell this fat Samoan asshole to take a flying fuck at a rolling donut. Instead, he held up his hands in mock surrender. He turned to Ed and Joe.

"I tried. You saw me. I came here in peace. I thought maybe we could work something out."

"We got nuttin' to work out."

"What are you gonna do when a third company comes over?"

"Dat ain' nevah gonna happen."

Jack turned to Joe and Ed with a helpless shrug. "I don't know what more I can say."

Jack pivoted with his walker and began to shuffle out of the warehouse. Sid called out after him.

"When you done wit' dis job, you leave your trucks and go home. Dat way fo' nobody get hurt den." And then, as an afterthought, "'Cause somebody will."

...

Joseph had spent most of the day oscillating between a kind of energized euphoria and a bloodless nagging malaise. In between the two extremes he just felt sick to his stomach.

He drove to the beach, found a place to park, and climbed out of his truck. He took some of the papaya with him and went and sat under a banyan tree. A light breeze was blowing, the swell in the ocean was building, and the surf was beginning to smack loudly into the sand and then rumble as it was being sucked back out. The tide was changing.

Not far away, the outdoor yoga class was in progress. Tourists bending and stretching in the tropical sun. For them this island was paradise, for Joseph it was a prison.

He sliced off a piece of papaya and considered his options.

Sid was wrong to fire him, no question about that. Joseph had built the business with Sid. It was half his. But Joseph knew better than to argue with his uncle about it. If he wanted to run the business on his own—well, that was his choice. Let Sid see how far he could get serving Spam sushi and cold cuts to a crew from Los Angeles, a crew that knew good food and expected it when they were working hard sixteen-hour days. Joseph knew they would have Sid's ass in a sling before dinner.

The issue with Hannah was more complex. Joseph could see that he hadn't done enough to make her feel special. Not just wanted, needed. But then Joseph had never been sure he needed her. He had to admit he'd taken their relationship for granted. He had lived his life the way he wanted to and she was always nearby, doing her thing, equal but separate, united but not legally, the two of them somehow staying together. Now that she was gone, all he knew for sure was that he missed her. When she took her yogurts and lip balm it left a big gaping hole in him. His life just wasn't the same without her.

It was different. But now, for the first time, he could consider all his possibilities. He could explore what he wanted without having to worry about what Sid would think, what would happen to the business, and what Hannah would want. Now he didn't have to think about anyone but himself.

Joseph watched as the yoga class ended. *Namastes* and thank yous sprang from the participants' mouths. He watched the yoga teacher shake hands and nod to a few of the students as she rolled up her sticky mat.

Then she walked over to where Joseph was sitting. He watched her coming toward him, her body lithe and lean like some kind of gangly jungle leopard in a leotard. She had her strawberry-blond hair pulled back in a ponytail to reveal a smattering of freckles across her face and an athlete's disdain for makeup.

"Excuse me, but aren't you Joseph Tanumafili?"

Joseph looked up at her. "Have we met?"

The yoga instructor blushed. "I was a couple years be-hind you in high school."

Joseph nodded, then held up the half papaya. "Want some fruit?"

"Thanks."

She sat down and crossed her legs in a loose half-lotus and smiled as Joseph handed her a slice of papaya.

"I'm sorry but I don't remember your name."

"Tamara Collins."

Joseph watched her as she sucked the meat off the pa-paya skin. Her lips were sensual and full, her face was tight and lean like a professional surfer, and she had an awkward-ness to her that he found completely charming. He shook his head in dismay.

"You'd think I'd remember."

Tamara nibbled on the papaya. "I was a freshman when you were a senior. And I was kind of a dork at the time."

"Did we ever talk?"

"In the library. You told me Edgar Allan Poe was your favorite American writer."

"How can you remember that?"

Tamara's face flushed. "I had a pretty big crush on you."

Joseph was surprised. "I didn't think anyone even no-ticed me."

Tamara's blue eyes flashed at him. "Can I ask you some-thing?"

"Sure."

She hesitated. "I mean—um, here, let me start this way. I heard that you and your girlfriend split up."

Joseph winced a little. "Small island."

"But it's true?"

"It's true."

"So . . . you want to go out with me? You know, like for a drink or something?"

Joseph felt slightly uneasy but then reminded himself that he was a free man and could go have a drink with anyone he wanted.

"That'd be nice."

Tamara jumped up. "How about the bar at Indigo, around seven?"

"I'll see you there."

He watched as she walked off, her ass so muscular and round it was almost intimidating. He was confused by his emotions. He thought he might feel sort of repulsed at himself; instead, he felt strangely relieved.

He was in this strangely relieved mood when Stanley called. Somehow, Stanley had heard that Joseph was no longer working with his uncle and he wanted a meeting.

It really was a small island.

...

Yuki had put it off as long as she could. She didn't know what she would say. She didn't even know how to begin to approach it. Should she file a lawsuit against Francis, the studio, and the network? Or should she just let it slide? What was the proper response to what Francis had done? What's the protocol when your boss tries to ejaculate on you?

Francis was hurt and in the hospital and she didn't feel bad about it. Not at all. How could she? If she was going to press charges, Lono had done that for her when he introduced Francis to a Tilt o' Whirl of violence. It was a more reliable and effective form of justice than filing charges and allowing Francis to purchase a defense courtesy of fancy lawyers. Why should she, the victim, sit in court and have her reputation, her sexuality, dragged through the mud when it was so much more satisfying to see Francis ass-kicked and sprawled on the beach?

Yuki was fully prepared to be an annoying bitch to Francis. Walk in, get him to sign some papers, maybe give him a golden shower courtesy of his bedpan. Perhaps she would touch his penis like he'd begged her to on the beach. Only this time he wouldn't want her to. This time she'd bring pliers.

But when she got to the hospital and saw the pathetic shape Francis was in, she remembered her vow to rid him of negative energy. Besides, her life coach had always told her to let go of negative emotions. Recognize them for what they are and then put them aside. The dharma teaches compassion, not hatred. The bodhisattva way is one of forgiveness, not revenge.

Yuki took a deep, cleansing breath and called up every last reserve of Buddha nature she had.

"Hi."

Francis opened his eyes and looked up. He was immediately filled with shame, regret, and remorse. His face flushed red, and he couldn't look her in the eye.

"I don't know what to say. I'm really sorry."

"You were pretty drunk."

"That's kind of you."

Yuki could see that something was wrong. "Are you okay?"

Francis shrugged. "They don't know."

"Why? What happened?"

"You saw what happened."

She nodded. "It was dark. I didn't really see much."

"It's not the beating. I got two cracked ribs and my jaw still hurts . . . but that's not it."

Francis pulled himself up, wincing as he did.

"At the risk of going Clarence Thomas on you, let me just say that there was something wrong with the equipment in my nether regions."

Yuki didn't want to talk about his nether regions. She turned her attention to the bouquets in the room. "You got some nice flowers."

Francis smiled ruefully. "They care a lot." Then he looked her directly in the eye for the first time. "You saw who did it."

She nodded.

"You want to tell me who?"

"No."

Francis took that in. "Fair enough."

Yuki pulled a file folder out of her bag.

"I've got some papers for you to review. And I need your signature on a couple of purchase orders."

Francis looked at her.

"Yuki. I really appreciate the way you've handled this, with the studio and the network. I mean . . . I really appreciate your discretion and professionalism."

Yuki smiled at him. It was not a friendly smile or a wicked smile. It was the expression of someone who knows she's owed a really big favor.

"You'll make it up to me."

It wasn't a question. Francis nodded. Yuki handed him the thick folder. He opened it with a sigh.

"It's boring, isn't it?"

"What?"

"All this stuff."

Yuki thought about that. She remembered when she first started out wanting to be in the film business. She took classes and weekend workshops. She read books. She bought those directories with listings of agents, managers, and executives. She sent résumés and cold-called everyone she could. With her life coach giving her encouragement and daily affirmations, she persevered despite the fact that no one once bothered to acknowledge that she even existed. She kept telling herself it was what she really wanted. Her coach would remind her. "If it was easy, everyone would do it."

And then the call came. It was her big break. She was going to be the assistant to the line producer on a big network pilot shooting on location in Hawaii. It was everything she'd ever hoped for and dreamed of.

And then she met Francis. Now she wasn't so sure that her future lay in the glamorous world of Hollywood productions. Now she wasn't so sure about anything. All she knew for certain was that she wanted to be with Lono, and if that meant forgoing Hollywood and becoming the girlfriend of a pimp—well, so be it.

"It's an okay way to make a living."

Francis sighed. He had all the energy of a condemned man waiting for the priest to come read him his last rites.

"Yeah. It's an okay way to make a living."

...

They had decided, for security reasons, to stay in separate hotels. The only problem was that both of them were staying in Outrigger hotels, and there were dozens of Outriggers scattered around Waikiki. It took them over an hour to find Reggie's. Bouncing from one Outrigger to the next, always with a little Xeroxed map showing how to get to the one they were looking for, always the yellow highlighter on the paper showing them how to go around the block, where they would inevitably sit in the ridiculous crush of traffic on Kalakaua Avenue.

Baxter was annoyed with himself that he didn't write down the full name of the hotel. They all had names like Outrigger Surf, Outrigger Village, Outrigger Reef, Outrigger Prince Somebody, Outrigger Royal Islander. Who knew there were so many Outriggers? Why name them all the same? That's just weird.

So around and around they drove, two men dressed in black, sweating like pigs, slowly roasting in their big pink dune buggy.

They did, however, pass a sports bar across the street from the beach and agreed to meet for dinner there later that night.

Baxter pulled into the circle drive to drop Reggie off. "This it?"

"Yeah."

"Lotta fuckin' Outriggers in town."

Baxter nodded. No shit, Sherlock. Reggie climbed out of the pink Jeep and went around to collect his bag. Baxter turned to him.

"We're cool?"

Reggie grinned. Now they were beginning to play the part. "As a cucumber."

"Watch your back, hombre."

"I'm going to be watchin' the hotties on the beach."

Baxter smiled. "Just don't fall in love."

And with that he drove off in search of his own Outrigger hotel. The one that looked like all the other ones and had the same fucking name.

...

Chad went down to the pool and lay out on a chaise longue. He ordered a protein shake from the waitress; he'd lost a lot of protein last night. He smeared some expensive French tanning butter on his body and adjusted his Speedo-style swimsuit that gave his crotch the illusion that he was endowed with an extremely large package. He'd ordered the swimsuit from the *International Male* catalog. Normally he didn't shop from catalogs but he'd seen this Speedo, and what it had done for the model in the photo, and decided to give it a try.

Chad lay out all buttery-shiny, his crotch looking like a Shakespearean actor's codpiece, and sipped his protein shake. He'd asked to have fresh banana in it and somehow, probably through complete incompetence, they'd chosen to ignore that fact. Still, he was feeling magnanimous, resplendent and irresistible in near-naked sun-worshipping mode, so he decided just to drink his protein shake and not sweat the small stuff.

He lifted his Persols, purchased on a shopping trip to Milan, and gazed out at his fellow sunbathers. He was looking for Keith. He'd had an exceptionally good time with the young man and wouldn't mind an encore performance.

Chad knew he should be going to the hospital to visit Francis. But hospitals smell bad and are, let's admit it, depressing. Still, it would've been the right thing to do. Chad thought about poor pathetic Francis lying in bed with his Smurf-colored cock. It made him feel guilty. He didn't feel guilty about spending the night with the guy he picked up by the pool, but he did feel guilty about not going to the hospital. It was typical of Francis to make him feel he was not doing the right thing, like he was somehow in the wrong. It was always that way. Francis wore his martyrdom well. Chad found it very annoying.

He did feel bad that he'd hurt Francis, but it was *his* life. He could do whatever he wanted. Why should he deny himself experiences just because he had a boyfriend? How does that song go? If you love somebody set them free—or let them go or look like you don't mind it when they go off and fuck somebody else? Wasn't that what love meant? You want the person you love to live their life to the fullest. To grab the brief time we have on this planet with gusto. So what if it means fucking around? It's not like he killed any-one. It's not like he's a bad guy. He loved Francis. He was here, wasn't he?

Chad vowed to himself that he'd go to the hospital later that afternoon. But first he was going to ask that handsome Cuban man across the pool if he wanted to have lunch.

...

He didn't want to go. Not really. And he knew, for certain, that he would never work for them. But he was curious. So Joseph took the elevator up to the fourth floor and walked into Jack Lucey's office like it was the most normal thing in the world.

Stanley met him with the kind of jangly enthusiasm and fake goodwill of someone who doesn't know if they're about to be treated courteously or punched in the face. He offered coffee, mineral water, a soda. Joseph politely declined and let Stanley get to the point.

"We want you to come work for us."

And that was it. Part job interview, part threat assessment. Joseph shook his head. "I don't think that's a good idea."

Stanley nodded. It seemed like he understood. "Your *ohana* wouldn't approve."

The Hawaiian word coming out of the haole's mouth caught Joseph off guard. "No. They wouldn't."

"I understand. My dad can be pretty difficult."

"Thanks for the offer."

"Will you consider it?"

Joseph shook his head. "Actually I'm thinking I might be leaving the islands."

Stanley looked surprised. "I love it here. I'd never want to leave. It's paradise on earth."

...

"You're a weird one."

Joseph looked over to see his cousin standing by his truck. "What are you doing here?"

Wilson shrugged. "What they say?"

"They offered me a job."

"Yeah?"

"I'm not going to work for them."

"You gotta do somethin', brah."

Joseph looked off down the street. It was true. He had to do something. "Not with them."

"What Hannah say?"

"She moved out."

Wilson's expression changed. He stared at Joseph, astonished. "She'll be back. She loves you."

"She wanted me to sleep with that guy."

"You think you suck some guy's dick dat makes you gay?"

"Doesn't it?"

"No way, brah. That just means you got a mouthful. Being gay is a whole other thing. It's a lifestyle."

Joseph studied his cousin. "What do you know about it?"

Wilson laughed. "I been workin' in da nightclubs. I know all about da gay thing and you don't got it. You all the way straight. I think it would do you good fo' to suck dat guy's dick."

"Thanks. I appreciate your opinion."

"That's just it. You always think you know wot's best. You not always right, brah. You not da only one dat's got some brain."

Joseph didn't know what to say. "What are you talking about?"

"Everybody treat you like you know fo' sure wot's right. Just 'cause you go fo' college. You not always right, brah."

"I never said I was."

Wilson stood there glaring at Joseph, but since they weren't having an argument, he didn't know what else to say. Joseph tried to change the subject. "How's your dad?"

"He gone."

"What do you mean? Where'd he go?"

Wilson pointed to his head. "He walkin' round wid a gun. Thinkin' people are watchin' him. He think somebody snuck into his house but real quiet, like some kine *akua lapu*."

"I'll go talk to him."

"He stayin' with some friend tonight. He say he got a feeling."

"What kind of feeling?"

"A Vietnam feeling."

...

Keith sat on the beach, watching the waves roll in and out, in and out. Sometimes they'd curl and roll to the left; sometimes they'd rise up like a wall of foamy glass and crash straight down. Sometimes they sucked up sand in big howling slurps, pulling it back out to sea. No two were ever the same. Like snowflakes, each wave seemed to have its own personality. There was the noncommittal one that couldn't quite decide whether even to be a wave, really just a sloppy wad of ocean banging into the shore like it'd made a wrong turn at the Gulf of California. There was one that was ambitious, really putting on a show, curling up and slicing off to one side, hitting the rocks at the end of the beach and erupting into the sky like Kilauea.

Keith understood that wave. It was water, but it really wanted to be air.

He listened to them too. They growled and shouted, snapped and sang. They were all telling him to pay attention. Something's coming. Wake up.

Keith wasn't sure exactly where he was. He knew he was on the island of Oahu, but he'd hitched a ride with some surfers leaving Honolulu and made them drop him off when he saw this beach. It was, he realized, the perfect beach. Like a beach in a dream. Like a beach in heaven.

He'd found a little grocery store and bought several large bottles of mineral water and a handful of beef jerky. Then he popped a couple more hits of ecstasy and ambled down to the beach.

He'd been there all day. Feeling his heart pound, the blood pulsing through his body, his chest glowing with a warmth he'd never experienced before. He felt his heart expand, growing larger and stronger with each wave, absorbing the energy from the ocean until it had become the ocean. The waves had become his teachers. He just had to pay attention.

He felt the light change. The sun had shifted behind the serrated green mountains and was casting a soft peachy hue across the sky. Just offshore Keith watched as a small pod of dolphins swam in the waves. They kept circling the same area. It took Keith a little while to understand—he was not versed in the ways of dolphins—but eventually he got it. He waded out in the water, surprised at how shallow it was, until he found the spot. In the water he couldn't see the dolphins. But he could feel them. They were close. They were protecting him.

The ocean had calmed, and he let the soft swells gently slap against him, his brain rolling with the waves. The water was warm; the air, scented by a thousand tropical plants, was just beginning to cool as twilight fell. Keith felt as if the whole universe had suddenly become unbearably delicious.

An hour later he watched the moon rise. It was a new moon, just a silver crescent hanging over the ocean, but it cast a bright blue line along the surface of the water, like a glimmering, luminous path.

Then Keith saw it: a shooting star. A vivid orange arc of searing light leaped out of the moon and fell toward a spot on the horizon. Keith roughly guessed that the spot was a few hundred miles away, 27 degrees left of moonrise.

He saw it clearly and instantly understood. He understood why the dolphins had told him to wait here. He realized what he had to do.

...

Jack was restless but he didn't want to go out. The thought of dragging his walker through the tourists to sit outside and drink fruity drinks while some crappy band played sappy music? Fuck that. Leave that for Stanley, who was suddenly getting excited by all the exotic Polynesian tribal stuff, spending his free time way up at the Polynesian Cultural Center watching fire-eaters and hula dances. Yammering on to Jack about the history of the various tribes scattered around the Pacific, squatting on any clump of land they could find, even the ones that were active volcanoes; their various cultures and languages springing from isolation and boredom. Jack would listen to Stanley recounting the history of the Pacific Islanders and nod his head. Right. Like he cared.

Jack didn't want to go to any cultural center. He didn't want to go to the bar. He didn't want to go to a luau or see a dance performance. He didn't want to leave his room. Jack wouldn't admit it, of course, but he was worried. Worried and nervous and a little scared. He thought the hitman might be lurking around the hotel waiting to pounce.

So Jack sat in his hotel room drinking beer, eating a cheeseburger, and trying to watch sports on TV. He was surprised to find Sumo wrestling on one channel, even more surprised that he had watched it for over an hour. It's not like the remote was broken. But there was something about giant-sized men grabbing each other's underwear and then trying to hurl each other out of a little circle. It was fascinating.

Jack even found himself rooting for the lone American in the tournament—not that the guy looked even remotely American; he looked more like a gigantic defensive lineman from Mongolia, but he was listed as an American—and Jack felt his patriotic spirit surge when the big American demolished some fierce-looking Jap.

Jack didn't understand the salt throwing, stomping, and hand clapping. But wasn't it kind of like baseball? The pitcher reaches down for that bag of stuff next to the mound, looks at the catcher, spits, and goes into his windup. That's almost the same. The stomping was just part of the Sumo windup.

Jack thought about Sid. He looked like a Sumo. Jack imagined himself in the ring against him: putting his walker to the side, throwing salt over his shoulder, grappling with the behemoth. Winner takes Oahu.

...

Baxter looked at the pineapple spear garnishing his plate. This must be how you tell you're not in Florida. In Florida they'd plonk an orange slice on the plate next to your cheeseburger. Otherwise, as far as he could tell, Hawaii was just like Florida. Nothing but beaches, chicks showing off their hooters, bars, strip clubs, and retarded-looking tourists buying crappy T-shirts and things made out of seashells.

Reggie came in from the beach. He'd taken off his black shirt and rolled his black pants up near his knees so he could wade in the water. Baxter could see the outline of where a wave had slapped Reggie in the crotch. It looked like he'd pissed himself.

"What're you doin', man?"

"I was at the beach."

Baxter remembered that contract killers were excruciatingly punctual.

"You're late."

"I met some chicks from Kansas City."

"Kansas or Missouri?"

"What's it matter, man? They were ready to party."

Baxter also remembered that contract killers were serious about the business at hand. They didn't party with girls from Kansas City, not while they were on the job anyway. They kept a low profile. Lived in the shadows like ninjas. You didn't see a fuckin' bad-ass Ninja assassin smokin' a fatty on a surfboard. You didn't see a cool hitman buying rounds of drinks for girls at Duke's Canoe Club. It suddenly occurred to Baxter that perhaps Lee Harvey Oswald had been a lone shooter for a reason.

"Dude, we don't have time to party. We're on a job."

"I'm ready."

"No, you're not. Go get dressed. Put on your game face."

Reggie looked at him, exasperated. "If we can't have a good time, what's the point?"

"You want to go back to Vegas?"

Reggie didn't like the edge that had crept into Baxter's voice. "No."

"Then quit fucking around."

"All right. Jesus. Don't freak out. I'll be right back."
Reggie walked off to the bathroom to get dressed.

...

The first thing Yuki noticed about Lono's apartment was the complete absence of chairs. There wasn't a single one. Not that there was that much furniture. There wasn't a table or a sofa either.

Yuki laughed. "Do you have kathisophobia?"

"What's that?"

"Fear of sitting down."

Lono smiled. "I've got a futon. That's where I sit."

He gave Yuki a brief tour. It was a lovely apartment: large and open, loft-style modern, with a new gourmet kitchen, a balcony, and big windows that looked out over downtown Honolulu and the ocean beyond. But it looked like he'd just moved in, plopped a futon on the floor, and hung his clothes in the closet. There was exactly one bowl, one plate, two coffee mugs, four glass tumblers, and seven wooden chopsticks in the kitchen cupboards and drawers.

"Don't you have a can opener?"

Lono shrugged. "I don't cook much."

"I'm not talking about cooking. I'm talking about opening cans. I would at least expect a bachelor to have a microwave."

"I've been meaning to get one. The thing is, I don't spend a lot of time here."

"I like it. You just need to move in."

But the apartment wasn't completely barren. There were several bookshelves filled with books, a TV set and DVD player, a small superexpensive stereo system with its attendant stacks of CDs, an Apple G4 Powerbook sitting on the futon, and a scattering of little fake mice.

"Do you have a cat?"

Lono nodded. "Yeah. He's around here somewhere."

Yuki looked around. It's not like there was anywhere for a cat to hide.

"You sure?"

"Maybe he got out."

Lono went over to the balcony and slid the door open. A large ball of tabby-orange fluff and fuzz came trotting into the house, hair flying off and drifting in its wake. Lono looked at the cat.

"What were you doing out there?"

The cat, naturally, didn't answer and headed straight for his food dish.

"What's its name?"

"Topaz."

Yuki bent down to scratch the cat's head. "Hi, Topaz."

Lono looked at Yuki. "I have a present for you."

Lono went to the closet and opened the door. He took a gift-wrapped box out and handed it to her.

"I hope you like it."

Yuki blushed. No one had given her a present, not like this anyway, since she was a little girl.

"It's not my birthday."

"I saw it and I thought of you."

Yuki felt slightly embarrassed by the way she tore the package open, just like a little kid at Christmas; she couldn't help herself. She lifted the lid off the box to reveal a super-cool, powder-blue vintage-looking Puma tracksuit with dark blue stripes running down the sides of the sleeves and pants. Lono grinned.

"It's kind of hip-hop. But, I don't know. I thought you'd look good in it. It's your style."

Although it was something that Yuki never would've got for herself—after all, she wasn't a professional athlete or mega-platinum rapper—it did fit right in with her new look. She liked that Lono thought it was her style. When was something this cool ever her style?

"I love it."

"Try it on."

Yuki slung the jacket over her shoulders and zipped it up. It fit perfectly and made her look totally street-chic savvy. Looking in the mirror, she realized, *This beats the hell out of a peasant blouse from Turkey.* Yuki stuck her hands in the pockets and bumped up against something metallic. She knew right away what it was.

"What's this?"

Lono looked sheepish. "I know we just met and everything. But I thought . . . you know, if you get tired of the hotel you can always come over here."

Yuki took the key out of her pocket and examined it. No one had ever given her a key to his place before.

"Does this mean we're going steady?"

"If you'd like to."

Yuki walked over to him, stood on her tiptoes, and wrapped her arms around him. "I'd like to."

She dropped her head to one side and gave him the hottest, wettest soul kiss she could muster. She kissed him like she meant it.

. . .

Joseph climbed the rickety wooden stairs, past clumps of ginger, banana plants, and hairy overgrown ferns, up to Hannah's apartment in an old Hawaiian house. Neo-Victorian but with tropical additions like a corrugated steel roof, the house rose out of an overgrown valley above Honolulu. It had been sliced up into six apartments, each with a view of the city and the harbor beyond. Hannah's consisted of two small rooms that had formerly been the library and study. A funky kitchenette, suitable for making instant ramen noodles or toasting bread, had been stuck against the wall of the main room.

Joseph didn't spend much time there, preferring the comparative spaciousness and cleanliness of his home, but he had to admit to a fondness for the old house. Especially when he would lie curled up in bed with Hannah and listen to a heavy rain hit the metal roof like ten thousand Taiko drummers on a wind-driven rampage. It was unbelievably loud and he loved it. Nothing else in the world sounded like that.

Joseph knocked on the door. Hannah answered it, still wearing her teaching clothes. She did not look happy to see him.

"I knew you'd eventually come around for an explanation."

"I was worried. I called."

"I didn't feel like talking."

Joseph nodded. "Do you feel like talking now?"

Hannah heaved a sigh. "I've got tests to grade."

Joseph looked her in the eye. "I'm just trying to figure out what it means."

Hannah shrugged. "You were leaving. I decided to go first."

"I hadn't made a decision."

Hannah shrugged. "I did."

...

Baxter had done his homework. Find yourself in a strange town in need of illegal items, what do you do? You ask a seedy-looking cab driver. Preferably one that doesn't have a Mohawk. Baxter strolled down Kalakaua Avenue, scanning the streets for a suitable cabbie. Reggie trolled along beside him.

"What're we doing, man?"

"We need guns."

"So? Let's go to a gun store. This is America, man. We can just go buy 'em."

Baxter shook his head in dismay. "We need some that can't be traced back to us. Jesus, get a clue."

"We buy 'em. Whack the dude. Throw 'em in the fucking ocean. What's the problem?"

"We have to register. There's a waiting period. And then the cops figure out that we used a .44 on the guy and they ask the local gun stores if anyone bought a .44 recently and then they give them our names and addresses."

Reggie shrugged. "We'll be back in Vegas, man."

Baxter shook his head. It was like talking to a brick wall.

"Besides, we don't have to use a .44."

"It was just an example. If we use a .38 it's the same thing."

"No it's not. A .44's much bigger."

Baxter looked at Reggie. He studied his eyes. "Did you toke up?"

Reggie shrugged. "A couple puffs."

"Fuck. I knew it."

Reggie shrugged. "What's the big deal?"

Baxter turned, grabbing Reggie by the collar, and braced him against the wall of a building.

"Dude, what're you doin', man?"

Baxter put his face an inch away from Reggie's. "We're here on business. I need you to be clear. Serious. We gotta focus."

"I'm focused."

"You're stoned."

Reggie dropped his head. Baxter released his grip.

"Dude, those chicks from Kansas City were sweet."

Baxter shook his head. From now on, he thought, I work alone.

...

It took about half an hour, but Baxter recognized the cabbie right away. It was the same type of guy he'd seen dozens of times in Vegas: the thinning hair, the deep bags under the eyes, the bloodshot nose and paunchy gut under the big floppy shirt. These were the guys, losers at cards, losers in love, losers in life. They were always dropping tourists at the strip club and then ingratiating their way in for a free drink, a free peek, maybe even a complimentary lap dance. The management tolerated them because they kept bringing people to the club.

They climbed into his cab.

"Where you wanna go?"

Baxter tried to feel the guy out. "I don't know. Chinatown?"

"Chinatown? What do you wanna go there for?"

"I heard you could have some fun there."

The cabdriver—the license laminated to the dashboard said his name was Don Kloots—looked at them in the rearview. "It's fun if you like smoking crack."

Baxter shifted. "We're not into drugs."

Don Kloots smiled. "You fellas here for a convention?"

Reggie shook his head. "No way, man. Why would you say that?"

Don Kloots shrugged. "You got matching suits."

"We could be musicians."

Baxter gave Reggie a look. He spoke to Don. "What would you suggest?"

"For fun?"

"Yeah. For fun."

Don Kloots thought about it. "You want some pussy? I know a couple of great places for that."

Reggie smiled. "That sounds excellent."

Baxter shook his head at Reggie. "What else you got?"

"Most of the gambling is Asian stuff. Pai Gow. Mahjongg. We do get the occasional cockfight. Sometimes some Muy Thai or Escrima."

"Escrima? What's that?"

"Filipino stickfighting. It's awesome."

"Is it legal?"

Don Kloots nodded. "The fighting is. The betting isn't."

"Sounds dangerous."

"You wouldn't want to face a pissed-off *Pinoy* with a couple of sticks in his hands, I'll tell you that."

Baxter folded a hundred-dollar bill and passed it up to the driver. "If I wanted some protection while I was here, what would you suggest?"

"I'd suggest you use a condom."

Reggie snorted. "Funny, dude."

Baxter plucked a second C-note out of his pocket and handed it to Don. "We need something a little stronger than rubber."

Don Kloots pulled his cab over to the curb near the Hilton Village. He turned around and faced Baxter and Reggie.

"Look. I don't deal with this kind of thing, okay? I'm strictly tourist-friendly. You want something like that, I can't help."

"Do you know someone who can?"

"Maybe."

Don Kloots looked like he was thinking about it. Baxter tried to help him make up his mind by handing him another hundred-dollar bill.

"You need to find a guy named Lono."

"Lono?"

"He's not a dealer, but he's connected. He'll know where to send you."

"Where can we find him?"

"That's the tricky part. He doesn't like to be found."

Baxter was getting annoyed. He felt like punching Don Kloots in the face and getting his three hundred bucks back.

"You got a suggestion?"

Don Kloots nodded. "Go into this Thai restaurant. Tell the hostess you're looking for someone named Lono. Then sit down and have a nice long dinner."

"Thanks."

Baxter and Reggie got out of the cab and walked across the street to the Thai restaurant. Reggie turned to Baxter. "I was gettin' the munchies anyway."

...

Nuʻuanu Street. Where the low, ramshackle buildings and slightly gamey atmosphere of Chinatown crashes into the modern high-rise bustle and polished chrome of the financial district.

The bar was outside on the patio, facing a small Japanese garden miraculously planted in the middle of urban decay. Joseph and Tamara sat at a table facing the garden, isolating themselves from the happy-hour hubbub, drinking mai tais. Normally Joseph would've just had a beer, but this particular spot was well known for its cocktails and Joseph didn't protest when Tamara ordered a couple of the potent drinks.

During the first mai tai they took turns recounting high school memories and talking about people they knew. During the second she told him about the benefits of a regular yoga practice and he told her how to use cellophane noodles to make an interesting vegetarian stir-fry. Halfway through the third, Tamara took the bold step of asking Joseph if he wouldn't like to finish his drink at her house, a proposition he accepted.

...

Reggie didn't even wait for the waitress to pour the beer into the glass. He snatched the bottle out of her hand and chugged half of it down as quickly as he could.

"Ahh. Fuck."

He slumped back on the banquette and ran the cold bottle across his forehead, hoping the ice-cold glass would staunch the copious flow of perspiration that was raining off his head. He let out a long, low, chili-scented belch.

"That shit is fucking hot, man."

Baxter nodded. Beads of sweat had formed along his forehead.

"Try some water."

"Water doesn't cut it. It's like a fuckin' snakebite in your mouth. Beer is the only antidote."

"That's your fourth one."

Reggie looked at him. "What? You're my mom now?"

"I want you to stay sharp."

"I'm sharp. Jesus."

"Try some rice."

Reggie spooned a scoop of white rice into his mouth. He cautiously chewed it, as if each grain was made out of wood and he didn't want to get a splinter.

"It fucking hurts, dude."

Baxter shrugged. "You wanted spicy."

"I wanted edible."

Neither of them had eaten Thai food before. They'd expected it to be like the Chinese food you get in Las Vegas, and they weren't prepared for the onslaught of chili, mint, lime, and lemongrass that made the dishes so provocatively pungent and confrontational. It was, without a doubt, the spiciest food either of them had ever put in their mouths.

Hotter than the Killer Nachos at the Hard Rock. Hotter than anything at Taco Bell.

"You want more of this duck stuff?"

Reggie looked at him like he was insane. "I want to live. Go ahead and eat all you want."

"I like it."

Reggie shook his head. "Duck in radioactive waste."

But while Reggie was writhing in agony, Baxter seemed to be enjoying himself. It was partly because he felt a kind of macho pride in being able to swallow the capsicum stew. His lips had become numb and swollen, throbbing from the continuous topical application of chilies, and the inside of his mouth had been thoroughly torched, charred and raw and in ruins. It hurt to chew, like rubbing a wound with salt, but he kept spooning it in.

"You can't get food like this in Vegas."

Reggie signaled for a fifth beer. "That's 'cause we're gamblers, not fire-eatin' maniacs."

The way Reggie said it was funny. Baxter laughed. The laughter was contagious and soon, even though it hurt, Reggie was laughing too. Laughing so hard that beer came out his nose and foamed up on his mustache, making him look like an old man. But the beer coming out of his nose was loaded with chili paste and fish sauce. It only took a second for Reggie to register panic. His face turned bright red and he began blowing his nose on the napkin as hard as he could.

"Fuck, man. My nose is on fire."

Baxter laughed even harder. This, he realized, was more like it. This was what they'd signed up for. Two cool contract killers having a laugh over some Thai food in an exotic locale.

"Stick some ice up it."

"Fuck you."

Even though tears were springing out of his eyes like a sprinkler, Reggie was laughing. He couldn't help it. It was funny.

"Wait until tomorrow morning, dude. Then we'll see who's stickin' ice up what."

Baxter laughed even harder. "That's a good one."

Then, all at once, Baxter stopped laughing. He felt his stomach catch fire, like a pilot light had just ignited a big gas burner. An acidic churning sensation began to rumble through his belly and climb his throat, burning its way upward toward his mouth. It was not at all pleasant.

"I'll have a beer too."

...

Yuki and Lono sat at the bar of the Thai restaurant sharing a plate of green papaya salad and sticky rice with a couple skewers of pork *satay* thrown in for protein. Lono picked up a large bottle of Thai beer and refilled his glass. As he did, he looked in the mirror behind the bar, checking out the two strange dudes in their matching black suits. It was hard to figure out just what they were up to. They were eating and drinking like they were on vacation, yet they were dressed like they were in town for a necrophilia convention. Lono thought they could be the horn section of some strange R&B tribute band or, perhaps, undertakers. They could be dealers, but if they were in the drug business they were obvious amateurs. Who wears black suits in Honolulu? And what was with the matching mustaches? It occurred to Lono that they looked like hitmen in some movie from the seventies, but he couldn't remember which one.

It had always amused Lono that people who wanted to be criminals often went out of their way to look like they were criminals. Which, as anyone who's ever been to prison will tell you, is not the smartest idea. Maybe they were wannabes; maybe they were from Kazakhstan; he didn't know. One thing he was sure of—they weren't cops.

Yuki sipped a cup of hot tea and wiped her hands on a napkin. She turned to Lono.

"What's up?"

Lono smiled at her. She didn't miss much. "Those two guys over there were asking about me."

Yuki looked in the mirror. "They look like alien hunters."

Lono chuckled. They did look like alien hunters.

"What're you going to do?"

Lono leaned over and kissed her ear. "Eat."

Yuki smiled. "You can't be too careful."

"Especially around alien hunters."

Yuki giggled. Lono munched on a skewer of spicy grilled pork and watched the two men. She was right; you can't be too careful. He wanted to try and figure these guys out before he sat down with them. He didn't want to walk into anything weird. But he had to admit he was intrigued. What could they be up to? If they wanted a girl, they would've called one of his numbers. Besides, no one gets to meet the pimp. He was merely a middleman in the transaction, a quality control specialist. If they wanted drugs—well, he wasn't sure he'd point them in the direction of any of the dealers he knew.

...

"This is a big waste of time, man."

Baxter hated to admit it, but Reggie was probably right.

"Those chicks from Kansas City are gonna be at this club. We should go hook up."

"Let's give him five more minutes."

"Fuck that. Maybe someone at the club'll know where we can score."

The waitress came over and cleared their plates. "More beer, sir?"

Reggie looked at Baxter. "Why not?"

Baxter held up two fingers. "And the check, too."

The waitress left with the dirty plates. Reggie turned to Baxter and playfully mocked him. "That's your third, dude. Don't you wanna stay sharp?"

"Yeah, well, fuck it, it's the only thing keeping my stomach from exploding."

Reggie laughed. "I knew you'd loosen up."

Baxter fixed Reggie with a serious look. "I'm not here to party. Understand that. I need this to work out. I really do. All my life this is what I've wanted to do. This is who I am, man. I can't afford to blow this."

"I'm cool."

The beers arrived along with the check. Reggie looked at the waitress. "No fortune cookies?"

She shook her head. "Sorry. Fortune cookies Chinese."

Reggie turned and looked at Baxter. "No fortune cookies."

"That's life."

Baxter examined the bill briefly and then threw a wad of twenties on top of it. He shoved the money across the table and that's when he noticed a large Hawaiian man standing next to them in a tank top and cargo shorts.

"You looking for me?"

Baxter was startled. He'd expected someone different. Like the little guy in the movies with the bugging-out eyes that's always looking over his shoulder and talking fast but knows everyone in town and can hook you up in a heartbeat. That's who he expected. He didn't expect a massive Hawaiian dressed like a beach bum.

"You Lono?"

Lono nodded.

"About fucking time, man," Reggie blurted out.

Lono gave Reggie a hard look. Reggie froze, not sure what to do next. He shrugged sheepishly.

"You know. We been waiting."

Baxter was still a little off his game. This guy definitely did not look like anyone who could hook you up with anything, except maybe a fishing trip.

"Yeah. What took you so long?"

Lono ignored that. "Let's talk outside. Your partner can wait at the bar."

Reggie made a squeaky sound of protest, but Baxter shot him a look. "It's cool."

"Fine. I'll wait at the bar. But then we are definitely going to hook up with those chicks from Kansas City."

Lono turned and walked out of the restaurant. Baxter followed. Reggie watched them go and then grouchily pulled himself to his feet and walked over to the bar. He sat down next to a chick that looked like a dude. In fact, focused through his beer goggles, he wasn't sure if it was a guy dressed like a chick or a chick dressed like a guy who dressed like a chick. Either way, he ordered a second beer and then turned to the guy chick.

"Know where a dude can score some Maui Wowie around here?"

...

Lono and Baxter walked out onto Kalakaua Avenue just as a bus went by. The street was busy, filled with traffic and tourists, all out looking for a good time. Lono scanned the street, more out of habit than anything else. Baxter looked at him.

"How do I know you're not a cop?"

Lono smiled. Amateurs. "You can't tell?"

Baxter thought about it. "Yeah, you're cool, man."

Lono didn't say anything; he just looked at Baxter, waiting for him to make his pitch. Baxter leaned forward and spoke quietly.

"We're in the market for something heavy."

"Heavy?"

"Some nines."

Lono stood there expressionless, trying to figure out why these two strange-looking men needed guns. Baxter took his expression for one of incomprehension.

"Ninas, you know? When I step up with my nina you'll know I'm straight-trippin'."

Lono looked at him blankly. Baxter tried again.

"Doctor Dre? Pop a cap? Bust a clip? Gats?"

"Guns?"

Baxter pointed at Lono. "Now you got it."

"You can buy guns at a sporting goods store."

"We need something untraceable."

Lono furrowed his brow. The last thing he wanted to do was set these two up with firearms. He rubbed his chin like he was really considering it.

"It's difficult on the island."

"We don't care how much it costs. We can pay. We're here on business."

"What's your line of work?"

Baxter gave Lono his version of a stone-cold glare. "I'd rather not say."

Lono nodded. "And I'd rather not supply guns for people who are gonna knock over a bank in my hometown."

"We're not into armed robbery."

And that was all Lono needed to know.

...

Keith didn't have a piece of paper. He didn't have a pencil or pen. But that didn't stop him. He found a nice patch of sand under a coconut palm, doused it with water to smooth it out, and began to sketch his plans. He charted his course using celestial navigation, drawing in the sand with a stick. He found some rocks to use as landmarks—one for the moon, another for his current position—and a seashell to mark what he believed was the approximate position of his final destination.

Keith was no stranger to working without a compass. He'd been on the ground in Afghanistan for a couple of weeks when the batteries in his GPS failed. He realized, after the fact, that he should not have used the batteries to run his MP3 player, but it was boring digging in and sitting undercover all day long. He needed some tunes. And somehow the tribal thump and drone of house music lent a texture to the steady aerial bombardments that were constantly shaking the ground and blackening the sky.

At night he'd switch the batteries back into his GPS and move to his next position. Traveling quickly and silently through the black Afghan night, occasionally crossing creeks or rivers, wending his way through pomegranate groves until he reached his next position and dug in for another day of lying immobile, smelling the stench of burning buildings, and grooving to the beats and samples.

His batteries died the day he was scheduled to move to an extraction point forty kilometers northwest of his position. Once the stars came out he was up and running, jogging at a clip, roughly figuring out which direction to head in. He knew that if he cut too far to one side he'd run smack into the Northern Alliance's front lines; a little bit to the other side and he'd be saying hello to the Taliban warriors. But some-how, guided by the stars or by simple dumb luck, he made it to the point and was extracted by helicopter without incident.

Keith checked the sky, his eyes running from one con-stellation to the next. He checked and double-checked his chart. He had to be careful. Sometimes he'd pick up phantom stars, really just optical illusions, his brain sending signals through his overheated synapses. Other times he'd locate a constella-tion, only for it to appear animated, dancing in the night sky.

The chart he was drawing in the sand was complex. To the untrained eye it might've looked like some kind of in-sane petroglyph, but Keith wasn't working in two-D. He was charting his course using three dimensions. It was important. After all, he'd be sailing through a three-D world.

. . .

"So, did they offer you a part?"

Lono looked at her. "A part of what?"

Yuki laughed. "A part in their movie. You'd make a pretty good tough guy."

"What makes you think those haoles are in the film business? Did they say something?"

"Why are you so serious? I was joking."

"I just wondered where they were from."

"Well, if you really want to know, they're from Las Vegas."

"Is that what they said?"

Yuki nodded. She could see from his expression that something was wrong. "Why are you so worried about it?"

Lono thought about what he could tell her. With the exception of Yakuza on vacation, it was unusual for contract killers, even amateur ones, to visit the islands. But these two were here, and it wasn't for pineapple and poi.

Lono thought about Las Vegas. He thought about all the gamblers and deadbeats he knew. He searched his memory for any clue as to why these guys were here. And then, as always, his unique talent for piecing disparate scraps of information into a clear picture of what was about to go down kicked in. He knew, intuitively, why they were here and why they wanted guns.

"I need to make a phone call."

...

The pubic hair went up his nose, tickling him like a snoutful of black pepper, and for the second time Joseph had to lift his head from between Tamara's strong, flexible thighs and sneeze.

She laughed. "I think you're allergic to me."

Joseph rubbed his nose vigorously, trying to suppress another sneeze. "No. I'm just . . . I don't know. Maybe you need a trim."

She laughed some more. "I'll take it up with my hairdresser."

Joseph put his head back between her legs, found the groove between her labia lips with his tongue, and began to suck gently on her clitoris. Tamara moaned and arched her back. She was enjoying herself.

Joseph was glad of that. He'd been unable to get an erection, no matter what they tried. For some reason—and he really didn't understand it because she was every bit as sexy with her clothes off as he'd thought she'd be—he just couldn't get it up. Even if his mind was elsewhere, thinking about Hannah and going to New York, he thought his body would respond. But it didn't. It let him down: literally. She'd been nice about it, saying "Maybe it's too soon," making excuses for him when he could see that she was disappointed. He was frustrated. This never happened to him with Hannah.

He went down on her to cover for his lack of turgidity. He was trying to be enthusiastic; he wanted to make her come. It was the least he could do for an old high school classmate.

...

Lono had called in some favors; he'd asked his friends to find out what they knew about these two jokers from Vegas. The answer came back loud and clear: Nobody had ever heard of them. They weren't connected to La Cosa Nostra, the Russian or Armenian mafias, any of the drug cartels that anyone knew, or any outlaw motorcycle gangs or local security companies. They weren't law enforcement. They were definitely freelance, probably amateurs.

Lono knew that it wasn't uncommon for friends or relatives of someone in dire straits to ask for a favor. People did it for love. They did it for money. Some of them even did it for fun. The general public seemed to be under the impression that being a hitman was easy. Blame it on Hollywood.

The one disturbing piece of information Lono learned was that someone in Las Vegas had actually put a contract out on Sid. No one knew who did the hiring or who'd been contracted for the job. Lono couldn't imagine why someone would hire these two morons to do the job. But it didn't matter. They'd be dead soon.

...

It had been a busy night at the discothèque. First there was some Japanese businessman, a big shot with Sony, who decided he'd had too much to drink so he took off his suit jacket, rolled it into a nice little pillow, and lay down for a good night's sleep on one of the banquettes. Wilson studied the sleeping businessman. He had a keen eye for details and guessed he weighed about 130 pounds. The man had short stubby legs. That was good; that would give Wilson some decent leverage. Then he tested the strength of the drunk's belt, making sure it was buckled securely. Wilson smiled. Things were lining up. Maybe tonight he could break his record and chuck this guy twenty-five feet into the street. That was the distance that had been eluding him for the last few years.

Unfortunately for Wilson, the businessman's friends must've realized something was going on, quickly hoisted the drunk to his feet, and got him the hell out of there. Wilson was disappointed but philosophical. There would always be another chance.

He forgot about chucking the drunk when his cell phone rang.

...

Wilson and Lono had been part of the starting defensive line for the Mighty Menehunes of Moanalua High School during the year they vied for the state championship. They'd been good friends ever since. Lono called Wilson and told him about the two haoles. He had excellent instincts about these things, an innate ability to read people, and he was confident that he was right. The two were hitmen from the mainland and they'd come to kill Wilson's dad. Why else would they need guns?

Sixteen

Joseph ordered a bowl of congee with dried shrimp and chilies for breakfast. He'd gotten up bright and early and gone for a run. He needed to think, and jogging on a beautiful beach was a good way to do it.

He spooned the spicy gloop into his mouth and looked out at the street. Businessmen and women walked by on their way to office buildings down on King Street. Other people were walking around too. Misplaced tourists wondering where they could find an Egg McMuffin. Workmen with dusty shorts and faded T-shirts on their way to repair something. Hotel workers cutting across town to get to the Hilton on time so they could spend their morning replacing spunk-stained sheets and picking up empty beer cans. Surfer dudes and dudettes, the real and the wannabe, all shuffling around on their way somewhere. Everybody was on the way somewhere. They all had lives. Places to go, people to see. It was Joseph who felt trapped.

But what was trapping him? Joseph realized nothing was holding him here. His girlfriend had dumped him. His family had abandoned him. He'd been fired from his job. The ties that bind had been severed.

He decided to call the chef in New York.

...

Keith had spent the early morning hours scouting the area around the beach. He'd found several small fishing boats, a couple of plastic kayaks, and some kind of church camp that had a dozen red canoes stacked up against a tree.

Since he didn't have an outboard motor, the canoes seemed to be the best bet for a long trip.

Keith popped another hit of ecstasy—he wanted to stay rolling—and walked into town for supplies. The morning was exceptionally beautiful. The sun rose over the ocean hot and golden, like an advertisement for pancakes. The blue of the water was deep and vibrant, like something spiritual. That's the best description Keith could come up with: spiritual blue.

Keith watched in amazement as the trees seemed to awaken with the light. He could see photosynthesis taking place. Or maybe that was just the trees' aura. The birds could see it. He heard them talking about it.

He stopped at a little hole-in-the-wall café and devoured a massive pile of fried Spam, eggs over medium, macaroni salad thickly bound with mayonnaise, and white rice smothered in gravy, all of it choked down with coffee that tasted like boiled dishwater. Although the textures of the food reminded him of molten whale blubber, the flavors were good, the fat and grease deeply satisfying as it settled in his gut like a quart of Spackle. He felt better, energized. He had work to do. The dolphins were waiting.

...

For the one thousand seven hundred and ninety-fourth time in his life, Chad woke up feeling guilty. Not that he was counting. It had been a long lunch with the handsome Cuban—he eventually left around three in the morning—and Chad never did find time to visit Francis in the hospital. Or call. Or send flowers. Or even think about him.

So here he was, lying in bed, feeling guilty. He considered the possibility that perhaps there was something vaguely dysfunctional in their relationship. He shouldn't feel guilty all the time, should he? Chad vowed he'd discuss this with his shrink when he got back home. He didn't like feeling guilty.

After a few minutes of rolling it around in his head, the guilt turned to resentment. Once Chad had a cup of coffee and started to check his e-mails, the resentment turned to anger. Why was he wasting his time here? Why couldn't Francis look after himself? He had important things to do. Studio heads needed to know what he thought of the script for a new action movie—Interpol's most dangerous prisoners unite and take over the Louvre. Chad had high hopes for this one. It was international—they could fill it with foreign stars and make a killing overseas—plus it was arty. Who wouldn't want to see someone shot to death and dying next to Michelangelo's *Pietà*? I mean, come on. That's classic. And Chad loved the line in the script where Dieter, the knife expert from Hamburg, says, "It's time to wipe that smile off the bitch's face," and slices Mona Lisa's lips with one of those razor-sharp kung fu throwing stars.

It had "hit" written all over it, and that meant he had work to do. There were dozens of meetings he'd had to reschedule. Sit-downs with hot young hip-hop directors, lunches with the new writers that everyone would be talking about, and drinks with their agents. Chad was annoyed; he was missing the flavor-of-the-month.

He suddenly came to the realization that Francis was a drag. He was like a big dead weight that Chad had to carry with him wherever he went. Sure, he was smart and fun and took care of the dogs while Chad was working, but he could always hire someone to do that. A dog walker doesn't care who you're fucking. A housekeeper wouldn't tell him to cut down on the martinis. Did the gardener ever sit around pouting because he couldn't go with him to Cannes? The answer was so clear, Chad was appalled that he hadn't considered it sooner. Who needs the wear and tear, the grief and hassle of a relationship? It's really kind of Old World when you think about it. Not a progressive situation at all. If he saved what he spent on a shrink to help him deal with his relationship, he could hire a personal chef. Why hadn't he thought of this? A staff is much better than a boyfriend.

...

Hannah stood in front of her class describing the early childhood-in-exile of Kamehameha. Fearing that a jealous kahuna would kill the future warrior king, his family kept him hidden, raising him in the forests of the Big Island. In his exile, Kamehameha studied hard, learning the myths and legends of the Hawaiian people and mastering the art of *lua:* bone breaking. He grew into a great leader and powerful warrior, eventually returning and uniting the islands into one kingdom.

She was interrupted by a shout as the normally attentive Keanu Cho decided to demonstrate his mastery of *lua* on George Onishi's arm. As the two boys scuffled between desks—and Lisa Nakashima loudly pointed out that this time she wasn't the cause of the disturbance—the bell rang, signaling recess.

The wrestling ended abruptly and the children tore out of the room. Hannah didn't even bother to tell them to walk. She was happy to see them energized and excited. She sat down at her desk and took a thermos out of her bottom drawer. She unscrewed the lid and poured herself a cup of hot green tea and thought about Joseph. Wondering if he would return. Wondering if they would be reunited. And as she sipped her tea, she began to cry.

...

Baxter was feeling good. Things were falling into place. The career switch from strip-club doorman to all-around international supercriminal cool cat had been surprisingly easy. Who knew? He should've done it years ago. All you need is to find the right person and he hooks you up. A, B, C: easy as 1, 2, 3. It's a done deal. The criminal underworld, he realized, was actually a very cooperative society. We're all on the same team here.

The Lono dude had called and arranged everything. He'd found some guns for a decent price and arranged a meet. He'd swing by the hotel later and take them out to meet the man. All Baxter had to do was kick back and be cool.

Baxter cringed when he thought about how uncool he'd been. Getting buzzed on beer when he should've been straight-up serious. Letting Reggie get stoned and act like a fool. It was definitely bush league; they'd have to do better.

They'd have to be more like Lono. Lono was ice cold. Baxter'd even offered Lono a C-note, but he'd refused. Who refuses free money? Only the coolest of cucumbers.

It made sense to him now. Lono would get a kickback from the gun dealer. That's how it worked. Everyone was cool. Everyone took care of the people who took care of them.

Baxter felt like he was a part of something big, something dangerous and exciting. It made him feel good about himself. And it beat the hell out of busting some asshole's arm because he touched a stripper's tit.

Baxter poured another dollop of fake maple syrup on his macadamia-nut pancakes and forked a big sticky glob into his mouth. He looked over and saw Reggie working the buffet line like a pro, coming back with his plate piled high with sausages and scrambled eggs.

"What's that, your fourth trip?"

Reggie sat down and grinned. "Number five."

Baxter shook his head in amazement. "You amaze me, dude. How can you eat that much?"

Reggie smiled again. "It's all about the order. You gotta sequence things. That's the secret. And you gotta take your time. You eat too fast, the buffet wins."

"The buffet wins?"

Reggie put his fork down and sipped his coffee. "Everybody pays like twenty bucks, right? All you can eat?"

"Twenty-nine."

"Whatever. Twenty, thirty, it don't matter. What matters is, you gotta eat more than twenty-nine dollars' worth of food. Otherwise the buffet wins."

"That's a lot of food."

Reggie agreed. "You gotta be scientific. Like it's easy if there's steak or lobster, because all you gotta do is grab a plate of surf-an'-turf, and blackjack! You win. But if it's like this breakfast thing, you gotta work in shifts. There's no way you can get thirty bucks' worth of bacon and eggs onto one plate. You gotta have a system."

"You figured this out? You got a system?"

"Exactly, man." Reggie warmed to his subject. "First thing, ignore the fruit. Fruit is cheap."

"It's good for you."

"Eat it at home. This is a buffet."

Baxter nodded. "Okay. No fruit."

"First, I hit the pastries. No muffins, unless they're super fancy. I'll have a couple of sticky buns or a Danish to kind of go with the coffee and kick my digestion into gear."

"That's plate number one. Worth maybe four or five bucks."

"Right. Then I move on to something like a waffle. Belgian waffles are my favorite."

"But that's got fruit on it."

Reggie nodded. "But it's more like a sauce."

"It's still fruit."

"Okay. But there's whipped cream."

Baxter nodded. "Plate two."

"Sometimes I'll have pancakes instead of waffles. How are those pancakes anyway?"

Baxter looked at the massive disks of fried batter mixed with chunks of macadamia nuts. "Nutty."

"The waffles are good for like seven–eight bucks. So now I have to get serious. I usually go for an Eggs Benedict or an omelet. Something like that. But not with too much meat. You know what I'm sayin'?"

"Plate three is eggs."

"Basically."

"So how much is that?"

"Figure ten bucks for the omelet plus eleven from the first two plates and we're up to twenty-one bucks."

"You're getting close."

Reggie nodded as he stuffed some eggs in his mouth and chewed carefully. He swallowed, then drank a little more coffee before continuing.

"Now, depending on the buffet, plate four is meat. Bacon or sausage."

"Link or patty?"

"Dude. It don't matter. Both, if they got 'em."

Baxter nodded. Reggie went on.

"Sometimes there's prime rib or steaks or a big ham or something. And that means you have a little prime rib and then go back for the bacon and sausage. That's how I got five plates today."

"I think you beat the buffet."

"I gotta eat it first, my man."

And with that, Reggie began to shovel the scrambled eggs and greasy meat into his mouth.

...

Jack clomped painfully into his office. Up the two goddamn steps that his idiot son didn't get a fucking ramp for—thanks, Stan—and across the floor. Jack didn't look at the view; he didn't admire the puffy clouds forming on the horizon. He shuffled past Stanley, the walker sounding like a chain gang's coffle, until he reached the door of his office. Jack wasn't feeling well; his stomach was upset. He'd spent almost an hour sitting on the john that morning, and it put him in a sour mood. Ever since he'd hired Keith to whack that fucking Samoan, his stomach had been acting wacky: bloated, gassy, and exploding one day; clogged like a sink with a hairball the next.

Jack turned to see Stanley sitting at his desk reading a thick book.

"What the fuck're you doin'?"

Stanley looked up. "Hey, Dad. How's it going?"

"Is that a Bible?"

Stanley closed the fake-leather-bound book in his hand and gave his dad an excited smile.

"It's the Book of Mormon."

Jack did a double take. "What?"

"Revelations given to Joseph Smith, the prophet, for the benefit of all mankind."

Jack didn't know what to say. His legs felt weak. He needed to sit down. "Why are you reading that?"

"It's interesting."

Jack found a chair and flopped into it, making a noise louder than he'd meant to. "You've never been interested before."

"I know. But I met some really nice people at the cultural center, and they told me about it."

"The Polynesian place?"

"Yeah. You should come check it out. It's great. You could sit in an outrigger canoe."

"They have Mormons there?"

Stanley nodded, a contented grin spreading across his face. It was the grin of the spiritually sated. Jack was not spiritually sated or grinning; his jaw dropped like the tailgate of a pickup truck, hanging open on its hinges. He couldn't believe it. Why of all people in the world did he have to have a son that would fall in with a cult of—well, he could hardly utter the words.

"Polynesian Mormons?"

"We're all sinners. Even Polynesians. But that's okay. It's how we learn."

Jack was from Las Vegas, and there was nothing he hated more than preaching. All the losers in the universe came to Las Vegas, blew their money gambling, drinking, and whoring, and then—possibly due to sunstroke—they'd find God and start preaching on any available street corner. They never said, "I'm a loser and the only thing I can do to feel good about myself is tell all of you that you're goin' to hell." No. They couldn't handle the truth. They blamed everyone but themselves. It made Jack want to puke. Sure, we're all sinners. Sinners, suckers, and whores. Big deal. Welcome to the fuckin' world. Jack looked at Stanley. He could barely keep the caustic out of his voice.

"Is that so?"

"Absolutely. God sent us down here to learn and to redeem ourselves by making the world better."

"That's God for you. Big on the self-improvement."

Stanley looked hurt. "I didn't expect you'd understand."

Jack looked over at his son. His first instinct was to rip the Book of Mormon out of Stanley's hands and beat him with it. But then, like all parents when they learn their children are involved in something they don't approve of, he decided it was probably just a phase.

"So you're a Mormon now?"

"I haven't been baptized yet."

"I thought that was Baptists."

"It's a commitment to Christ; they all do it."

"I'd be careful, you know. It's a religion started by a guy named Smith."

"He was a prophet, Dad."

Jack nodded solemnly. Mormons? Who knew? He wondered how his son, admittedly a dork, could keep several wives satisfied when he'd never even had a girlfriend. He was practically, although not technically, due to thirty-five seconds of intercourse his freshman year, a virgin.

"You're serious about this?"

"Yes."

"Do me one favor. Get some pussy before you convert and go all Jesus-freak on me."

"I don't think that has anything to do with it."

Jack pointed to the Book of Mormon. "It says in there that God wants you to learn, right?"

"That's what it says."

"So you should learn what it's like to get boned by a pro. These churchy girls are just gonna lay there. They may not even get naked. It'll be over in two minutes. You gotta promise me you'll try it with some wild-ass chick who won't stop until your well's run dry."

Stanley looked at his father. "You're insane."

"I'm insane? You want to be a Mormon. Just do this for your old man before you commit to Christ. Even Jesus got down before they nailed him to the cross."

. . .

Yuki had always lived by the maxim, *When life gives you lemons, make lemonade.* She believed that she was smart and resourceful and that if she kept a positive outlook she would make the most of her life. Yet she had no idea what to think of her current situation. There was no maxim that starts with "*When life gives you a pimp . . .*" And yet life had given her a pimp and she found she was okay with it. She rationalized it to herself because Lono wasn't like any pimp she'd ever heard of. He was special.

The door to the office opened and Francis, looking slightly gray, came limping in. Yuki turned to greet him.

"Hey, welcome back."

Francis looked at her, seeing her smile beaming at him, and shook his head. "You're a fucking saint, you know that?"

"Let me get you a cup of coffee."

"How can you be so nice to me?"

"Because I don't want to be filled up with anger or fear or any negative emotions. I want to stay positive."

Yuki flashed him another smile and headed off to the coffee room. Francis didn't know what to say, so he hobbled into his office and looked around. It was still shit brown, but it had been cleaned. Papers organized on his desk just the way he liked them. Some fresh flowers in a vase. Yuki's efficiency and affability only made Francis feel small and awful, like he was the lowest life-form on the planet. Then he remembered Chad. Chad was the lowest.

Francis had spent most of yesterday, the brief times between visits from the residents who were constantly palpating and measuring his dick, waiting for Chad to arrive and cheer him up.

At the end of the day, when it was obvious that Chad wasn't going to show up or call or send flowers, when it was time for the night nurse to tuck him in and turn out the lights, Francis had lain in his lumpy hospital bed and wept. He cried because he was scared, afraid his penis might never be hard again; he cried because no one loved him, he was all alone in the world; and he cried because he was mad at himself that he even cared about Chad.

Yuki came back with a cup of coffee for him. "Here you are."

Francis took the coffee and looked her in the eye. "I hate to say this, but I've got to let you go."

Yuki was stunned. She could hardly bring herself to blink. "What?"

"I know, it's ridiculous. But I can't work with you. I'm sorry. I'm too embarrassed. I'm ashamed of what I did."

"But—" Yuki stammered.

"You can fly home first class. I'll give you one month of severance pay and a letter of recommendation. Whatever you need."

"I don't want to go. I like it here."

Francis sighed. "It's not about you. It's about me. I'm sorry."

And that's when Yuki decided to call a lawyer.

...

Keith organized his supplies. He had several gallons of drinking water, two dozen papayas, five coconuts, a pound of beef jerky, and twenty-seven little cans of Vienna sausages with the EZ-open lid. He'd also bought a serious-looking fish-gutting knife, some hooks, and some line. He figured if he got sick of eating Vienna sausages he could use them for bait, maybe land some yellowtail, have a little sashimi.

Keith squatted down in the shade of a palm grove and rested. He checked his ecstasy supply and found he still had twenty-two little pills. That, he figured, ought to get him where he needed to go. He'd seen the dolphins. They were out just past the reef. They were waiting for him. Waiting for the moonrise.

He closed his eyes and lay back on the sand. Its warmth relaxed his muscles; he melted into it, feeling the earth's chi flowing from limb to limb. He was filling up with life force; it was coming up out of the earth itself and into him in a kind of profound osmosis. He heard the wind whipping through the palm fronds overhead, the sound of the planet breathing. Without trying, Keith found himself matching the planet's breath with his own, and for a brief moment he felt he *was* the planet. He was one with the life force. He drifted off into a kind of exhausted sleep, floating on the energy of the universe.

The revelation flashed through Keith's subconscious and jolted him awake. For the first time in his life, he felt as if he understood why he was here, the purpose of his particular existence. Keith could sense the presence of death in the life force. He'd been around it enough to know it when he felt it. It was there, all around him, like a pungent dusky scent drifting in the wind. Keith had sensed it, smelled it, and tasted it in Afghanistan, Colombia, Las Vegas, Chicago, San Francisco, and Omaha. He had sniffed it drifting on the wind. He had felt its warmth and stickiness in his hands. But now he understood that death is just a part of life. The two are one. Life does not exist without death, and vice versa. Breathe in, breathe out; yin and yang.

In the past, when Keith had killed someone, he'd always experienced a slight pang. It wasn't guilt, really. He didn't feel compassion for those he dispatched. But it was a pang. Maybe it was his humanity speaking. Maybe it was empathy. He didn't really know. But the pang was always there, sharp and sweet and sad. Sometimes he thought his soul was trying to tell him that killing wasn't okay, that it was bad. But now he realized that what he had done wasn't so bad after all. He was, in his own way, reaffirming the beauty, the value, and the power of life. The only thing he'd done that was bad was to take money for it.

Keith vowed to himself that in the future, he wouldn't accept payment for killing. He'd do it because it was the right thing to do and he had the expertise to do it well.

Keith sat up and opened one of the plastic bottles of water. He popped another hit of ecstasy and washed it down with the cool clear liquid.

Seventeen

Joseph carried several flattened cartons into his house, along with a tape gun and a couple rolls of tape. He had to figure out what he was going to take, what he was going to put into storage, and what he was going to give away. Joseph leaned the cartons against the wall and tossed the tape gun onto the couch. He looked around, trying to decide where to begin. Earlier, he'd called a friend who worked for a real estate agent and discussed renting out his little house while he was gone. No sense paying a mortgage in Honolulu and rent on a place in New York. And— you never know—he might really hate living in the city; this way he'd keep his options open. At first he felt he was being chicken. He should just sell everything and go, make a real commitment to his new life. But he found he wasn't comfortable with that. Maybe it was because that's what his parents had done. They'd sold everything, moved to the mainland, and never come back. Now, when he talked to his father on the phone, the conversations were always about their getting back to the islands: how the fish was better there, the air, the water, the people, the weather. Everything was better in the islands, and yet his parents couldn't move back because the cost of living was so high. It was definitely better to keep his house. He could always sell it later.

Joseph began to take a mental inventory of the place. Part of him thought he should pack everything. He didn't want to leave behind his Plate Lunch sign or his tiki-mask lamps. Another part of him wanted just to throw some clothes in a suitcase and take nothing but his prized set of professional-grade Henckels knives and his running shoes.

In the end, he grabbed a beer out of the refrigerator and sat on the couch, unable to decide, emotionally paralyzed.

...

Chad sat in the first-class lounge at the airport. He'd grabbed a prefab turkey sandwich and a Diet Coke from the hospitality bar and was plopped in an overstuffed club chair watching CNN as he chewed. He was supposed to be reading a screenplay but had only gotten through ten pages when he shoved it aside. Not that it was bad. He was just having trouble concentrating. He wondered briefly about Francis—if the doctors had managed to save his penis or if, as he feared, they'd been forced to amputate. Chad couldn't imagine what Francis would do without his cock. Go all the way and have a sex change? Become some sort of freakish eunuch? Smile and try to live a normal life?

Chad knew one thing. Whatever Francis decided, it would be without him. He'd already had his lawyer draft up a settlement and FedEx it to Francis. It wasn't generous. He wasn't going to buy him a house or anything. Fuck that. Francis was damaged goods as far as he was concerned. Besides, they weren't married and Chad hadn't done anything wrong. He just wanted to give Francis a little severance pay. He was purchasing some guilt relief. Hopefully, it would be enough to keep him from hiring a lawyer and going after palimony or something stupid like that.

Chad wished he had some drugs. Anything was better than the boredom of waiting for a flight. He didn't like to drink on airplanes because it dried him out and left his skin looking terrible. But there were no drugs to be had; the handsome man with the pale blue eyes had seen to that. Chad let his eyes wander over the other passengers: men dressed in business suits or those god-awful Hawaiian shirts. Some were even wearing shorts and sandals. They were all straight, overweight, and out-of-date. Chad heaved a sigh and went back to his turkey sandwich. It was going to be a long flight.

...

Keith had been waiting for nightfall. He sat under a tree and watched as the sun began slowly to ease its way behind the mountains and the few sunbathers who bothered to come to the beach packed up and went home. The birds fluttered around; they seemed to be more excited than usual. It seemed to take forever for the sky to get dark.

That's because Keith was anxious to get going. His heart was pounding; he didn't have much time; he had to be ready to hit the water at moonrise. He moved stealthily to the church camp, running in that lethal crouch he'd been taught at the base in Okinawa. He quickly picked up a canoe, hoisted it over his head, and began jogging down the beach toward his staging area.

There was a line of clouds on the horizon, so it took a little longer than usual for him to catch a glimpse of the moon. But there it was, rising above the clouds, into the night sky.

Keith had his canoe ready, loaded with supplies and hidden in the tree line. The last thing he wanted was for some nosy park ranger to come around and ask him where he was going at night in a stolen canoe. Once the moon seemed set, Keith popped a couple hits of ecstasy and dragged the canoe out across the sand and into the surf. He struggled with it, the waves seeming heavier and stronger than they were before, but eventually he jumped aboard and began paddling through the surf out into the ocean.

Once he was clear of the reef the water settled down, the hard-breaking waves turning into smooth rolling swells. Keith would paddle up one swell, reach the top, and check his position with the moon. He'd have a few seconds before the canoe tipped over the crest and gravity sent him sluicing down the hill of water. It was fun. Like a roller coaster.

He kept one eye out for the dolphins. He knew they'd appear sooner or later. He kept paddling. Bearing 27 degrees left of moonrise.

. . .

Baxter was nervous. He'd counted his cash three times already: one thousand dollars for each gun. That's what they told him to bring. The price didn't seem outrageous. After all, these were untraceable, with the serial numbers burned off. And that, as he understood it, costs extra. He rolled the wad of bills up and rubber-banded them together before jamming them into his pants pocket. Then he thought better of it.

Carrying a big wad in his pants like it was milk money and he was going to his first day at school? No way. It would be cooler if he kept it inside his jacket, so he could reach in and take the money out like he was going for a gun or something.

He took the wad out of his pants pocket and couldn't help himself; he compulsively counted it again before putting it in his inside jacket pocket. Then he practiced taking it out of his pocket a couple of times until he looked really smooth.

Baxter went into the bathroom and put some product into his hair, really shaping and defining his mullet. He wanted to look sharp for his first big gun buy. He even took a little brush and smoothed his mustache out. He caught his reflection in the mirror as he primped and it made him laugh. He didn't do this much grooming when he had a date.

He brushed a dusting of dandruff off his shoulders. That was the problem with black. It made his dandruff look worse than it really was. He checked himself in the mirror and then impulsively decided to button the top button of his shirt. It gave him a look. A kind of New Wave vibe. He liked it. Then he thought better of it and put on a tie. Don't be too distinctive. Blend. Be smart. Maybe when he got more established he'd try that top-button look.

He met Reggie out on the street. Baxter was pleased at how they both looked, although he thought Reggie's sunglasses at night were a little over the top and told him so.

They didn't have to wait too long before Lono showed up. The big Hawaiian ambled toward them with his hands in his pockets like he didn't have a care in the world. He wasn't smiling, but he wasn't frowning. He looked like he hooked contract killers up with gun dealers every day. And who knew? Maybe he did.

Lono stopped in front of the big pink Jeep and stared at them.

"This is your car?"

Baxter was trying to think of a cool comeback, but Reggie beat him to it.

"Yeah, it's pretty fuckin' sweet, man."

Lono sighed and climbed into the back of the pink Jeep. "You ready?"

Baxter nodded.

"Let's go."

...

Francis was watching TV. The plumber character had been there for a few minutes checking the water pressure in the sink when a UPS deliveryman, a really handsome Freddy Mercury type, knocked on the back door and saucily asked the plumber if he'd sign for a package. The plumber, who peeled off his jumpsuit to reveal a body as articulated and firm as chiseled marble, was more than happy to oblige and now had the deliveryman bent over the kitchen table while he pneumatically rammed his glistening cock in and out of him. Which is right when the owner of the house, a long-haired blond, came back from the gym. He grinned when he caught the two on his table and said, "I see you're accepting deliveries."

Francis sat naked on the bed in his hotel room. He shoved the remains of his room-service cheeseburger off to one side and looked down at his crotch. Nothing was stirring. He tried gently stroking it, but his cock was still tender from the recent traumas and injustices perpetrated on it. Francis looked at the TV and watched as the long-haired blond ripped off his clothes and let the deliveryman blow him while the plumber was banging away on the other end. He looked back at his dick. Nothing was happening at all.

...

Baxter piloted the Jeep down the road. He was trying to follow Lono's directions but was having trouble hearing. Lono would have to lean forward and shout to be heard above the wind and the roar of the engine as Baxter fumbled his way through the gears. Baxter wished Reggie had sat in back so Lono could've ridden shotgun. It would've been easier to hear, and it would've been cool to talk to a consummate professional like Lono. Maybe Lono could help hook him up with more jobs down the line. I mean, who knew? It's good to network. Everybody knows that.

Reggie leaned forward and whispered to Baxter. "Dude, check it out." He pulled a tightly rolled joint out of his pocket. "I scored it off those chicks from Kansas City."

Baxter looked at him, his irritation growing. "Not now."

Reggie pocketed the joint. "I'm saving it for after. We can celebrate."

Baxter nodded like a bobble-head doll. Why couldn't this fool just shut up? "Great."

Reggie turned and looked out the window, watching the countryside whiz by. Lono had explained that they were going way out into the country so they could fire the guns and make sure they worked. That was so smart. Baxter wouldn't've thought of that. He would've just trusted that the guns worked and the ammo was live. He could've busted in on the old guy with a starter's pistol and a load of blanks. How would that look? Stupid, that's how. They were lucky they'd found Lono. Who knows what kind of trouble they'd be in if they hadn't?

...

Wilson was waiting by a big white van in a little scrap of clearing surrounded by dense tropical forest. It was pitch black out in the jungle, the only light coming from the van's interior, and they were well off the main road. Baxter hadn't seen a house or a streetlight for miles. He had followed Lono's directions perfectly, bouncing down one muddy lane after another until they'd arrived at this desolate spot.

Baxter was so excited he could hardly contain himself; he wanted to jump out of the Jeep and try out his new gun. But he also wanted to be cool, so he forced himself to adopt a languid air, moving slow like that guy in the movies.

Wilson waved to them. "Hey. Cut your lights."

Baxter nodded and turned off the Jeep.

Reggie turned to Baxter. "I want a .44, man."

"Let's see what they got. They might not have a .44."

Reggie got out of the Jeep with a swagger. He looked over at Baxter. "Dude, I want a fuckin' .44. The customer is always right."

Lono had already climbed out of the back of the Jeep and was standing over by Wilson.

"Just don't fucking say anything. Okay?" Baxter hissed at Reggie. "Let me handle it."

Reggie recoiled a little. He was surprised by Baxter's ferocity. "Relax, man. You sure you don't wanna toke up now?"

Baxter ignored him and walked over to Wilson. He extended his hand.

Wilson shook it. "You good?"

Baxter nodded. "I'm good."

Reggie had to open his mouth. "I'm good too. Scored some Maui Wowie from these chicks from Kansas City. You guys wanna fire up a joint?"

They ignored him. "You got the money?"

Baxter nodded. "Let's see 'em."

Baxter was pleased with himself for not just handing the money over. He wanted to wait until he saw the guns. It's not that he didn't trust Lono and the other guy, it was just the way cool dudes did business.

Wilson reached into the van. He pulled out a couple of handguns, a .38 snub-nosed revolver and a Beretta 9 millimeter semiautomatic.

"You said you'd like a nine millimeter."

Baxter nodded. "Yeah."

Reggie saw the guns. "Awesome. I got dibs on the nina." He stepped forward to grab the Beretta out of Wilson's hands. "I wanna see if it works, man."

Wilson held the gun out. "It works."

That's when he pulled the trigger. Twice. Pumping two shots into Reggie's chest, aimed to tear into his aorta and cause him to die instantly without a lot of bleeding. Reggie was dead before he hit the ground.

The shots took Baxter by surprise. He couldn't believe it. Was it some kind of accident? He wanted to say something. But he heard the gun go off a couple more times, maybe three or four more, and couldn't really think of anything to say.

Baxter fell to the ground too, his face slapping into the soft Hawaiian mud.

...

Keith had been paddling for hours but he wasn't tired. He'd stopped and coasted down a swell for a minute and guzzled some fresh water, but otherwise he was jamming straight through, staying right on course. He was far enough away from shore that when he cranked his head around and looked back he couldn't see any sign of civilization. No lights. No distant glow. Only a big ship on the horizon and a couple of planes in the sky.

It was quiet out there on the water. The only sounds were the soft slap of the paddle and the deep primordial rumbling of the waves. The pull of the swell going down, the push of it rising. It was a Jurassic sloshing, life and death in all its fantastic spin-cycle glory. It was the in and out of copulation. It was positive and negative, yin and yang. It was the universe, constantly changing and thrusting and unkempt.

Keith was in it. On top of it. Under it. He felt like he was napping on a dragon's belly. Rising and falling. Bigger than anything he'd ever seen, stronger than he could ever describe. It took Keith a little while to get in tune with it; he had to work hard to control his breathing. But as he pushed on into the moonlit blue-black world of the ocean at night, he kind of synched up with it.

And that's when the dolphins appeared. He didn't know how long they'd been with him. They arrived without a sound. He caught a glint of moonlight off the back of one of them, like a living piece of obsidian moving silently through the water. The pod embraced him, closing in around the little canoe and leading him onward.

The first flash of lightning was beautiful. It left latent images of silver-white tracers in the sky. The image of Zeus standing on Mount Olympus hurling thunderbolts sprang into Keith's consciousness. Bolts of energy delivered direct from a god. That's really what it looked like. The flash was followed by the electrical crackle and crunch of the atmosphere being torn in two. The shock wave resounding from the thunder shook Keith's stomach, and the air around the canoe sparkled alive with static electricity. His hair stood on end, like an electroshocked Einstein.

Keith was surprised that the rain wasn't bothering the dolphins. He thought they might dive deeper under the water to avoid getting pelted. But there they were, right alongside him, taking him along. It was a good thing, too. The sky had grown dense with clouds, and Keith couldn't find the moon or stars to guide him. He just plowed ahead, confident in the dolphins.

The first big wave woke him up. Keith realized he'd fallen into some kind of ecstasy trance. He'd been cruising along, stroking his paddle through the blackness. Dipping it in, pulling as hard as he could, repeating again and again. But the wave snapped him out of it. It descended on the canoe like a down comforter, gently billowing above him, blotting out anything but its roiling curls, and then it swept over him. It felt like a truck had been dropped on him. It knocked the wind out of him and swept his canoe clean of supplies. Keith held on as tight as he could, but the wave got his paddle and sent it swirling off toward Australia.

The canoe got heavy fast. But before Keith could react, he was rising up on the tip of a massive swell. The ocean lifted him up, high, to its apex. Keith looked over the side. It was a mistake. He saw that he was maybe forty feet up in the air and there was nothing to do but fall.

The canoe broke in two on impact. Keith felt the ocean grab him and yank him down, sucking him deep under the surface. The water was warm and felt surprisingly good, although Keith wished he could breathe. In fact if he didn't get back to the surface pretty soon, the breathing issue was going to become critical. But the ocean loved him and pushed him back up to the surface like he was rocket propelled.

Keith burst to the surface, gasping for air. He treaded water for a moment, trying to think what to do. One of the dolphins came up to him and gave him a nudge. They wanted him to follow them. Keep going. Keep swimming. Keith did a reasonably good breaststroke and followed the dolphins as well as he could.

Then he remembered the ecstasy. It wasn't going to last long in all this water. He stopped, kicking hard to keep his head above the waves. He opened the little plastic bag. It appeared that the pills were still dry but Keith didn't want to take any chances. He emptied the entire bag into his mouth and washed them down with an accidental swallow of seawater.

Then he checked his position. He could see a sliver of moon breaking between the storm clouds. He was right on course. Keith ducked his head under a wave and began to swim. He followed the dolphins.

. . .

Lono had never seen a dead body before. Not really. Not one freshly executed right in front of him. It was something, he realized, that unnerved him. He'd never wanted to be involved in any kind of homicidal endeavors. It wasn't the way he did business. It wasn't his thing at all. But in his heart of hearts Lono knew there wasn't any other way to deal with these guys. What could they do? Beat 'em up and send 'em home? Lono had thought about turning them in to the police. He had some friends who were detectives. But what proof did he have? It was their word against his, and he knew from experience that in battles between tourists and pimps the tourists always won. The killers would just make bail and be back on the streets. They would persist and eventually find someone to buy a gun from. They weren't the type to back down and go home; they were too stupid.

Lono helped Wilson strip the bodies and load them into the back of his van.

"What're you going to do with them?"

Wilson shrugged. "I don't know, brah."

That wasn't what Lono had expected. "You don't have a plan?"

"I'm gonna get rid of dey clothes an da guns an' stuff."

"What about them?"

Wilson turned and looked at the two corpses stacked in his van. "Chop 'em up?"

Lono put his hand on Wilson's shoulder. He did it in a friendly way.

"Listen, brah, you got to be smart about this. You can't just chop 'em up and make a big mess. Why don't you ask Joseph to help? He'll figure something out."

Wilson nodded. "Okay."

...

Joseph had just finished packing his CD collection into a box when Wilson and Sid knocked on his front door. The two men peeped in through the screen.

"Look like you goin' den."

Joseph could only nod; he really didn't know what to say to his uncle.

"You got a job somewhere?"

"New York."

There was an awkward pause, Wilson and Sid unsure whether or not they'd been invited in.

"So we *pau*?"

"You fired me."

Sid nodded. Joseph thought about saying that Sid would always be his uncle, they were his family; they would never be *pau,* finished, done.

Wilson broke the uncomfortable silence. "We need to talk."

"Door's open."

Wilson and Sid entered, and that's when Joseph could tell something was wrong.

"Do you guys want a beer or something? You look terrible."

"No, thanks, brah."

Wilson flopped onto the couch. Sid kind of paced, turning his massive hulk one way and then another.

"Is everything all right?"

Wilson snorted. Sid tried to figure out a way to explain the situation.

"You know dat guy from Vegas, Jack Lucey?"

Joseph crossed his arms. "Of course. You know that."

"You know he hired some guys to come fo' whack me?"

"What're you talking about?"

Wilson spoke up. "Killers, brah. Murderers for hire."

Joseph laughed, shook his head, and started for the kitchen. "You sure you don't want a beer?"

"It's fo' sure true. We got dey bodies in da van."

Joseph stopped in his tracks. "What?"

"We had to kill 'em fo' dey kill us."

Joseph turned and looked at Sid and Wilson. He could tell they weren't joking; they were serious as a heart attack.

"You wanna see 'em?"

...

Lono drove the pink Jeep into the airport car-rental return lot. He pulled into a specially marked spot. A young man in a baseball cap and knit shirt bearing the logo of the rent-a-car company came bounding out of a little kiosk holding some kind of computer thing. He had already typed in the license plate number when he got to Lono.

"Did you fill up the tank?"

"Just did."

Lono handed the kid the keys. The kid walked around the Jeep, looking for damage. Then he put the key in, started the car up, and checked the gas gauge. Satisfied that everything was in order, he pushed a little button on his hand-held computer and a receipt came rolling out.

"Thanks for choosing us. We appreciate your business." He handed Lono the receipt.

"Thanks."

"Have a good trip home."

Lono nodded and walked off toward the terminals. He'd catch a cab back to Waikiki and see how Yuki was doing. He needed her. He wanted to feel human again.

...

Joseph didn't want to go out and look at the bodies. He didn't want to see them; he didn't want to have anything to do with them. But Wilson and Sid were obviously in over their heads. They hadn't known what to do so they'd turned to him. Joseph considered their options. They could go to the police and try to explain themselves, but the guys from Vegas would deny it and Wilson would go to jail for murder. They could take the bodies out and sink them in the ocean; that would get rid of them for sure, but what about Jack Lucey? Wouldn't he just hire someone else?

Joseph needed to figure out a way to dispose of the bodies and, at the same time, send a message to Jack. And then he remembered the story of how the ancient King of Maui tricked an invading army. It wouldn't be easy, but it had worked back then and maybe it would work today.

"We had to do it, brah."

"I know."

Joseph stood up and headed for the door. Wilson and Sid looked up from the couch.

"So where you goin' den?"

"I'm gonna dig an *imu*."

He couldn't think of any other way.

Pau

Eighteen

Hundreds of blackflies swarmed the pile of bones laid out in the sun on Sid's roof. The bones, long slender femurs with ball joints at the end, stubby ribs, a mishmash of vertebrae, tangled tibias, fibulas, and a couple of slightly dented skulls, were arranged to maximize their exposure to the sun, accelerating the drying process.

Sid stood on a ladder and nodded his head. "A couple days den. Should be good to go." He looked down at Wilson, who was steadying the ladder. "You boys done good."

Joseph wasn't feeling that great. He stood in the kitchen drinking a cup of coffee, hoping the images would fade from his short-term memory. He'd barely managed to strip the meat off the bones, but he got through the process by imagining that they were butchering a couple of pigs. Getting a meal ready for a crew. He was a chef. He was just cooking. That's what he kept telling himself.

Wilson, on the other hand, seemed to enjoy the work. Stripping off the meat, ligaments, tendons, and fat with genuine gusto, throwing it all back into the hole, turning the *imu* into a prefab grave. Joseph kept a close eye on him. He was sure he'd seen him sneaking another taste or two.

They'd had to beat the skulls against a rock to get the brain to come gushing out. That was the part that made Joseph vomit. But the other organs—liver, heart, kidneys, and intestines—separated from the bones without much fuss. They were able to shove the majority of the guts back into the hole without having to sort through them.

It was just like making kalua pig for a luau.

Joseph didn't know why he was drinking coffee. It wasn't helping him relax—he had begun trembling a few hours earlier and it wouldn't stop—but he didn't want to drink any alcohol, figuring that might push him over the edge and send him sobbing to the nearest police station to confess.

Wilson was the opposite. He was positively preening. Strutting around with that unique kind of gladiatorial testosterone swagger that only comes from having vanquished your enemies and tasted their flesh.

Sid came into the kitchen and saw Joseph sitting at the table, staring off into space. Sid slapped a reassuring arm across Joseph's shoulder.

"You did right. Eat or be eaten."

Joseph simply shrugged. "We're Hawaiians." With that he got up from the table. "I'm going to go take a shower, Uncle."

Joseph took his mug of coffee and padded out of the room.

...

Yuki carried a couple of small cardboard boxes into the office. On the advice of her lawyer, she was here to clean out her desk and leave without saying too much to anyone. She wasn't supposed to give two weeks notice; it wouldn't be good for her to stick around working in such a sexually hostile environment. Not that she had much stuff. Just a few things: an atomizer filled with diluted lavender oil—for when she felt stressed—and some assorted Tibetan incense, a collection of healing crystals, a small reproduction of a Buddhist painting, several books on self empowerment and positive thinking, a collection of inspirational poetry that she liked to look at, and a Magic 8 Ball she kept around for laughs.

Francis entered the office and stopped when he saw her. He knew immediately what she was doing.

"Save a box for me."

Yuki was surprised. "What?"

"Your lawyer didn't waste any time."

"They fired you?"

Francis nodded. "Don't worry. I've already admitted to everything. I'm claiming a nervous breakdown, which isn't far from the truth."

"I'm sorry."

"Don't be. You'll get a nice fat settlement. You deserve it." Francis felt a lump in his throat. His voice caught. "Look, Yuki. I'm the one who should apologize."

Francis couldn't help himself; he slumped into a chair, put his face in his hands, and burst into tears. Yuki didn't know what to say. This, she realized, was some catharsis he needed to go through. A natural emotional and spiritual cleansing. He was letting it all out. He was healing. Yuki realized that her mission had been successful. Somehow, through the threat of a lawsuit, she'd managed to touch his inner spirit and transform him.

Francis sobbed. "I'm so sorry. I don't **know what**'s wrong with me."

Yuki handed him a box of tissues. "It's okay. You're going to be better now."

She reached for her atomizer and sprayed a light lavender-scented mist in the air. He looked up at her, his eyes burned red from crying.

"I don't think I'm ever going to be better."

"Why do you say that?"

"It's true."

"Healing is painful, but it's necessary."

"It's not that . . . it's—"

Francis couldn't finish his sentence. He was too embarrassed, too scared of making it true by saying it out loud.

"Is there something I can do?"

"Not unless you're Mother Teresa and can raise the dead."

Yuki didn't know what he was talking about.

"Nobody died."

"My penis did."

If Francis hadn't appeared so genuinely distraught, Yuki would've just walked out the door and asked for an even bigger settlement, but Francis was so sincerely overcome with grief that Yuki couldn't help herself; she had to stay and show him some compassion.

"What happened?"

Francis began sobbing. "Long story."

"Did the doctors tell you it's dead?"

"No. But I can tell. When a Dick Ryder movie doesn't do anything for you, you've got one foot in the grave."

Yuki nodded like she understood. "Have you thought about a holistic approach?"

Francis blew his nose. "What's that?"

Yuki thought about it. "Well, if it's your penis, then it's connected to your root chakra."

"I'll try anything. Voodoo, cryptic mumbo-jumbo, whatever. I'll walk across burning coals barefoot for a hard-on."

"You should get a piece of black tourmaline."

"A rock?"

"A crystal."

Francis resisted the urge to call her a fruitcake. He was desperate.

"Okay. What do I do with it?"

"You put it on your root chakra. Black tourmaline stabilizes your root chakra and dispels negative energy."

"Where's my root thing?"

Yuki turned around and showed him. Francis shook his head.

"You want me to shove a rock up my ass?"

"You place it on the outside."

Francis nodded. "Then what?"

"Then put some patchouli around and relax. Let the energy in the crystal do its thing."

Francis recoiled. "Patchouli? Like a hippie?"

Yuki shrugged. "It works."

...

Finally he had it in his hands: a signed contract. A good one, too. The network and the studio were paying full freight and they weren't skimping; they wanted steaks, lobster, ahi tuna, fresh pasta, a smoothie bar, the works. They wanted him to keep a cook on call just in case the director or one of the stars needed a grilled cheese sandwich or a bowl of tomato soup in the middle of the night. They even gave him a 15 percent contingency, in case he had to fly something special over from the mainland. He knew right away he'd have to arrange to get some decent prime rib sent over. Otherwise what was he going to do, serve prime rib of snapper?

After all that dilly-dallying, now he could get down to brass tacks. He could start hiring drivers, cooks, assistants, maybe a cute girl to work in the office. He could start opening accounts with suppliers: the butchers, bakers, and greengrocers. From what he could tell from the locals' eating habits he'd probably need a warehouse full of Spam and a fleet of his own fishing boats. It seems like that's all they ate over here.

Jack was happy. Stanley's driving didn't even bother him today. Finally he was going to see some return on his investment. It had been a gamble, bringing all this gear over to Honolulu, but Jack was a gambler. He lived in Vegas, didn't he? But now that they had their foot in the door—well, it would be difficult to get them out.

He grinned at his son. "What did I tell you?"

Stanley smiled. "You were right, Dad."

"From here on in it's smooth sailing."

Stanley cleared his throat. "So, Dad?"

"Yes?"

"When we set up the payroll accounts, I want to tithe ten percent of my money to the church."

If Jack had been driving he would've driven off the road. "Are you out of your fuckin' mind?"

"Why does it bother you? It's not your money."

Jack turned and looked out the window. "Can't you

blow it on booze or drugs or something? Why give it to the church? Why don't you take up scuba diving?"

Stanley looked straight ahead. He wasn't going to get into this with his dad. In fact, he was going to do what he thought was right, and he didn't care what his father thought.

"Why don't you mind your own business?"

Jack did a double take. "What'd you say?"

"I said mind your own business. I don't tell *you* how to live."

Jack wanted to say something but thought better of it. In fact, he realized that Stanley was right. It wasn't his business.

Jack didn't say anything for a long time as the rental car crawled slowly through the streets of Honolulu. After a while, he turned to Stanley.

"Could you drive faster, please?"

...

In the old days, when someone was discovered to be an Ai-Kanaka, a man-eater, he was hunted down and, as tradition tells it, chucked off the nearest cliff. They were clever, those original Hawaiians. They didn't mess around. No judge, no jury. No lawyers, no reasonable doubt. You're a man-eater; off you go.

Joseph didn't think Wilson would be thrown from a cliff, but he worried about him. The gods don't think too highly of cannibalism either.

And then there were the gods of law enforcement. Joseph could just see some well-meaning high school kid coming over to clean the gutters on Sid's roof. What would they think of a pile of bones? Even if the authorities overlooked the cannibalism, Joseph was pretty sure that murder was still against the law.

Of course *he* wasn't a murderer or an Ai-Kanaka. He was just the cook. Joseph understood that this didn't let him off the hook, either judicially or culinarily. He was still guilty.

Joseph sat on the couch in his little house and stared out the window. He wasn't thirsty. He wasn't hungry. In fact, he hadn't been able to keep any food down except the occasional papaya. He'd even tried a simple bowl of rice. It didn't stay down long, so he'd given up trying to eat for a while.

Although Joseph hated himself for what had happened, barbecuing the hitmen had done something good for him. He'd gotten in touch with some deep tribal emotions when he'd pitched those two haoles into the *imu*. It made him realize that he was Hawaiian. It was who he was. Nothing could change that. It was a primal impulse that he felt deep in his core, as if it were stitched into his DNA. He was Hawaiian, and moving somewhere else would never take that away from him. He could go anywhere. Do anything. He would always be who he was.

He realized that a people can only take being conquered, living as virtual servants in their own land, for so long. Joseph knew what the ancient kahunas would've said. The haoles are *pau*. Let's luau.

...

Jack lurched his walker into the foyer of the Teamsters office and stopped dead in his tracks. Sid turned and looked at him.

"What wrong wid you den? You look like you seen a ghost."

For a brief, heart-stopping second Jack did think he was seeing a ghost. Sid loomed in the office in all his tattered T-shirt, beer-gut glory. But he wasn't a ghost. Not yet anyway.

"Get out of my way, asshole. I have a contract."

Sid chuckled to himself and started to walk away. Then he turned back to Jack.

"Remember, when da show's over, leave da keys in da trucks an' go home." Sid wagged his finger at him. "Don' forget now."

"I had a stroke. Not Alzheimer's."

Sid laughed. "Dat's a good one."

He walked out of the building. Jack craned his neck and watched him go. The big man in his gym shorts and flip-flops, lumbering out the door, sweating like a hog but still very much alive. That annoyed Jack. It pissed him off. How many hitmen did it take to whack this fucking guy? Sid should've been dead, gone, disappeared by now. Jack didn't understand it. Maybe the creepy hitman had scammed him, but Baxter should've finished the job. I mean, how hard could it be?

...

Francis thought he was going to barf. The patchouli was assaulting his system, causing his olfactory glands to recoil in terror, his mouth to salivate, and his brain to release an infomercial's worth of bad memories.

A few of these memories had to do with a girl he'd gone out with in high school. Her name was Amanda and she dressed in a kind of post-hippie-world beat style. She wore multiple bracelets and bangles on her wrists, which jingled and clinked whenever she twirled her long hair. She did this compulsively, so the overall effect was like sitting in a wind chime store during a storm. But it also had a kind of charm and complemented her uniform of peasant blouses and big flowy skirts with combat boots.

Amanda claimed to be addicted to patchouli, which she dabbed behind her ears and dribbled down her wrists. The cloud of perfume floated around her like a protective force field, spreading the magic of patchouliness wherever she went.

It's not that she, herself, was a bad memory. He had been in love with her. But when they kissed he felt uncomfortable, like he was kissing a sister he didn't have or, worse, like he was Frenching his mom. It was through Amanda and the power of her patchouli that Francis discovered he was attracted to men. So that now the smell of patchouli rekindled all those adolescent feelings of shame and self-loathing that went along with the discovery that you are just a little different from everyone else.

Francis lay down on the bed and placed the black tourmaline on his lower back in a close approximation of where he thought his root chakra should be. He didn't feel anything right away. He didn't know if he should. He thought about calling Yuki and asking her if he was supposed to be feeling something. But instead he closed his eyes and fell asleep.

...

Jack hoped the Korean stripper was working tonight. He'd been thinking of her, off and on, since the night the Sumo and his kid had threatened him in the club. Why did they do that? Didn't they know who they were fucking with? Not only did they keep Jack from getting up close and personal with that hot Korean chick, they forced him to take drastic action. Jack comforted himself with the fact that they brought it on themselves. They really did. They pushed him too far, forced him to make some hard business decisions. As far as Jack was concerned, they had to pay a price for their actions. It was all their fault. But he'd paid a price himself. Jack realized he hadn't shot his wad once since that night.

He hadn't really been in the mood for a lap dance. But he hadn't been able to relax in his hotel room, either. He was too excited about the contract, too nervous about the fact that Sid was still alive. Jack wasn't naïve; he didn't just fall off the turnip truck. Even with the contract signed, sealed, and delivered, the Sumo could cause problems. He could jam things up, make them look incompetent, so Jack and his company wouldn't be able to work in Honolulu again. It would be easy. An outbreak of salmonella that shut production down would be enough to destroy Jack's reputation here.

And what was with Sid's cryptic comment about seeing a ghost? Did he know something? Had the plot been discovered and now the FBI was working with the Sumo to torture Jack and drive him crazy? Was this some unique Hawaiian revenge plot? Or was Sid really dead and Jack was now seeing visions? Just thinking about it gave him the creeps.

He had to get out. He had to burn off some of this nervous energy. It's not like he could take a stroll on the beach, painfully hobbling in the sand with his walker. Fuck that. He needed to blow off some steam. That's why he was here at La Femme Nu.

Jack had asked the bouncer if the Korean chick was working tonight. The bouncer had just looked at him and said, "Which one?" What was Jack going to say, "The one with the big tits"? They all had big tits. So he sat at the edge of the stage watching a parade of women strut out in spike heels and stroke their asses up and down a big metal pole.

Not that they were bad strippers. Not by a long shot. They could hold their own with any of the girls at the Spearmint Rhino or Cheetah's in Vegas. But Jack was looking for one special woman.

He almost fell over when she came out. Even though she was wearing a pink wig, he recognized her right away. He hoisted himself to his feet and began stuffing her G-string with ten-dollar bills. He whooped and hollered, applauded and screamed. He wanted her to know he wasn't fucking around. He wanted her.

After her number she came and got him. Helping him navigate the dark space with his clunky walker, she led him to a private room in the back. Even with the air bags keeping him constantly erect, Jack felt a little stirring in his penis, an organic throb all his own.

He had been under the impression that the stripper was from Korea so he was surprised when she spoke excellent English. She informed him that her parents were Korean, but she was born and raised in Sacramento. Jack was just beginning to process this new information when she plopped him down on a chair, shoved his walker over in a display of passion, and started dancing.

She didn't hold anything back. Her bikini top came off immediately and she wasn't shy about jamming his face between her breasts as she thrust her crotch against him. Her breasts were big, packed to bursting with saline pouches. She danced in a frenzy; Jack thought his jaw might've been dislocated when she spun around on his lap and one of her tits whapped him upside the head.

Unlike other lap dances he'd had, there was no tease to this one. She went right for his cock. She banged her bulging vulva against it with violent and aggressive thrusts and grinds, really digging in. Jack had never felt anything quite like this. He couldn't tell if it felt good or was some new form of senior abuse.

The pain was immediate and intense. Jack's eyes rolled up in his head as he unleashed a feral howl and flopped onto the floor, curling into a fetal position, screaming in agony. The stripper knew something was wrong and, being a consummate professional, she grabbed his wallet and fled the scene as quickly as possible.

…

Stanley raced to the emergency room as soon as he heard the news. It took him about twenty minutes to get there and another half hour to find parking, but eventually he made his way into the ER and found out what had happened to his father.

The doctor, a young Japanese-American woman with a taste for raunchy humor, met him in the corridor and gave him a quick diagnosis.

"Is my dad going to be okay?"

"He's stable."

"What happened? Was it a heart attack?"

The doctor suppressed a smile. "No. The EKG came out perfect. His heart seems unaffected."

"Did he have another stroke?"

She shook her head. "Were you aware that your father suffered from erectile dysfunction?"

Stanley had not been aware.

"It appears that, after his initial stroke, your father had some inflatable erection devices inserted in his penis."

"You're joking."

"According to what he's told me, the devices never worked properly and he has suffered from a constant erection ever since."

Stanley was confused. "What does this have to do with whatever's happened to him?"

"Apparently your father was getting a lap dance from a young woman who, we've now learned, had several piercings."

"What does that mean?"

"She has a stainless steel bar connecting her labia lips." The doctor tried to draw a diagram in the air to help Stanley understand. "It's common nowadays. Everyone's getting metal stuck through their genitals."

Stanley felt dizzy. He leaned against the wall. Now more than ever he was committing himself to the Church of Jesus Christ of Latter-day Saints.

"What happened?"

The doctor again struggled to suppress her smile. This was, after all, a story she would tell at parties and medical conventions for the rest of her life.

"It appears that repeated impact with the metal bar caused your father's air bags to rupture."

When Stanley still didn't register comprehension, she spoke in the vernacular.

"His penis got popped."

Nineteen

Sid plopped the sizzling teriyaki steak down on a plate in front of Joseph. "Dis is new."

Joseph looked at the meat. There was no way he was going to eat it. "Smells like you added pineapple juice."

"Taste dis."

Joseph shook his head. "I'm not hungry."

Sid wasn't about to take no for an answer. "C'mon den. Try it fo' me. Da haoles are gonna love it. I call it North Shore steak, Haleiwa-style."

Joseph pushed the meat away. "I'm thinking about becoming a vegetarian."

Sid looked at him like he was insane. "Why fo' you do dat den?"

"Look, Uncle, I'm just here for the bones."

"Dey on da roof."

"They ready?"

Sid nodded. "Dey ready."

Joseph took a cardboard box and a pair of disposable rubber gloves up to the roof and began packing the bones. The maggots and the sun had done their job, stripping the bones of any remaining tissue or marrow and drying and bleaching them so they looked like something you would find in a science lab or doctor's office.

Somehow, as just a pile of bones, they didn't make Joseph feel nearly as queasy as when they were part of a viscous, bacon-smelling, steaming heap of cooked flesh. He packed them in the box and carried it down the ladder.

Sid was waiting at the bottom with a roll of packing tape. Joseph looked at him.

"Wait. I want to add something."

"What fo' den? Dis is enough."

Joseph put the box down and went into the house. He came back with a pen and a slip of paper. Sid looked worried.

"I want to send a message."

"A box of bones is fo' sure plenty message."

Joseph scrawled the message on the paper and held it up for Sid to read.

Sid laughed. "You da crazy one in dis family."

He followed Joseph over to his truck and watched him put the box of bones on the passenger seat.

"You wanna taste the North Shore steak Haleiwa-style now?"

Joseph shook his head. "I'm going to go away for a while."

"You goin' fo' mainland?"

Joseph nodded. Sid patted Joseph on the shoulder.

"We catch some work soon, dat fo' sure. Don' worry. I call you when we got work."

"Thanks."

Joseph gave his uncle a hug and climbed into his pickup. Sid gave him a long look.

"I'm sorry 'bout da gay guy. You wuz right."

Joseph nodded. "I'll be in touch."

"Dis your *ohana*. Don' forget."

"I won't."

Joseph smiled, started the truck, and drove off.

...

It is difficult to sleep balancing a stupid rock on your root chakra.

Every time he moved, even if it was just a tiny twitch, the rock would roll off. Francis wondered if the constant rolling would interrupt the curative powers of the crystal. Maybe he should just tape the thing on.

He'd grown accustomed to the stench of the patchouli, he hardly smelled it anymore, but now he worried that he'd corrupted his nose and would never be able to smell anything else. Then Yuki came over with a new mix of aromatherapy insanity and began spritzing it around his room. Francis wanted to be annoyed with her, but he couldn't. For all her New Agey weirdness, she cared about him, something he couldn't say about his ex-significant other.

Francis had received the documents from Chad's lawyer. A sizable sum was being held in an escrow account for him. All he had to do was scribble his initials in six different spots—little plastic stick-on arrows pointing the way—and sign at the bottom.

Francis didn't even think twice. He signed it and dropped it in the return pouch. It wasn't because of his sudden unemployment; it was because he didn't want to dwell on it. He didn't want to think about his relationship with Chad. All the lies, infidelity, and negativity: Francis was past that. He was moving in a positive direction. He was ready to start a new life.

He prayed that the stupid crystal balanced on his ass would do the trick.

...

He should've come home a hero. A man who had stood up for free enterprise, for the American way of life. A man who had gone to battle against a Sumo and a tribe of savages and returned triumphant. A man who didn't just talk the talk, a man who actually walked the walk.

But he didn't feel that way. Jack felt deflated. Victory was not ensured. The situation in Honolulu was more complicated than he thought; his only living relative had run off and joined a hula-dancing cult of Mormon freaks, and here he was sitting in his urologist's office learning from the fucking quack who'd put the air bags in that they couldn't be removed without permanent tissue damage and the loss of all penile function for the foreseeable erection-free future.

Jack sat there wearing one of those stupid paper gowns and listened as the quack reeled off a laundry list of bad news. It appeared hopeless. The only light at the end of the tunnel was a risky procedure that a team of doctors in Bangkok had developed. Something about Thai marital relations made it a somewhat common occurrence for cheating husbands to get their cocks chopped off by angry wives. Thai doctors had become the world's leading penis reattachment specialists. The idea the urologist had was to actually remove portions of Jack's penis and reattach them through microsurgery.

It would take a few months for Jack's penis to heal enough to be removed, so he'd just have to sit tight. This was the best Western medicine could offer.

On the one hand he was relieved. Having a constant boner for years on end can make you a little—well, edgy. Aggressive, even. It was like the air bags kept a testosterone engine pumping away in his brain. Once his penis was popped, after the initial excruciating pain subsided, Jack felt relaxed for the first time since he had the stroke.

It was almost as if he were a different person. When Stanley told him he was quitting the business and staying on Oahu permanently as some kind of missionary, Jack just nodded. He didn't even feel like yelling. How could he? When Jack thought about it, Stanley's conversion seemed inevitable. His son was a follower looking for a leader. Jack wasn't mad, only disappointed. He consoled himself with the knowledge that at least Stanley was in a place with nice weather.

Jack thought about selling his business. Retiring. Maybe he could dump the Hawaiian headache and the Vegas operation on some sucker. But then what would he do—collect Social Security and hang around Las Vegas? Sit glassy-eyed and limp-dicked in a strip club? Rot away in the sun like some leathery old lizard? No fucking way was he doing that. Retirement is for people who can't think of anything better to do. Retirement is for losers.

Jack decided he needed to spend more time in the office. Get some work done. Be responsible. And save up for a trip to Thailand.

. . .

Lono had heard about a woman's touch, but he'd never actually seen it in action until Yuki moved into his loft. The first thing she did was paint the walls a series of pinks, purples, and soft greens. Then she went out and bought furniture. Lono tried to warn her that Topaz might make a scratching post out of some of the things, but she didn't care. She was making a comfortable home for both of them. The cat would have to adjust.

Lono would have to adjust too. He'd come to the conclusion that now would be a good time to get out of the sex industry. In fact he wanted to sever his ties with the criminal underworld all together. It had something to do with seeing those two chumps in their matching black suits lying dead on the ground. Not that they hadn't deserved it; Lono wasn't feeling guilty; it was something else, something he couldn't put his finger on. He'd begun to feel uneasy. Started looking over his shoulder when he knew no one was there. It was a warning from the island spirits. It was time.

He'd saved up plenty of money and was thinking of investing in a farm on the big island. Organic baby lettuce. Why not? All the tourists want it. And if there was one thing he knew how to do, it was give the tourists what they want.

Yuki, expecting a sizable settlement from her sexual harassment suit, was all for it. It was, she said, part of her life mission to help the planet and the human race by doing something productive and beneficial. What could be better than organic farming?

...

Joseph wrapped the box as carefully as possible. He felt a little bit like one of those mad bombers you see in movies. He didn't want to leave a hint of anything on the package, no fingerprints, marks, or telltale hairs that could be traced back to him. It had to be clean, totally generic. He put down the Beretania Street address of the Honolulu Police Department as the return address. He didn't use a name.

Not that he was worried that the guys in Las Vegas would call the cops. What would they say? We sent some hitmen to kill these guys in Hawaii and look what they did to them? It was more likely they'd just throw the box in the trash and get the hell off the island. That was the hope anyway.

He filled out the address forms at the Federal Express office, declined insurance, and paid cash.

Then he went home to finish packing.

...

He had called; he wanted to see her before he left. But Hannah had decided that she didn't want to say good-bye. She didn't want some tearful scene at the airport, didn't want to have to come home to her messy little house and deal with the fact that he was gone. She was hoping that by putting it off, by delaying it, maybe it wouldn't happen. At least maybe it wouldn't feel real.

So she didn't return his calls. Instead she graded tests, prepared classroom assignments for the coming weeks, and drank a six-pack of beer. She was hoping she wouldn't cry, she really tried not to, but she did anyway.

Twenty

Mary Sue Meaker was having a bad day. She just wasn't built for kicking habits she loved. It was the third time this year she'd tried to quit smoking. She'd stopped drinking caffeinated coffee, sodas, and tea a couple of months ago and had just barely managed to do it without taking an ax to her lazy-ass husband, Bert. She'd managed to give up the bacon and eggs for breakfast and the double-whammy cheeseburgers for lunch, somehow lowering her cholesterol seventy points without having to eat like a rabbit.

Now her doctor was telling her she had to quit smoking. So she crawled out of bed, brewed up a big cup of decaf, and set about fixing her hair without her customary cigarette smoldering like incense in the ashtray on her vanity.

She was trying to get her hair to stand up, have a little body like that country singer she admired, but it was almost impossible. Mary Sue had to spray half a can of lacquer just to approximate the effect, and all the hair spray she inhaled had given her a weird little buzz. She needed a smoke just to get back to normal.

Mary Sue pulled a box of nicotine patches out of her purse and slapped one on her arm. She thought for a minute about putting another one on, just to be on the safe side, then decided to save it as a backup. She said good-bye to Bert, who was busy reading the sports page while he irrigated his colostomy bag at the kitchen sink. Bert nodded in her direction and asked her to get some real bacon on the way home tonight. The turkey bacon just wasn't cutting it, and it was tomato season. How the hell can you have a proper BLT with turkey bacon? Mary Sue knew he was right; she didn't know if she could quit smoking and not eat bacon at the same time, so she said she'd pick some up on the way home.

She walked outside and climbed into her Toyota, rubbing the nicotine patch to kick-start whatever the hell it did, cranked the air conditioner all the way up—her hair, it should be noted, did not move in the breeze—and headed to work.

She had been working for Jack Lucey Production Catering for almost fifteen years. She liked it there. Jack was a good guy to work for, when he wasn't trying to get her to spend the afternoon with him at the Silver Mine Motel just outside of town, and she thought Stanley was a super kid. Real neat.

She'd been with them through good times and bad. Mary Sue classified this Hawaii escapade as one of the bad times. She'd never seen Jack or Stanley acting so strange.

Her doctor had told her that stress was a killer. Naturally, she worried about Jack. She was glad he was coming back. She didn't know the nature of his emergency, but she was getting lonely in the office.

Mary Sue had been at work a couple of hours when the FedEx guy arrived. She'd already drunk half a pot of decaf, checked the fax machine and found out it had run out of toner, answered several inquiries by e-mail, read the paper, skimmed the latest issue of *Weekly Variety,* taken a couple of phone messages, spoken briefly with Stanley about sending some money to the Honolulu bank account, and slipped a second nicotine patch onto her ankle.

The FedEx guy was cute, and if Mary Sue had been twenty—make that thirty—years younger she would've thought about asking him to meet her for a cocktail after work. Instead, she signed for the box and began scouring the office for some scissors so she could cut the thick tape that bound it.

It was from Hawaii. She was hoping Stanley had sent her some fresh pineapples. That's all he could talk about in their phone calls, how good the fruit was.

She sliced through the tape down the middle of the box and then had to cut the tape at both ends before she was able to pop it open.

Mary Sue Meaker opened the box, looked inside, and started screaming.

. . .

When Jack pulled his specially built van up to his office, in an industrial park just outside of the city, he saw Mary Sue sitting on the curb smoking a cigarette. He knew her well enough to know that something was wrong.

"What's goin' on?"

"I'm not goin' back in there."

"Why not?"

She gave him a strange look and shuddered. "I thought it was pineapples."

Jack patted her shoulder. "Sit tight."

He clomped his walker up the specially designed handicap ramp that led into the building. Mary Sue called after him.

"You want me to call the police?"

He turned toward her. "I'll handle it."

Jack found the box sitting open on Mary Sue's desk. He looked inside. For a fraction of a second he thought he'd vomit, either that or just start screaming like a freaked-out toddler in a haunted house. But he shakily held his shit together long enough to collapse into a chair and take a few deep breaths.

Oddly enough, he wasn't surprised. When he'd seen Sid still alive at the Teamsters office, he'd thought something might've gone wrong. Jack looked at the skulls, the bones; there were two sets of everything. Baxter and the weird hitman with the sweater. The Sumo and his pals got them both. They knew he'd hired them and they'd gotten them. Apparently they'd eaten them. Jack saw a note stuck to a femur. It said: *Delicious. Send more.*

Twenty-one

The trucks, neat and shiny and hardly used, stood in a row at the back of an abandoned warehouse, the Lucey company logo still painted on the cab doors. Wilson and Sid stood there, admiring them.

"He not so bad."

Wilson turned to his father. "Who?"

"Jack Lucey."

Wilson couldn't hide his surprise. "He tried to kill you."

Sid shrugged. "But he kep' his word, fo' sure. He give up da trucks."

"What're we gonna do with 'em?"

"Giovanni up da North Shore can turn one into a shrimp truck. An' I was thinkin' we move a couple over to the Big Island; dey's sometime work in Hilo."

"Let's send one fo' Joseph in New York."

Sid looked at his son and laughed. "Dat's a good one."

...

The kitchen was crazed. It was Saturday night, nine o'clock, crunch time. Joseph stood at his station, grilling fish, as the sous-chef called out the orders. The kitchen was filled with cooks, men and women from all over the world. Half of them spoke Italian, the other half spoke French. For some reason they all spoke Spanish. Every now and then Joseph would speak Hawaiian as a joke. But at crunch time, there was no time for jokes. It was all about pure concentrated lucid movement.

Joseph loved it. The chef was an exuberant, demonstrative fellow with a real affection for his crew. Like all great artists he could sometimes be arrogant and demanding, but he returned the loyalty of his cooks by teaching them unique techniques and innovative combinations. He encouraged boldness and experimentation. He taught them how to smell, how to taste, how to pay attention to the nuances and connections that food and flavors brought into the consciousness.

Flavor is memory. Food works with your mind to transport you to places you've been, places you want to go, and places in your imagination. Taste is emotion. You might hate one kind of food, love another. A certain taste or smell might remind you of a lover and all the emotion—good and bad—the memories bring with it.

Eating is a sensual experience. If a flavor excites the senses, caroms through your consciousness until it collides with memory and ignites the imagination, it is delicious. If it's delicious enough, you can fall in love.

When Joseph wasn't cooking, he was eating at other restaurants or drinking late into the night with his fellow cooks. There was a whole universe of them. They had a unique camaraderie, like police officers or emergency-room workers, individuals who understand the collective stress.

He'd found a small apartment in Long Island City, one stop on the number seven train from Grand Central, that was classic New York. He wondered what Hannah would think of the claw-foot bathtub sitting in the middle of the kitchen. He'd thought of her when he signed the lease. Even though she was only coming out for the summer, he knew she'd like it. She'd be impressed that he'd started a new life in the big city. She might even want to stay. He didn't know. He hoped she would. He thought about the islands a lot, but the only time he got homesick was when he saw the sorry shape the pineapples and papayas were in when they got to New York. They were nothing like the ones he'd picked off the tree in his uncle's backyard.

In the height of the crush, when Joseph had four sea bass, twelve salmon, and three orders of scallops all sizzling on the grill, the chef came rushing up to him.

"I just got a call from the cultural attaché at the UN. The president of some country is coming for a dedication, and they want me to cook a goat."

He looked at Joseph.

"Can you cook a whole goat?"

Joseph smiled.

"I can cook anything."

Acknowledgments

This book would not be possible without the intelligence, energy, and enthusiasm of Mary Evans, Morgan Entrekin, Kevin Jones, and Daniel Maurer.

A big mahalo to my Honolulu crew: Detective Mike Cho of the Honolulu Police Department Narcotics/Vice Division; Walea Constantinau of the Honolulu Film Office; the Kahala Mandarin Oriental Hotel; Det. Mike Church and Det. David Brown of the Honolulu Police Department Criminal Intelligence Division; and a shout out to Lee A. Tonouchi, "Da Pidgin Guerrilla" whose books were invaluable research.

I'd like to thank Olivia and Jules Smith, Tom Boyle, Paula Shuster, Gerald B. Rosenstein, Sheldon MacArthur, Janet Baker, Kristine Larsen, Adam Schroeder, Elizabeth Beier, and Barry Sonnenfeld for their kind words and support.

And thanks to my team at Endeavor: Tom Strickler, Christopher Donnelly, Bill Weinstein, and Brian Lipson.